Philip Hensher's novels include K[...] Somerset Maugham Award, Ot[...] Empire, which was longlisted fo[...] shortlisted for the WH Smith 'People's Choice' Award. Chosen by Granta to appear on their prestigious, once-a-decade list of the twenty best young British novelists, Philip Hensher is also a columnist for the *Independent* and chief book reviewer for the *Spectator*. He lives in south London.

For automatic updates on Philip Hensher visit harperperennial.co.uk and register for AuthorTracker.

From the reviews of *The Fit*:

'It will be interesting to see what Hensher writes next. Nobody saw this one coming – like many of the best things in life, it fell from a clear sky, and is all the more intriguing for that'
The Times

'Philip Hensher's novel is that staple of English comedy: the gleeful dismantling of an orderly life . . . a novel as painful as it is funny'
PATRICK GALE, *Independent*

'It's a sharp novel, full of deft dialogue, ridiculous moments, enjoyable sallies against contemporary stupidity; it also has depth and compassion, especially in the stark and moving conclusion'
Literary Review

'Hensher has a singular voice . . . exquisite'   *Mail on Sunday*

'Combines sharp comedy with bitterness and a melancholy that catches you by surprise'
A.S. BYATT, *Guardian* Books of the Year

By the same author

OTHER LULUS
KITCHEN VENOM
PLEASURED
THE BEDROOM OF THE MISTER'S WIFE
THE MULBERRY EMPIRE

PHILIP HENSHER

The Fit

HARPER PERENNIAL
London, New York, Toronto and Sydney

Harper Perennial
An imprint of HarperCollins*Publishers*
77–85 Fulham Palace Road
Hammersmith
London W6 8JB

www.harperperennial.co.uk

This edition published by Harper Perennial 2005
1

First published in Great Britain by Fourth Estate 2004

Copyright © Philip Hensher 2004

Philip Hensher asserts the moral right to
be identified as the author of this work

A catalogue record for this book
is available from the British Library

This novel is entirely a work of fiction. The names,
characters and incidents portrayed in it are the work of the
author's imagination. Any resemblance to actual persons,
living or dead, events or localities is entirely coincidental.

ISBN 0 00 717482 9

otherwise circulated without the publisher's prior consent
in any form of binding or cover other than that in which it
is published and without a similar condition including this
condition being imposed on the subsequent purchaser.

'The pluck of women! The optimism of the dear creatures!'

– Conrad, *Chance*

For my mother

1

A man who has nothing is nothing. A man who exchanges what he has for what no one could want: he learns to become even less than that.

When I woke up, my wife had gone. The night before, there had been three suitcases lined up at the foot of the bed in order of size. They were gone, too. They had looked like giant wallets: I now thought I could have asked about them before we had argued and gone to sleep.

Where my wife's head should have been, on the pillow, there was a letter. It had been put there squarely, carefully, like the chocolates luxury hotels leave for their guests. Janet had sealed it, though no one else would be likely to open and read it: I opened it, I read it.

It was a clear bright morning in May. May the first: a clean blue day, laid out for you behind glass. Janet must have opened the window before she left. The thin curtains flapped in the breeze. I lay down again, my hands behind my head, and stretched myself, thinking.

After a time, I jackknifed out of bed. When I opened the wardrobe doors, I saw that most of her clothes were gone, too. I pulled out a crimson shirt with ruffles; a pair of green velvet trousers; a pair of cartoon socks I bought at an airport once; and a pair of pale blue underpants. All these I laid carefully on the end of the bed, ready for me to put on when I had finished my breakfast.

A man whose wife has left him: he can become a bachelor, can breakfast in his pyjamas.

The clothes I had set out, they were not my normal clothes. They were unlike everything else in my orderly wardrobe of grey suits and white shirts. That was why I laid them out. I never needed to hunt for pairs of socks, since all my socks were exactly the same, this cartoon pair aside. I don't wear pale blue underpants, and couldn't tell you why underpants should be manufactured in a colour so perfectly designed to show up skidmarks, if any.

I went downstairs into the kitchen. The house was empty. 'Hello? Hello?' I called, almost as if summoning the dog we don't have. Irrationally, I wondered whether there would be another letter from my wife in the kitchen – in case I'd missed the one on the pillow. But there wasn't one. I switched on the kettle.

'Breakfast,' I said in a reasonable voice. 'Breakfast, in the garden.'

Why not? I unlocked the back door. I made a cup of coffee. I poured a glass of orange juice. I put them on a tray, and went outside, still in my pyjamas. It was quite warm enough to breakfast outside. The sun was shining. My wife had left me. I had an entire day in front of me. 'This is the first day of –' I thought. I had an outfit of unforgivable lunacy awaiting upstairs. I looked at the garden. It struck me with astonishment. I didn't look after it and my wife didn't look after it, but here it was with the blossom foaming over the fruit trees, the blossoms round and weighty as Japanese chignons in the sun. I had carried out many boring and inexplicable tasks in my life. I had passed grade three clarinet with merit. I had compiled indexes to the memoirs of elderly ex-ambassadors. But today I felt as if every one of those pointless tasks had gone towards qualifying me for my present ambiguous state. Millions of candidates had been examined, but only I had been selected to sit, wifeless, in the lovely garden in the sun.

It was then that I began to hiccup.

'!' I said.

When one strange thing happens, others soon follow, like ducklings after their mother.

A shadow fell across the white-painted iron table. I looked up, squinting in the dazzle, to find a stranger in my garden. There was a small girl standing in front of me, observing me with open curiosity. I hadn't seen her coming. She was just there. For a minute or so we examined each other closely, as if each of us was in possession and silently quizzing an intruder. When she spoke, her head tilted on one side, she took the tone of any housewife who had found a pyjamaed stranger taking a leisurely breakfast on her terrace.

'What are you doing?' she said. Her voice was surprisingly husky, and I took another look. At first, I had thought she was a girl of eleven or twelve. But now I looked, her face was lined, as very thin faces are. She was thin; she was tiny; she could have been twenty or forty. Her face was still stranger than her question.

'It's my garden,' I said, collecting myself. 'I'm not doing anything.'

She shrugged.

'I meant what are you doing showing off your doo-berries like that,' she said. 'It shouldn't be allowed.'

It was an old pair of pyjamas, overdue for replacement. I had wondered why the breeze was so refreshing, and hastily covered myself up with the only thing to hand, a saucer.

'I often come through here,' she said, conversationally. 'It's ever such a useful short cut, through your garden. Never seen anyone here before, though.'

For a moment we were at a loss for words. I looked at her; she looked at me; I had a saucer over my genitals.

'You don't mind, do you?' she said. 'Using your garden as a short cut, I mean?'

'I'm not mad about it,' I said. 'I can't stop you. It's a right of way.'

'There's a right of way through your garden?' she said.

'!' I said.

'You've got the hiccups,' she said dispassionately.

'It's just started,' I said.

'My name's Susie,' she said. 'Have you tried drinking a glass of water backwards?'

'!' I said.

'It doesn't really work, that one, anyway,' she said. She narrowed her eyes, inspecting me, then slowly as a consultant she walked round me. 'Hmm,' she said.

'What's this plant called?' She indicated a pot on the terrace.

'It's a bay tree.' She went on. 'That's a dahlia,' I said. 'It's a pelargonium – wistaria – fuchsia –' and on she went, for five minutes. She circled the whole garden, indicating each plant in turn, nodding kindly at each correct answer, and then she was back by my side.

'And finally to score one hundred bonus points and win that two-week holiday in Baghdad what –' she said, pointing downwards like a dowser – 'do you call this?'

'That's called grass,' I said.

'Hmm,' she said. She flopped down quite abruptly on the lawn. She seemed to have finished her game for the moment. 'I've phoned in sick today,' she said. 'It's shocking, really. I do it all the time. I'm not sick at all. I never am. Have you thrown a sicky, too, or do you count hiccups?'

'No,' I said. 'I work at home mostly. My wife left me this morning.'

This did not appear to interest her enormously; she nodded slowly.

'Why do you call in sick when you're not?' I said.

'Because if you go to work you don't learn anything, and if you call in sick, by ten thirty in the morning, you've learnt the names of twenty plants, and they'll pay you anyway. Listen, I know what'll fix your hiccups, a nice glass of champagne.'

'I don't drink,' I said.

'I'll be back in a tick,' she said. 'I only live over there. It's medicinal, it doesn't count.'

'But I don't drink,' I said.

'Do you know why she's gone, your wife?' Susie said.

'She left me a letter,' I said.

'Right,' Susie said, walking off. 'Back in a tick.' As she went, I heard her murmuring with concentration, 'Dahlia, pelargonium, grass, tree, wistaria, hydrangea . . .'

She had not asked about the contents of Janet's letter. I would not have known what to say: it was not her business. It had been a short letter, and a strange one: it had mentioned my wardrobe; it had spoken about the fact that I had taken a part-time job working for an old lady in Hampstead without telling Janet about it; it had spoken about needs of my wife's which I had no conception of; and it had misspelt the word 'possessive' twice. Imagine: I was married to someone who could not spell the word 'possessive', and never knew it. It was not Susie's business, or yours; though, reader, you will either send or be sent precisely the same letter at some point in your life, and you can imagine or remember it.

The word 'sanguine' means 'bloody' if you think about it. Well, actually, if you think about it, the word 'sanguine' doesn't mean 'bloody' at all.

The girl whose name was Susie had gone away. I didn't see her come and I didn't see her go. In a garden in Wandsworth, a man sat in his pyjamas with a saucer over his groin. That was me. I sat and thought about the events of the last twelve hours. I had gone to sleep and woken up. When I woke up, I had lost a wife and three extremely nice suitcases.

'!' I said, to the empty garden. The tock in my throat

was immodest, unmuted, raucous. Seventeen seconds passed. '!' I said.

Wife, suitcases. I had laid out my clothes. I had made a cup of coffee. I had met a girl called Susie who was too thin, with hair like a swatch of yellow silk. I had started to hiccup. Those were the things which had happened in the previous twelve hours. I thought about them in a sanguine way.

I am an indexer by profession. I write, or extract, indexes from what other people have written. Their labour is anguished and mine is calm. There is a poet called Wordsworth who said that indexes are emotion recollected in tranquillity. Well, of course he did not, but that is quite a good thing to say and I am saying it.

At this moment I examined my life in an indexing sort of way. I looked at it in the way I would look at a fat tormented manuscript someone else had written.

Girl called Susie, I noted.

Hiccups, I noted.

Suitcases, I noted.

Wife, departure of, I noted.

It all seemed more or less equally significant as I sat in the garden with a saucer on my groin. I supposed that, in time, some of these things would become more important than others. With a certain effort, I made myself consider some of these things, made myself imagine the subheadings which in time would be attached to these headings.

My wife, I acknowledged, had gone. I considered ejaculations of grief, none of which seemed quite suitable to produce to an audience of dahlias. My wife has gone, I said again, as serious as a wardrobe. Something had led up to that and perhaps I ought to try to understand what had happened. And then after that perhaps I ought to try to think in a responsible way about the future. When your wife leaves then it changes your life, mostly. How should one continue with a life, having once made a tragic ejaculation in an empty garden?

'!' I said.

It is so hard to be distraught and heartbroken if you have the hiccups. That's what I think, anyway.

Susie was coming up the path now with a bottle of champagne in her hand. She was so tiny that it looked like a magnum.

'Not got dressed, then, I see,' she said.

'I don't drink,' I said.

'Oh, this isn't drink,' she said. 'This is medicine. Think of it like that. Listen, I predict that you'll have two glasses and your hiccups will have gone. They've not gone, have they?'

We both listened, like naturalists waiting for the call of the tawny owl.

'!' I said.

'No,' she said.

'Predict some more,' I said.

'That's a hydrangea,' she said knowledgeably. 'I predict – I predict –'

'!' I said.

'Plop,' the champagne went.

'I predict that you'll make some money this week. That

you'll meet a dark stranger with blue eyes who will tell you three lies and one true thing. If you follow a cat tomorrow week, it will lead you to an old friend. And I predict that your wife will come back on a rainy Friday. There. Drink two glasses of that, and they'll have gone.'

'I like your predictions,' I said.

'Oh, I'm good, I'm very good,' she said. 'You won't forget my name, will you? Susie? I'm going now. I like you, you teach me stuff.' She was skipping away now, and I watched her going, not knowing whether she was old or young, irritating or enchanting, right or wrong. 'I'll tell you something else,' she called over her shoulder, her thin voice fading as she went. 'The next time we meet, it'll be in my garden and not yours . . .'

The strangest thing was this: I did not see this girl again through all the events which followed that month. I only saw her again when it was all nearly over. Her predictions were all wrong, and I had nothing to guide me through that hiccupping month. No, not quite nothing; it seemed to me that two things stayed with me, all that mad month: her voice accompanying me everywhere, promising me that when we next met, it would be in her garden. Her serious voice, that was the first thing. The second were my hiccups.

2

I have said something about the house we lived in but not anything very interesting. I have said that there was a right of way through the garden and the names of some of the plants which were in the garden. I could go on and describe the house: I could tell you that the bedroom was upstairs and the kitchen was downstairs; I could describe the different colours which the different rooms were painted; I could tell you that there were means by which water could be heated for baths and the rooms, in winter, could be warmed; I could inform you that there was a window in the bedroom, and indeed in most of the other rooms, if not all.

This is not very interesting or surprising. Because, for instance, most bedrooms in most houses do have windows, and there is nothing to exclaim about if your bedroom is upstairs and your kitchen is downstairs and in the kitchen is a kettle. That is not very interesting or surprising.

But the way that we came to be living in this house and how it came to be ours is interesting. And this is how it happened.

My wife is called Janet and I am called John.

[ ]

That is a space inserted for anyone who feels like it to indulge their merriment. If, on the other hand, you are a kind person, you may take the opportunity to reminisce about the pastel adventures of nicely-turned-out Janet and John. Everybody our age learnt to read from these adventures. Yes, yes, we are called Janet and John. We know.

Well, Janet before I met her was a girl who drudged in a bank. Not a real bank with cashpoints. The other sort. Everyone else in this bank had red braces and the sort of money which is called serious. Serious money; the sort which makes its monthly beneficiaries laugh incredulously. Janet did the typing for them. She did not wear red braces, and she did not laugh when she saw what the bank had paid her each month. The men in red braces worked through the daylight of a summer solstice, they worked in winter from darkness to darkness; they were working many hours before any London shop opened its doors and many hours after every London shop rattled down its shutters. The money they had could not be spent. There was no time.

Occasionally they bought a house. That was about the best they could do in the expenditure line.

Janet and the people like her had better lives, but less money. They went in at nine and they left at five. They had £2,000 a month which is not a great deal, not in London. But at least they could have told you what daylight looked like.

I am terribly interested by the certain knowledge that

my wife was extremely attractive. This fact occurs to me now. She is attractive still, I expect, but she is my wife, of course, and that is just the face of my wife. Some people have blonde hair which falls like a swatch of silk and a face which is slightly too thin and a quizzical gaze and a husky voice. But my wife does not look like that at all. She is very attractive, to me and to others.

In the place where she worked the men with the money called her baby to her face. They referred to her as a babe when she was not there. That is quite a different thing. After a while my wife found herself alone with one of these men. As the others did, he called her baby. But then after a while he told her that she was a babe. When that happens – well, then she did what women do and he did what men do. It is not very interesting to tell the story of the next four years, because everybody knows the story. It is the story of a woman who has a strikingly substantial differential between her breasts and her waist, and her waist and her hips; it is also the story of a man who is thirty-seven years old and ulcerous as a crocodile who earned £763,000 last year. Seven hundred and sixty-three thousand pounds – but in any case, that man, you aren't going to see a great deal of him.

You know how the story goes. It is not a bad one to find yourself in, I shouldn't wonder. His name was Gareth, I think.

Well, that was the story. As with all these people, from time to time this man examined his position. He discovered that he had a great deal of money languishing unspent. He did what they all did, whenever they discovered this.

He went out and bought a house. With a house you can get rid of any amount of money if you look hard enough. The lucky thing was that one of these Oh God My Millions crises in Gareth's life happened when Janet was going out with him. So he bought a house and about a week later gave it to her. What do you say, giving a house to someone? Did Gareth say, 'Darling, I tell you what. You go and live in this house and it is your house because I love you that much.' I find the scene impossible to construct.

The house Gareth bought is a very nice one, but I suspect it was rather a bargain, for two reasons. The first was the fact that anyone could walk through its garden at any time. There was a long-established right of way, dating from before the house was built, which could not be got rid of. Few people took advantage of this; in fact, nobody, as far as I know ever had, apart from Susie. The other was that when he bought it, it had been converted into a bed-and-breakfast establishment, and it needed to be gutted before anyone could live in it. When he bought it, it had twenty bedrooms, a hardboard conflagration waiting to happen. When he had finished with it, there were five bedrooms, which is more like it.

It makes you feel dizzy when you think about giving your girlfriend a house, like looking directly up a great cliff of love. I guess that the reason he loved her so much was that whenever they went to bed together she would agree to do whatever he asked her to do. If you earned £763,000 last year then I expect your girl will make herself generally available without being too difficult about it. I mean, you know, up the bum, or really anything at all.

At this point, I met her. You will want to know something about me. Before the party at which I met Janet, I had been born in Bromley. I had two sisters. One of them is dead now and the other one is still alive. I worked hard at school and was quite good at it. Sometimes girls came up to me with a strange directness in their eyes. I always knew what they were going to say. They always told me that they loved me. It was as if they could not help themselves. Sometimes they blushed, or wept, when they had said this. Sometimes they did not. That does not happen to everyone, I've found out.

I went to a sort of university for people who worked hard and achieved what they achieved through labour, not native wit. In my last year I had no idea what to do so I went to the career adviser. She was a woman in her forties; she was not attractive; she had invested a great deal in what she could like about herself. Her nails; her hair. Her hair was piled up with two blonde wings hanging down. Her dress, on the other hand, was khaki and woollen.

To hand over your future to the suggestions of a fat woman in a khaki woollen dress! The pathos of it!

'You like books,' she said.

'You don't mind whether you work with people or not,' she said.

'You're diligent and methodical,' she said.

'Have you thought about indexing as a career?' she said.

I agreed three times and dissented once. She had a roneoed information sheet in her hand. She held it out to me. I took it. She did not let it go, and we seemed to be holding the thing over the desk. I looked at her.

'I love you,' she said. She looked absolutely appalled.
'Yessssss,' I agreed.

So I became an indexer. It suited me. From time to
time a computer disk would arrive from a publisher
containing an entire book. Over the next couple of weeks,
I would fillet and bone it, pulling out names and themes
and events and placing them where they belonged, in
alphabetical order. It was soothing and easy, like
unpicking embroidery. The only thing you had to make
sure of was that you got dressed in the morning, and did
not start indexing in your pyjamas. That was easy for me.
I was bloody good at it; but even if nothing else, I was
never late with an index and I was never difficult.

Lady, you think an indexer can't be a prima donna
about his work?

I had been doing this for four years when I met my wife.
I had left home, and in four years had lived in five different
flats, as the lodger of someone richer. 'Don't let them get
their feet under the table,' that's the advice landlords get; I
went from house to house, taking my work with me. Out
of the blue, I had an invitation from a girl I had been at
school with, an invitation to a party. She, like me, had struck
out, though less adventurously; she had moved from
Bromley to Catford, where the dogs race in circles.

I went, and I met my wife. It was not a very successful
party. Perhaps people from Catford aren't tempted by the
idea of staying there on a Friday night; perhaps no one
who didn't live there would have wanted to go there to
kick-start a weekend; perhaps she had fewer friends than
she thought. In any case, the party happened in one of

those double lounges, the dividing doors thrown back wantonly, an extended table piled high with food, so cruelly showing the numbers expected. The orgy of bulimics did not materialise. I talked to the girl's father, and then to her sister, and then to the lady who lived next door, and by that time I more or less had to talk to my wife. Everyone else was comforting the hostess in the kitchen.

'He said he loved me only Tuesday last and where is he?' the hostess was saying, her cadenzas of grief drifting through into the sitting room where Janet and I stood face to face.

'Oh, I used to work with her,' Janet said briskly, heartlessly.

'Poor girl,' she said.

'Well, she worked for my boyfriend,' she said, her eyes dancing all over my face.

'No, he works late.'

'Well, I say my boyfriend.'

'To be honest, it's not so much a relationship, more of a business agreement.'

'He's a good man, don't get me wrong.'

The walls of the room were brown, and her eyes were blue, figure-of-eighting over my features, and the voices in the kitchen were shrill, were soothing, and Janet might as well have been saying that she loved me. So I married her; and by the time we married, poor rich Gareth was such an abandoned wreck that he said she could keep the house, he having no use even for the money which he had. And that is where we live.

3

By the afternoon, I was so exhausted by the hiccupping that I did what anyone who is like me would do. I went upstairs and fetched a medical dictionary, the relevant volume of the *Oxford English Dictionary* and, for good measure, the *Guinness Book of Records*. It probably would not have occurred to me to fetch the *Guinness Book of Records* normally. By now – it was about half past two – I had drunk a whole bottle of champagne in a steady, nursed sort of way. As the last time I had had an alcoholic drink was on my eighteenth birthday, this was not proving a very good idea. It had had absolutely no effect on my hiccups. My sober hiccups had turned into stage-drunkard hiccups, that was all. After the second glass, I had had the sense to go and get dressed. It would have been beyond me now. I yawed from the banisters to the wall, laden with books, in my nightmare gear, and wondered, in a peculiar, emphatic way, how drunkards coped. It seemed terribly demanding to me.

I stood at the French windows, and leant my head against the frame. The books fell from my damp hands.

I don't know how long I stood there. Presently, I heard the grunty diesel noise of a taxi drawing up at the front of the house, and someone getting out before it drove off. I closed my eyes. When I opened them, there was a man in front of me.

He was large and raw and shining – I couldn't quite see how he had lugged the three rucksacks lying at his feet up the drive on his own. He had evidently had a history of being blond – his head was shaved, but the stubble gleamed menacingly gold in the sun. His glasses were a triumph of ocular engineering. He was evidently German.

'I would like to see a room,' he said clearly, as if preparing for an argument.

'Well, you can't,' I said. The guidebook he was clutching looked a good fifteen years out of date to me. 'This isn't a guest house any more.'

This sort of thing happened from time to time. The worst of it was that the guest house had never been very successful. It was in a dull remote suburb. It would never have been anyone's first choice. So about once a month a pair of French girls turned up at their absolute last resort, and we turned them away weeping.

'You are full?' the German said.

'No,' I said patiently. Just then the phone started ringing in the house. I ignored it.

'I would like then to see a room,' he said. Decisively, he stepped past me and walked into the house. I hardly resisted, beyond making a faint whimpering noise. I suppose he thought, as he stomped upstairs, that he had put one over on an obstructive hotel keeper unwilling to let his guests see the rooms before they signed in. Far too soon he was down again.

'!' I said.

'This is quite satisfactory,' he said. 'Now, how much per night?'

'Oh, fuck off,' I said.

Now this is a strange thing, because I said 'Oh, fuck off' to this man as clearly as I could manage. But in some way he did not hear me say this at all. I expect that like many people he only heard what you said if it was what he thought you were going to say.

'Fifty pounds? Sixty pounds?' he said.

'Five hundred pounds,' I said. 'Per night.'

For some reason he heard that. It is widely thought that Germans have no sense of humour, but I now saw that this wasn't true at all. He became unbelievably hilarious. He slapped his bald head and he slapped his stomach and he slapped his thighs. He opened his mouth wide and retched with silent laughter. He bent double and stretched over backwards and then, like a child's toy, came slowly back to an upright position. The whole pantomime took about a minute. I watched it with hiccupping interest.

'Now listen here, my friend,' he said when he was serious again. 'Let me tell you I have travelled a great deal in your country. I have stayed in many of your beds and your breakfasts. And I know how much such a bedroom should cost. I shall tell you that I stayed in a house which was in your Dorsetshire for thirteen pounds per night. And then there was a house in Scotland which cost fifteen pounds per night and it was a very comfortable and a good hotel in which to stay.'

He went on for a while. Of course, after a small amount of this, I stopped listening entirely. Drunkenness was a new and an interesting sensation to me. Germans were not new or interesting, on the other hand. So I preferred to listen to my drunken thoughts. I was thinking that this was something I had never done. I had never turned up, alone, with three rucksacks, at the door of a hotel which was not really a hotel in a foreign country. I had never stood and argued about the price of a room and first pretended to be amused, and then pretended to be angry. It seemed an extraordinarily stupid thing to do.

In fact, I had never really travelled at all. When I was a child, my family all went to the seaside for a week in the summer, by car. We always set off at five o'clock in the morning. I don't know why. It was something to do with the bank holiday traffic, though the end result was that we always got to Littlehampton by ten in the morning and had to drive round and round the ring road until the bungalow we'd rented was cleaned and ready. (My father is one of those people who will not leave a car with luggage in it.) And then after my sister died we didn't go on holiday at all for some years, for obvious reasons. When I was seventeen we did go to Paris, the four of us, on a 'city break'. But because there were four of us my parents tried to save money and we found we had booked a hotel in a street which was not very much like Bromley and not very much like Paris either. It was more like the sort of place where Arabs stand around and seem to think that an English family wearing brown suede shoes might be interested in buying some heroin. So that was not a great success. And then, when I was at university, I found that many people my own age had travelled a great deal, and whereas they could talk for many hours in the university canteen about the times they had had in Cambodia and China and Kazakhstan, I felt shy and sad, as anyone would if they had seen no more of the world than the rock arch at Durdle Door.

But it was hard for me to turn myself into a traveller. Perhaps I was just not the type. At the end of my first year at university, a Dutch girl on my course said to me 'I love you' when she was drunk and I was sober. This time I decided that I would say 'I love you' back. It was a terrible thing to do. She had dyed ginger hair and the perm of a prize-winning hound. But I thought I should travel. So that summer, when she went back to Holland, I went with her. It struck me as a reasonable start to a more adventurous future. But she lived in Utrecht, which is a town where every house has perfect double glazing and everyone speaks much better English than you do and there are four old buildings. We looked at those from the outside and then we went away again. She wanted to introduce me to all her friends, and I somehow failed to persuade her to take me anywhere more interesting. So I had a week in Utrecht and then I came home and wrote her a letter telling her that she was a very nice girl but I didn't think I loved her really.

That, more or less, is the extent of my travelling. I was very unlike the sort of German who was standing in front of me. Of course, my wife and I had had a honeymoon, but that is not travelling. It is just spending enough money to show that you love each other. You sit in a plane for a long time. Then you are in a hotel with lots of other people also on their honeymoons, like some kind of sanatorium. It could be anywhere at all. And you don't dare show your face between lunch and dinner because you are supposed to have endless amounts of sex all the time. So, as I say, that is not really travelling.

The German seemed to have finished by now. I hiccupped.

'Five hundred pounds,' he said.

'Well, you don't have to pay it if you don't like it,' I said.

The phone in the house, which had been ringing steadily, had stopped a moment before. Like a bird returning a mating call, my mobile phone started up. I took it out of my pocket. The German was about to say something. I held up a hand, authoritatively, and answered the telephone instead.

'Hello,' my wife said.

'Oh, hello,' I said.

'Listen,' she said. 'I haven't got much time. I'm at the airport.'

'What are you doing there?'

'Didn't you read my letter?'

'Yes, I read your letter. You can't spell "possessive".'

There was the sort of silence that is not far from a groan of contempt.

'So what can I do for you?' I said with the utmost civility.

'I'm at the airport,' she said. 'I don't know where to go.'

'Well, it depends where you feel like going,' I said.

'I could always –' she said.

'Yes,' I said. 'I suppose you could. It wouldn't be much of a running away, though, would it? If you just came home again now?'

'I wasn't going to say that,' she said. 'I'm sorry I phoned.'

I took the telephone away from my ear, and addressed the German by my side.

'Where should my wife go?'

'Hello, excuse me?' the German said.

'She's left me. She wants to go somewhere, somewhere out of the country.'

'There are many interesting cities in Germany where she could travel to,' the German said. 'With interesting modern-culture-scenes which she could like maybe, I think.'

'Who the hell is that?' my wife said, as I put the phone back to my ear.

'It's a German,' I said. 'I don't really understand what he's saying, though. I think he meant that you could go to Germany.'

'You've got German O level, haven't you? Doesn't that help you to understand Germans? Or is it some more general problem you have? Shouldn't you ask yourself that?'

'No,' I said. 'I got a B in Italian but I didn't do German. My school didn't do it. I got an A in English though.

The rest were Bs mostly. Well, there were two Cs, in physics and –'

'Oh, God, John, please,' my wife said. She was somewhere busy and public; her voice was close to the phone, but behind her was the noise of a crowd, of bongs and indecipherable announcements, the noise of an impatient city. 'Spare me the CV. OK, I don't know why I phoned you. It won't happen again. I'm leaving now, goodbye.'

I switched the phone off without saying goodbye.

'Your wife, I think,' he said. 'She would have a good time if she goes to Germany and its many interesting contemporary-culture-city-scenes. In Düsseldorf which is where I live there is so a scene and it is important and fine. So she can in Düsseldorf travel. Or she can – ha! – if she is not so interesting in these things be like a tourist who I think will like the picturesque landscapes of Germany, but that to me is not so interesting. And that is my advice which I offer to her.'

'Thank you,' I said. 'That was kind of you.'

'Not at all,' he said. Then he remembered that he was in the middle of a fit of rage. 'But your five hundred pounds –!'

He hoisted up the first rucksack, back to front, so that it hung over his stomach. He hoisted up the second, bigger one – I was interested to see that it had three small cooking pans hanging festively from it, which clanked as he installed himself into the straps. The third he took in his left hand. When it was all done, he was bent double, like a glistening, blond, enraged chimpanzee.

'And for five hundred pounds,' he said.

Clank, his pans went.

'For that –' he said.

'!' I said.

'– you get in my country a hotel where the owner is not drunk,' he said.

Fair as the denunciation was, I was glad to see him go. My wife was at the airport and considering going abroad. Germany, it seemed – no, it had just been the German who had recommended that. I sat down and dutifully considered this. It was very unexpected. As far as I knew, she didn't know anyone in Düsseldorf. The only thing I knew about it was that it was a town with a large Japanese population. Someone Janet used to work with had once told us that when we had had dinner with him.

(The things you find out if you are an indexer who can never think of anything interesting to say in company! The interesting facts people will wheel out for your entertainment!)

I was drunk. But even if I had been sober as an indexer, I wouldn't have been able to make myself think seriously about all this. The fact that my wife had left me and was now on her way to – she didn't know where – somehow didn't hold my attention. It was a background thought, a gas-bill sort of thought. I kept thinking 'Oh, God, yes, of course' about it all. But then there didn't seem much more to think about it.

I turned instead to my reference books. The medical dictionary explained what hiccups were. It told you a good deal about trapped air and spasming diaphragms. It suggested drinking vinegar, or holding your breath. I put the volume down. The H volume of the *Oxford English Dictionary* was not much more use. The book, which came in twenty volumes, had been our wedding present from rich Gareth. He had not come to the wedding itself, naturally. I had rather admired him for his choice of present. It was fantastically expensive, and therefore unfaultable, but perhaps not something which would give either of us a great deal of pleasure. It would have been too bad to complain. After all, he'd converted a hotel into a house and then given it to us without quibbling.

According to the *Oxford English Dictionary* – but no, you don't want to hear that. I start to sound like a sixth-former performing in a debating society. I thought you could spell it 'hiccough' if you liked. But the book was very strict about this. Apparently, this was just someone poncing about. It is not a cough at all. The first time anyone talked about it was in 1580. I don't know what they called them before that. You always imagine the Middle Ages as being one long orgy of belching and drinking and hiccupping, so they must have called it something. Perhaps if it is just something everyone does all the time, though, people don't have a special word for it. Perhaps they just thought of it as just another thing you could do with your tubes, like breathing in through your nose and out through your mouth. And then suddenly, in 1580, some people stopped hiccupping all the time, so they had to have a word for it. I considered all this, in deep interest.

The *Guinness Book of Records* was my favourite book when I was a boy. That tells you everything about the sort of boy I was. The idea of fame I had when I was eight was the name of a man who ate fifty-four sausages in five minutes in Austin, Texas, in 1973. I used to read it devotedly, particularly the anatomical parts – when I had become riper, I devoted hours of contemplation to the question of why the book showed no interest in adjudicating between claims for the man with the biggest penis or the woman with the largest breasts. I had a faint memory, shaken loose from its moorings by the champagne, that among the book's medical curiosities was something to do with hiccups. I was right. There is something called bibliomancy, the art of telling the future by opening books at random and reading what you first see. It was with an obscure sort of bibliomancy, then, that the *Guinness Book of Records* fell open at exactly the right page. Through a fog of bewildered unfamiliar drunkenness, I read my fate without understanding, then read it again, and a third time. The true horror of it slowly came over me.

'From 1934 to 1951, Mr Tod J. Hastings of Birmingham, Alabama, hiccupped without ceasing for a period of 17 years, 2 months and 28 days.'

4

I don't know how long I sat there with the book open on my lap. When I got up it was getting dark. I went inside, turning the light on in the kitchen. I put the book down on the kitchen counter and started to go upstairs heavily.

At the first landing in our house, there is a full-length mirror. I had a shock. My hair was upright and raucous; my skin was pale and fleshy; my eyes red. Anyone would have thought that I had been weeping because my wife had left me, and not that it was my first bottle of champagne which had done this terrible thing to me. Interrogating myself, I tried to make quite sure that it was the champagne which had done it. But my wife had left me. There was no questioning that. I seemed, too, to be wearing some extraordinary clothes.

I stopped there and looked at myself in horror. I looked at the outfit I had on. It was very unlike my usual dark suit and white shirt. Something terrible had happened to me. I might have been a figure in a gigantic computer game. My life had been handed over to the control of some invisible eight-year-old, stabbing and nudging at the invisible controls, choosing what humiliations and disgraces he should inflict on this twitching 2-D figure. At any moment the game might be switched off and then it would all be over. In front of the mirror, I stood and looked at myself, and watched myself disconsolately hiccupping.

'!' I said. '!!!'

There was only one thing for it. It was probably not very late. But it seemed sensible to go straight to bed, and see what sleep would do.

Pink Suit Five

With a towel around my waist, still wet from the shower, I opened the wardrobe door and reached in for a suit. If your suits are all the same, you don't need to choose. But my hand met an unexpected texture: rough, nubbly, stiff. Janet, of course, had not taken all her clothes with her; this suit she had left. I paused, and brought it out. She had hung it carefully on its hanger, still the same hanger which the suit had come with, the celebrated designer's logo stamped centrally; though the suit had been expensive – I knew exactly how much, I had paid for it – the hanger was cheap and plastic, not worth hanging on to, and certainly unlike all the other hangers in the wardrobe, which were wooden and identical.

She had hung the skirt by those ingenious silk loops on the hanger's hooks; she had placed the jacket carefully over the top, and buttoned it up so that it would hang properly. It was a good suit; she took care of it. It was pink, a sort of rough tweed, with threads of quite different colours hairily running through it, one an electric green, another in some sort of metallic glitter, rasping as you felt it. The cut was now a little out of fashion, with a round neck, stiff big shoulders and a skirt shorter than most women now wore; but it was quite an old suit, and Janet's were the sort of looks which didn't depend on fashion. She made you wonder, wearing that suit, whether in fact you weren't wrong in what you thought about fashion now. I knew this for a fact, because Janet had worn this suit the day before she had left. But she hadn't taken the suit with her. Slowly, I put it back and started to dress myself for the day.

6

Looking back, it all started to go wrong with the wet fish.

The first rule of indexing is the same as the first rule of nursing, or indeed of anything else. Don't let your emotions get involved. Old indexers told me that when I was starting out in the trade. Miss Johnson passed on this wisdom, for instance, the first time I went to the offices of *Indexes and Indexing*. Her wavering squint was redolent of emotion. Mr Roy said exactly the same thing, come to that, the last time I went there, two weeks ago. 'Don't let your emotions get involved,' they both said. 'Always remember that.' I looked at them on each separate occasion, both smugly holding a cup of cold tea, and thought, Not me. I'm too tough. You can believe this for a while about indexing. You can believe that whatever you are sent to deal with, you are going to be able to switch off your own feelings, and deal with it as just another index to be written, another job to be done. It was the wet fish that got to me.

I was a good indexer. Everyone said so. From day one, I was one of the best in the trade. I expect that strikes

you as funny, since you probably suppose that indexers
are much the same. As if all there is to the job is the
ability to put stuff in alphabetical order. Far from it. I
didn't find it that difficult, but that's because I was
damned good at it. A born indexer. You could hand me
a seven-hundred-page manuscript in green ink about
numerology, the Holy Grail, the Knights Templar and
the secret alien sects which control freemasonry – a manuscript only a mother could love, a manuscript only a
lunatic could make sense of. I would return it with an
index of beauty and clarity, a clean diagram of the principal
points. I never met the authors I improved like this. I
wouldn't want to meet most of them. But occasionally,
an editor at one of the publishers I dealt with would pass
on a comment from the author. The author never knew
my name, of course, so couldn't write to me directly. The
comment was always this: that the author hadn't understood his own book properly until he'd read the index
I'd made of it. You bet you didn't, sonny.

I'd only done three or four indexes when I got my big
break. That sounds incredible. No one is as good as that,
surely? But those three or four indexes were the only
ones I'd published, you see. I'd done more than that, for
practice. My first indexes were to the sort of books which
aren't going to break your heart. Military history, polit-
ical history, that sort of thing. The sorts of lives where
experience comes in boxes anyway, leaving nothing much
over for the indexer to tidy up. I could see that if I
wanted to get anywhere, that wasn't going to stretch me.
I took to doing indexes to tax me, not for publication, in

my spare time. I'd take a book at random, perhaps one that already had an index, or one that didn't obviously need one. I'd read the book, and make an index of my own. Lives of writers are hard; those of women are harder; those of painters are impossible. You can't work out what the rules of such lives are, where one heading starts, another one finishes. But I did it anyway, writing indexes to impossible books. Once I wondered if you could write an index to a novel, and did it just for the hell of it. The novel was *Martin Chuzzlewit*. My index began 'Architectural adornments, charm of'. It knocks me out, that index. The beauty of it, like a landscape of fields stretching to the horizon, of clean oblongs of green and yellow, wheat and hay.

When my big break came, then, I was more ready for it than you'd have thought. I'd trained myself for the challenge to come, and I was calm as a boxer at altitude. You always know when the big one comes, from the way the phone rings. It rang in the same way every day, but not then. It sounded to me like a songbird at dawn. I cleared my throat. I stretched out my hand. I picked up the receiver. I'll always remember that phone call.

'John,' the editor said.

'Yes,' I confirmed, my voice deep and firm.

'I wondered how busy you were at the moment.'

'I could clear some time,' I said steadily. 'For the right project. For an important project.'

'Well, perhaps,' he said. 'We have a biography just in. We need an index for it.'

'A biography,' I said.

'Yes,' he said. Did I imagine it right? Was there some kind of tremor, there, in his voice, wondering whether this was too big a task for me? 'Yes, it's a biography of – of Krafft-Ebing.'

Anyone else might have thought that the way he paused, it was just an editor recollecting Krafft-Ebing's name. In reality, it was nerves. Krafft-Ebing! The windily impalpable, blustering, shapeless biography of Krafft-Ebing! Even I wondered whether I could do this. I squared my shoulders.

'I can do it,' I said. 'Two weeks on Thursday.'

'That'd be grand,' he said, and rang off. You probably know the rest of the story.

When the book came out, my Krafft-Ebing index became legendary among indexers. At the offices of *Indexes and Indexing*, the austere professional journal, long discussions were carried on, enquiring who this young man could be who had made so beautiful and lucid an index out of such a book. In the popular press, my index was commended strongly, though in passing, in a review of the book in *The Tablet*, to name but one. (They love sexual perversion in *The Tablet*; I don't know why, but it is so.) My professional status was assured. Within a matter of months, I was installed at *I and I*, as we call it, as the resident anonymous reviewer of other people's lamentable indexes. They promoted me, *nem. con.*, from nothing to the board of management of the journal. The others on the board were Miss Johnson and Mr Roy (sex-starved sticklers for accuracy, both of them, one with a squint, the other with a limp). I was besuited, immaculate, invincible. 'Never let your emotions become involved with a book,' Miss Johnson was to say to me, her voice trembling, the first time she made a cup of tea for me. I looked back at her ironically. Her emotions were engaged by nothing that was not on the radio. I was the young man who had turned Krafft-Ebing, his perversions and patients and obsessions and fetishes, into so beautiful an index that the book became supererogatory. Daft old bat, to say such a thing.

Of course, I had my enemies. Of course, if you rise so quickly in any profession, you acquire enemies. One anonymous contributor to the journal – I suspect that it was really Mr Roy himself, but would not stoop to demonstrate this fact – actually submitted a ludicrously embittered review of my next index. The index was to a history of the Heidelberg school of painting in Australia, and as good as anything I had ever done – incisive, unforgettable. The book was a mess. Mr Roy's review went straight into the editorial bin.

Perhaps now I can admit that I cared more than I thought that Janet took no interest in my work. She treated what I did as a job, no more than that; exactly like the job she now had. She worked for another bank in the same square mile of London, starting at nine and ending at five. I worked at home, and didn't earn so much, but my job was different in other, more important ways. It wasn't a job; it came close to a vocation. I was the best in the business.

As I say, it was the wet fish that did for me. The first fish book arrived a year and a half before the day my wife left me. It was a cultural history of haddock. 'Haddock,' it was called. 'The Story Of The Fish Which Changed The World.' My habits of work were unchanging. I always began by reading the manuscript from beginning to end, without taking any notes. I read the book on the computer screen. They had never touched or affected me before, these books I was sent. But this one touched me. It touched me because it was so crap. I read all day. It was one of those dark wet days at the beginning of December. By the time I was over, the room was lit only by the dimly glaucous light of the computer screen. I might have been a haddock myself, wriggling after krill in the briny depths of my terrible life. Haddock. The Fish Which Changed The World. It was no part of my job to wonder why a publisher should publish such a book; no part of my job to wonder who would buy such a book once it was published. I could see the book, the object, already, with an artistic cover and at a size slightly smaller than the usual for hardback histories. I wondered about these things, however, and about the life and interests of a man who could devote any time at all to writing about such an idiotic subject.

I compiled the index. It was a cinch. But I couldn't get those questions to go away. This book made the rocklike façade of my professional probity start to crumble. I couldn't help it. It might have been all right still if I hadn't breached – in a serious way – the indexers' code of conduct. I corrected a mistake. The index took me two weeks to compile. It was no worse, really, than many books I had worked with – it was certainly no more stupid than *Martin Chuzzlewit*, which is complete bollocks from beginning to end. The index was as good as anything I had ever done. But for the first time, I slipped a note in when I sent my work back to the publisher.

This is what the note said. *'I see that on p. 276 of this book, the author explains that halibut, in Italian, is called "ippoglosso", a word he translates as "the language of rivers". Well, I have looked this up and it actually means "horse's tongue". Perhaps this is a common mistake. I don't know.'* I never had any acknowledgement of this from the publisher and the book came out uncorrected. But at the peak of my powers I had let two parts of my personality overlap, for the first time. That was to prove disastrous. From that moment, my downfall began.

Correcting is not what an indexer does. He does not pass judgement on what he is given. He does not rebel against the unfairness or the absurdity of what arrives through the post. He does not rejoice like a lamb in springtime when something marvellous arrives. He reduces and reports on what is there, unjudgingly. He does not mark his references to truths with * an asterisk. He does not warn the reader with a dagger † when his author has said something preposterous. He does his best with what he has been given. The moment when you start warning publishers that an American academic does not know what the Italian word for halibut literally means – the moment when you remark to a publisher that you enjoyed working on a book, that it inspired you, that your eyes rose entranced at the end of each day's labour, full of light and poetry and truth – that is the day you are done for. You might not know it at the time, but you've committed a terrible sin. Your punishment follows shortly.

My punishment was unexpected, unmistakable. It was like watching Grendel's mother rising from the Anglo-Saxon mud. About two months after submitting the Haddock index, I had a telephone call from a publisher. Not the Haddock publisher, another one. He remarked pleasantly that I'd been strongly recommended by an acquaintance of his 'in the trade'.

'Which one?' I asked, knowing the answer.

It was the Haddock one. The man had heard that my Haddock index had been an exceptionally professional piece of work and that I had delivered it on time. 'The author had no complaints to make at all,' the publisher remarked, as if that had anything to do with the matter at hand.

It seemed, he said, that I could be of use to him on a different book. Different, but involving some of the same expertise which I'd apparently displayed. The book in question – well, yes, the book in question. It was about squid. It was a historical study. It was Squid Through The Ages. In Poetry And Prose.

I accepted the assignment without letting any irritation or fear into my voice. Squid Through The Ages. What was happening here? Was I, like a wretched drunken actor, being typecast by the outside world? It was an absurd feeling, but all at once, I saw my future stretching out, indexing one popular wet-fish history after another.

I put the telephone down and stared at the wall. It was clear how this had happened. I had yielded to the temptation to comment on a book. I had let my emotions get involved. I had explained what Italians meant when they said 'halibut' in their everyday conversation. And now people thought I was interested in nothing but indexing fish.

I dispatched the Squid index with swift repulsion. I must have broken the English under-thirties record for speed indexing. I hurled the thing from me complete with the exuberant distaste of a caber-tosser discovering that his caber had been resting deep in a cowpat. For two days I trembled nervously, awaiting the next assignment. But my luck seemed to return. The next job was a life, a harmless life of Mme de Pompadour. For six months I heard nothing more of fish.

It could not last. It's best if I don't give the constant impression that there was nothing worth respecting about me. So I won't explain in detail how it came about that I was engaged, one hot afternoon in August, in making the preliminary notes for an index to a light-hearted, popular history of the social function of whelks. It was so hot, that day; I unstuck my shirt from my back; I unstuck my back from the leather chair. I might have been peering into the abyss of my future.

For two days I made no progress on the index. I sat and stared at the wall. When Janet returned from work, she asked me if I'd had a nice day, and I asked her if she'd had a nice day. Neither of us answered. I was avoiding it. She took the answer for granted. There was a sort of unfamiliar jealousy in me, towards anyone who went daily into the world. For the sake of convenience, that jealousy was directed towards my wife and her ordinary job. I saw clearly that a life spent as I spent it was a life secluded from the world. Everybody I knew, everybody I dealt with, were people very much like me, or people very much related to me. How could one put that right? How could you expose yourself to the world, like Spartan infants on the Spartan hillsides? It seemed almost impossible, the idea of inserting yourself into a life so different from your own that you would begin to understand something other than yourself, something of the world, anything but the deep grooves of your own habitual life. It did not occur to me then that you might do this by trying to understand what your own wife did, and thought, and felt; by listening to what she said. I started to believe in the possibility of finding another sort of existence altogether, almost as depressives start to believe in the possibility of suicide. On the third day, once Janet had left, I put on a pair of comfortable old shoes and went for a walk.

It was the sort of walk which men undertake every day in London – men at the end of their tether. It begins with them announcing to their wives – perhaps even to themselves – that they're just popping out for the paper. A hundred yards down the road, the full horror of their secret fear hits them. That secret fear – it could be debts. It could be bigamy. It could be your embezzling habits. It could be the cold fishy gaze of computer disk after computer disk, looking at you with a single metal eye. Yes, indeed, it could be fish. That day, I could have kept on going and the next anyone would have heard of me would have been an abandoned hired car at Beachy Head, an incompetently failed suicide. Or apparently so – well, let's finish the story – five years later, you can see how it works out – Janet on holiday in a sealed-off resort in Bali, orders a cocktail from the hotel barman who looks so strangely familiar . . . Yes, I suppose so, sooner or later you have to explain why you ran away. I wouldn't have been able to explain that.

In the end it was Janet who ran away, of course. But that day it might well have been me. I walked away from my beautiful wife's gift of a house. The sun was shining and the streets were empty. It was the sort of day which always reminds me of those happy childhood days. The days when you are ill, but not so ill that your mother can't take you shopping. The streets look different on those weekday mornings when you're not supposed to be on them. Even the high street in Bromley did. I remember that. (You can tell from this what sort of boy I was – not the sort of boy who plays truant. I will explain why when I get to it.) I might have kept on going, on a morning so festive, Wandsworth might overnight have become a seaside resort, the pier just over the gull-garlanded brow of Putney Hill.

But I got to the newsagent's shop, and went in. I had said to myself that I was just popping out for a paper and that is what I was doing. I stood in front of the rack of newspapers, and instead of simply picking up our usual newspaper, I started considering the options. Which would suit me best today? I might never have seen an

English newspaper before. I weighed them up by the look of the paper, the patterns their different types made on the page. I considered them generously, in the way you might judge an old aunt who had made herself so successfully unrecognisable with small changes of clothes and hairstyle that you had nothing more to go on than the most superficial and outward aspect of her appearance. Every single paper had completely different words and pictures from the words and pictures it had had the day before, and yet it was the same paper. I tried to puzzle this one out. Each of them seemed already old. They were all about yesterdays, they always would be. Standing there, trying to understand what I perfectly well understood, I realised that now my life must change. By now, I meant now; the next five minutes, somehow.

I bought all the newspapers, every single one, every daily newspaper. I didn't want to exercise choice. Mr Patel is the newsagent. He gave me a satisfied, Mughal sort of nod. He seemed to approve as I paid. 'Yes, I thought so,' his nod seemed to say. I had no idea that my fish-fronted breakdown was so obvious to everyone around me. Mr Patel – I liked him well enough – he noticed if I didn't go in for a couple of days, but I wouldn't have anticipated that knowing nod. Mr Patel's nod seemed to say that he had expected exactly this for some time. He had seen many breakdowns among his Wandsworth clientele. He knew that that was how they first show themselves, in irrational and helpless buying of anything or everything in sight. Maybe, one day, a man walks in and buys *What Car?*, *What Computer?*, *What Mortgage?*, *What*

Pension?, *What Hi-Fi?*, *What What Magazine?* Buys them all at once – yes, then you would see, there is a man who wants to change his life and can't find the magazine which would help him. Yes, reader, your newsagent knows. There is a terrible sort of pathos about that. The day when I reached rock bottom, the only person who knew about it was Mr Patel, who I had never said anything to but 'Turned out nice again'. He knew, because one day I went in and bought every newspaper and every headline, from the *Independent* saying GREENS' PLEDGE TO SUPPORT BOSNIAN PEACE PLAN FOUNDERS to the *Daily Star* saying JADE TAKES US UP EYE-FULL TOWER – FULL STORY AND PICS, PAGES 2 3 7 8 9 11 13. He had been waiting for some time now for exactly such a sign from me. 'I thought so,' his nod said.

(Of course, the day would come when I would look back at my rock-bottom moment in the newsagent's and give a hollow laugh. What the hell was wrong with me? I mean – it wasn't as if I had *hiccups*, was it? But that is by the by.)

I don't know why, but just as I was paying, I asked him for a black biro, a cheap one. It was just an instinct. It was a good one. 'Here you go,' he said. 'On the house.' And that is strange because Mr Patel does not do on the house. But I took it anyway, the 12p biro, and out I went with my load of flapping yesterdays. I didn't even know what I was looking for until I got outside. I turned back, and there, in the window, was a plastic holder, half full of handwritten domestic advertisements. Some of them were for mature black prostitutes and some of them were for house clearances and some of them were from people who wanted to be left alone in charge of children. These I did not look at. But there was one which I read. *Sarcastic old lady could do with company during the day, to bully and chide. No one ugly or boring, please.*

That is what it said – well, no. It's only what it ought to have said. Even at the time, I got the general gist, however, so there's no point in not improving the advert I read that morning in accordance with the known facts. I wrote down the details, and the phone number. Later, when I was safely home, I called her; I went round the same afternoon. Her name is Mrs Grainger, and we suited each other. I brought the world into her immobile existence; I tried to go on thinking that the observation of her life had pushed me out into the world, the world outside indexes. After that, there was no more talk of Beachy Head. For a year, twice a week, I would go round to Mrs Grainger's and do for her, and the other days I would index. I am going to get round to her in time. Janet had no idea. It was only the week before she left me that she found out about Mrs Grainger. It was the week after she found out that she left me, and the hiccups descended on me.

7

When I left the house the next day, the world looked fresh as a lettuce on television. Of course it did. I was looking at it with the eyes of a convalescent. I just didn't waste days in the way I had wasted the day before. I certainly didn't spend whole days getting oiled up to the uvula, whether for pleasure or in a vain attempt to cure the hiccups. It hadn't worked. I had woken up, and gazed at the ceiling sleepily for some minutes. They were such ordinary minutes, not at all the sort of minutes you might want to congratulate yourself on. But then I hiccupped brassily; once, twice, three times. It infuriated me that I hadn't remembered to enjoy the few stolen minutes before they came back. It had just seemed like the normal state of being.

I didn't waste days. So, the first thing to do was to leave the house, and do something. I didn't know what, exactly. Though I strode off with my briefcase under my arm, in a respectable grey suit and a respectable white shirt, my face as determined as Napoleon's returning from Moscow, I actually had much more to do at home. It wasn't my day for my old lady. I also had an index to be getting on with.

The road where I live is overhung with trees and buckling with their roots. In wet weather you make your way down the pavement hunchbacked or ducking, so as not to be hit in the face by the drooping branches. Every five years, a pair of yokels come along with a chainsaw and give the trees a savage GI trim, or just chop them down, to save time in the long run. (What do they do in the intervals, the chainsaw yokels? Sit around drinking tea, probably.) As I turned right out of the drive, a branch had half broken, and was hanging horizontally across the way, blocking my path. On it, there sat a single magpie. It didn't seem alarmed by me. It just beadily eyed me. I stopped and eyeballed it back. One magpie is terribly bad luck – one for sorrow, two for joy, three for a girl, four for a boy.

I put it down to sorrow. But then there was the noise of something heavily collapsing through the tree, like a wet towel falling, and all at once, the first magpie had flown off and there was a replacement magpie, imperturbably observing me. What did this mean? Was that joy or sorrow doubled? I am not superstitious in the slightest. In any case, I wasn't someone who was going to be taken in by magpies; they are just crows with a desultory makeover. I turned round and went off in the opposite direction.

The idiotic thing about the magpies was that I was pretty sure that it was not really a proper superstition at all. When I was a boy, there was a television programme called *Magpie* on the television. It was one of those programmes which try to get children to stop watching so much television and do something healthy and outdoors instead, like construct their own catapult or something. A curious sort of ambition – I mean, you don't see theatres putting on plays about what a waste of time going to the theatre is, and you'd be better off leaving at the interval and going to have dinner. It's obviously true, but telly and theatre and books, they all keep going because of the conspiracy of silence, not encouraging the feeling that the punter is wasting his time. Maybe that's true about everything; love, for instance. But this programme's theme tune was the song about magpies; sorrow, joy, girl, boy, silver, gold, secret never to be told . . . Everyone knows the sequence, but they know it from the theme music to an old television programme. I had no idea whether it was a real country belief, or if it had all been made up thirty years ago for commercial television. It would be sad to think that any aspect of your life, however tiny, was being influenced by a song written in a couple of afternoons at a London recording studio in 1971.

They had sent me in the other direction, and after a few minutes, I realised that I was automatically walking towards my sister's house. It must have been the thought of superstition that did it. My sister – the one who's still alive – is the most superstitious person I know. You could tell Sarah that it was bad luck to put a hat on a bed, or to open an umbrella indoors, or to pick up your own glove if you dropped it, and even if she had never heard of such a thing before, she would instantly change her behaviour so as not to break the taboo. Once I was walking with her in the street, and she stopped dead in her tracks. It was the high street on a Saturday morning; half a dozen people behind her cannonaded into her, but she just stood there with an impatient look on her face, gesturing with her face at the pavement. She had dropped her glove, and someone else had to pick it up for her. (You're not allowed to ask someone directly, either, it seems – she explained all this afterwards.) You could tell her anything you liked in the superstition line – 'Never wear green on Tuesdays' – and she would accept it. She had great energy, I suppose; it would, after all, keep you fit if you never let yourself tread on a crack in the pavement.

Sarah lived half a mile from me, but we weren't close in other ways. Janet didn't much like her, and I never asked myself whether I liked her or not. She lived in a flat where the only clutter was a huge pile of interior decoration magazines and her fiasco of a fiancé. 'Don't mind him,' she'd recommend when you went round. It was our house that came between us. Their flat was perfectly reasonable, but she used it to measure me, and from both directions it made me seem not very admirable. It had cost exactly two and a half times their combined salaries, and was much swankier than anything Janet and I could have stretched to. On the other hand, it was no bigger than one floor of the four-storeyed house we actually lived in, and the fact that Janet had just been given the house, and I had basically been given a house by someone I'd never met – Sarah devoted long sour hours to this. The first time she came round, she went over the house minutely, like a bailiff, finally taking some comfort in the sympathetic reflection that it would be improved by what we could not afford, like a decent picture or two. I didn't blame her. It was deplorable that we lived in such a house.

It wasn't until my sister opened the door to her flat that I remembered that she wouldn't be at home. But then of course she was at home. It was a Friday, when to the best of my knowledge marketing executives like my sister are generally marketinging away in their offices. I was about to comment on this, but she beat me to it.

'You're late,' she said. 'I thought I said ten thirty.'

She turned unwelcomingly, and slumped back into her flat.

'That's right,' I said. '! I'm sorry. Someone phoned just as I was leaving.'

I meant most of this. When my sister opened the door, I had no idea that I had been supposed to come round at all. As soon as she said 'You're late', I had a conviction, if not a memory, that she was right. She usually was. I had forgotten agreeing to come round, but had come round anyway on what I thought was a whim. I followed her.

'Is that hiccups you've got?' Sarah said.

'Yes,' I said as I sat down in a chair. 'They won't go away. ! They started yesterday.'

'They can't have started yesterday,' she said accusingly. 'They'd have stopped when you went to sleep.'

'They didn't,' I said. 'I went to sleep and they were still there when I woke up.'

'That's ridiculous,' she said.

I wondered now what I was there for. Dogs, they say, can always tell when a journey or a holiday is imminent; they get agitated and nervous even before their owners start packing the suitcases. Like them, I could smell some kind of upheaval in the air. My sister has always been a tidy woman – I have an early memory of her organising her stuffed animals in order of size. It can't be accurate, but I have the distinct idea that her infant brother was the largest one, and placed firmly at the far right. Now, though her flat was as bare and tidy as ever, her appearance was unfamiliar and even mildly slutty. At eleven in the morning, she was still in a black Japanese dressing gown, and her hair was apparently under some process of construction, piled up lumpily, curling around amputated foam fingers, pink and purple and green, dotted with foil strips like an ice-cream sundae. Her face was covered with some sort of thick browny cream like the patsy in the custard-pie joke; her fingers, which she was spreading out witchily as if about to pounce, ended in just-painted nails. She looked a sight, and seemed to me to be preparing to be disagreeable.

'It wouldn't occur to you to drink a glass of water backwards, I suppose, like normal people?' she said.

'I tried,' I said. 'It didn't work.'

'Of course, the thing which does work –' she said, but then, as she was speaking, all at once, I remembered exactly why I was supposed to come round here. It wasn't, as I had been wondering, that in the course of my drunkenness I had invited myself round to tell her that Janet had left me. That hadn't crossed my mind. The reason I was here was that my sister and her boyfriend were getting married the next day. I had completely forgotten when it was.

'– the thing which does work is smoking a cigarette,' she said. 'You don't smoke, do you, though?'

'No, I don't smoke,' I said.

She fanned her hands around impatiently.

'How's it going?' I asked.

'Oh, God,' she said. That seemed to cover it. She went blank for a moment, before remembering that she had some instructions for me. As she spoke, her two unbodied eyes gazed into the middle distance from her savage mask of mud like a patiently hunting animal. She might have been reciting from a prepared script – Things to say to John the day before – and probably was. 'Listen, I just wanted to say – we both wanted to say, only he's out dealing with the florist – I only wanted to say that you mustn't feel left out because you don't have anything to do tomorrow. I mean, it's nothing personal, only I know, everyone else, Mummy and Daddy, everyone, they've been involved and they'll have things to do tomorrow, and I worried that you thought we were leaving you out, because, you know, you're not even an usher, not that we're having ushers. And he would have had you as his best man but. Well, let's not go into that.'

'Well, it's nice of you. !' I said. 'I don't mind being left out, though. Not that I am being left out.'

I had thrown her now. Her lips gummily retraced her lines *had you as his best man* before going on. 'But you

really are an important part of all this, and I want you to
do an important thing for us tomorrow. I want you to play
a very important role.'

'What?' I said. It was true that, as far as I knew,
weddings, whether in registry offices or in churches, had
established no very clear role for the brother of the bride.
I had hoped to get away with loitering.

'I want you to keep an eye out. You know what I mean
– I mean, I love everyone who's coming, or I wouldn't
ask them, but I think if I saw Mr Tredinnick or even
Daddy going over to talk to Clarissa, my boss's wife – I
told you, my boss is coming, and he's bringing his wife,
too. I just want you to do something if you see anything
like that, anyone embarrassing making an embarrassment
of themselves. I really want you to be a part of this, you
know that.'

I left it. My sister was a maker of lists, a holder of
grudges, a self-improver. She was so snobbish, she looked
down not only on her fiancé, her family, her surroundings, but even on herself. Her lists were all for the future,
of things to do. If, on the other hand, you make a
different sort of list, of her past, you could map her
dissatisfied history. The list – there would have been
many – would have gone like this: Mummy, Daddy, Dad,
Mum, Father, Mother, Pop, Mom, Ma, Pa, Papa, Pappa,
Fa, Ma. You could list the different words she'd tried
out and discarded, in the course of her life, for the most
ordinary things. She took the words up when she heard
they were the thing to say. She dropped them when she
heard a hint that they might be low or vulgar.

Did she trust or mistrust the world? The way she looked at it, sideways, assessingly, was full of mistrust. But then she openly believed whatever she was told. She let her life be shaped by the beliefs of acquaintances, by comments she overheard at parties. You could tell her that it was bad luck to see three nuns together, or that it was vulgar to pronounce the h in 'honey', and she would believe you. If, reader, a man like you took her tiny hand in your great paw and said with your eyes swimming that you loved her, her gaze would narrow suspiciously. She wasn't going to be made a fool of by love. Only by umbrellas, gloves, ladders, broken mirrors, black cats and the word 'pardon'.

Like a lot of people her age, she had seen *Brideshead Revisited* on the telly and was never the same afterwards. If you asked her, she would say she had grown up not in Bromley, but in Kent. (Of course Bromley is in Kent, I know that. But growing up in Bromley is not the same thing as growing up in Kent. Orchards don't come into childhoods like ours, for one thing.) She had taught herself to say 'sofa', 'lavatory', 'what', 'drawing room' and said them even to us. Perhaps she was trying to teach us to say them, too. We couldn't get the hang of it, somehow. We just looked at this prodigy in awe. It seemed wasted energy to me. I could see perfectly well that you might go out to dinner with twelve daughters of dukes, you could spend the whole evening explaining that you enjoyed nothing better than putting your *bag* on the *sofa* under the *looking glass* before going to the *loo* after *pudding* and all would be well. But then right at the end, if you slipped and said, 'Thanks ever so much for having me to a lovely meal,' they would all start chanting, 'Prole from Bromley, Prole from Bromley,' and the pretence would be over.

Mummy, Daddy, Dad, Mum, Father, Mother, Pop, Mom, Ma, Pa, Papa, Pappa, Fa, Ma. She had called our parents all these things with various degrees of sincerity or irony. Now we seemed to be back to –

'Mummy said to me –' she said.

'Who?'

'Mummy!'

– back apparently to Mummy again. It made an odd list.

'– she said the oddest thing to me. I said that we would start trying for a baby as soon as we were married. And she said something so odd. She said, "If you wanted one, you should have started straight away. No point in hanging about for what you want, hanging about for –" these were her exact words – "for a bit of paper." So I said, I have no intention, thank you, of going up the aisle six months pregnant. But she meant have the baby first, and then get married. Well, you can imagine –'

'Was it – ! – just the two of you talking?'

'Yes, it was. We went over last Sunday, and Daddy had taken Richard and Mr Tredinnick off into the shed. They'd have stared, I can tell you. Well, no one could call me a *conventional* sort of person, but I did point out, I can assure you, that the usual way of arranging these things is marriage first, babies afterwards.'

'What did she say to that?' I said cosily.

'She didn't say anything for a moment. She just sat there with her mouth open. You know how she does when she's thinking. Then she said the oddest thing. "Babies are important. Weddings aren't so important." Then she said, "Look at John."'

'Look at me?'

'Yes, look at you. I was completely lost by now, not the foggiest, and sort of said, "What?" But then Daddy and Richard and Mr Tredinnick came back, so –'

'Look at John?' I said.

My sister softened. It is a hard thing to describe, but she did it. Her eyes in their waste of mud took on an anxious look, her shoulders loosened as if she were about to give me her comforting hand. It was the first movement of an orthopaedic patient when the heavy cast is first removed from his soft shattered arm. I felt, as always, that she didn't care for these intervals and movements of vulnerable tenderness in herself. She'd rather have seemed perfect and judicious for every one of her waking hours, and most of her sleeping ones too. She didn't seem to appreciate that it was these stretches of failure in terms of her ambitions for herself that made most people like her. They did like her. I liked her myself. She believed that if only she could turn herself into glass, and the world could look through and see that she had no heart, not even the heart of a bug – then and only then would she have triumphed. She never understood that the cheerleader the crowd likes best is the one who drops her pompoms and giggles.

'Do you think she wants them?' I said. '! Grandchildren, I mean?'

'Who, Mummy?' she said. 'Are you *joking*???' She made an incredulous rolling movement with her eyes and, forgetting the face pack, smacked her forehead with the palm of her hand. 'Fuck –' with her fingers out for the wet nail polish, she had got the face pack all over her hand. She made the expressive gestures of a foreign conductor in a heart-rending slow passage. 'Fuck,' she said again, before hopelessly wiping her hand on her dressing gown. 'Does she want grandchildren? John, you haven't watched her. It happens to old ladies. They get broody. You go for a walk with her, anywhere, and watch what she does. She can't help it. She sees a baby coming in a pram, and she wants it. Last week I was with her, walking down the street. I was talking about the wedding, and then all at once, she'd disappeared and left me talking to myself. Do you know what she'd done? She'd seen a girl with a pram on the other side of the street and she'd crossed over – she didn't say anything – she'd gone straight through the traffic to have a look at a baby. Yes, she wants grandchildren.'

'Do you want – ! – children, then?' I said.

She looked at me. It was a strange look; even without the mud from which her eyes started, it would have been strange. 'I've got to clean this stuff off,' she said, getting up. 'Amuse yourself.'

It was hard to amuse yourself in my sister's flat. It was so terribly tidy, and in the middle of it, today, a ruined human pile of mud and plastering, my sister; she had turned herself into a squatter for a day. She and her husband-to-be kept no books in her sitting room – there was a shelf of impossible cookbooks in the kitchen, and a random shelf or two in the bedroom, but that, I think, was that. I suspect she threw books away when she had finished reading them; they were things for her holidays, things she bought at the airport on the way out, and left wherever she happened to stop needing them. Like sun oil, or insurance. I could have switched the television on, but it was still before noon, and there would be nothing on for anyone who didn't lead a life of quiet desperation. The hi-fi system was magnificent, and the rack holding the CDs was a magnificent piece of chrome design, but half empty. Mr Tredinnick, our parents' best friend, believed on the basis of the hi-fi and the CD rack that the two of them were interested in music, and routinely gave them records for Christmas and, if he remembered, birthdays; their collection was half made up of such do-nations, and not tempting. There were no invitations on the mantelpiece, even, to read. I satisfied myself by removing a couple of wilting tulips from the vase on the coffee table, and shuffling the remainder around a little. That was the best you could do in the amusement line, in my sister's sitting room. I was just wondering what to do with these two tulips – they were hardly dead, only just wilting, and there was no bin in the room in any case – when I heard my sister coming back. I stuffed them into the pocket of my jacket.

Her face was stripped, and the foam fingers and strips of foil which had held her hair up discarded; the wet strands hung over her forehead. She looked, if anything, less familiar; her skin was red and raw and wrong.

'I'm interested in what you said,' she said. It was

apparent that she had been working herself back to prepared conversation while rinsing all her gunk off.

'Why are you doing all this stuff today?' I said.

'All what stuff?'

'The mud and the hair stuff,' I said. 'It's tomorrow, isn't it?'

'You do it in advance,' she said. 'Then it'll be OK by the day. I've got the make-up lady to go to tomorrow and the hairdresser, tomorrow morning, it's all booked. Don't you worry yourself.'

'But the nails.'

'They look best with a series of coats. This is the fourth coat this week I've given them. Don't interfere with what you don't understand. No, I was thinking, it's interesting, what you said.'

'What did I say?'

'About the children.'

'What children?'

'What you said was "Don't you want any children yourself?" What you didn't say is "Don't you want any nephews and nieces?" And I think that's quite interesting.'

'I don't understand.'

She went over to the vase of flowers. With shame, I felt the damp crushed tulips leaking into my pockets. But even my sister did not know exactly how many tulips she had in a vase.

'We were talking about Mummy wanting grandchildren. If you have children, that counts as grandchildren, too, doesn't it?'

'I suppose so.'

'But you just assume it's up to me to have the children.'

'I suppose I do.'

She looked at me firmly. She looked as if she wanted to make some cutting, dismissive, non-verbal sort of noise – 'Durr!' But of course she didn't. I didn't know what she meant at all.

'Janet's terribly ill,' I said, to change the subject. 'I hope she's going to be able to come to your wedding tomorrow. I don't know if she will be able to.'

'Of course she'll come,' she said confidently. 'It's my wedding. It's not going to be like your wedding. Everyone's going to come.'

'If you say so,' I said. It was very odd, but at this moment I didn't feel like telling my sister that Janet had left me. To put a good face on it, you could say that I didn't want to spoil her big day with my worries. But that wouldn't be true. She wouldn't have been deeply concerned. I wasn't worried about it, or indeed very interested. It was simply that I didn't feel like explaining anything very much to anyone.

Silence seemed to fall between us. Something more was expected of me. I realised that she had asked me round this morning not just to give me my instructions about keeping the embarrassing guests apart from the non-embarrassing ones. She wanted to give me the opportunity to say something deep and conventional, something family. I could not think what this could be. In the end I did my best.

'I wish Franky could have been here for your wedding,' I said.

She stared at me. 'You always spoil everything,' she said. 'I don't know why you always have to say something horrible. I wish you'd go away now.'

I went away. As I went down the stairs of the block of flats, down the Wandsworth streets towards my house, the tulips mulched in my compost pocket. It was quite a pleasant sensation.

Pink Suit Four

It was late in the afternoon, one day before the hiccups. It was not my day for Mrs Grainger, and, as indexers say, I was between indexes; I had had nothing to do, and by the late afternoon, I had subsided warmly on to the sofa, like a collapsing soufflé. At some point, I must have turned the television on; at another point, I must have fallen asleep; and I woke up hearing the noise of the key in the front door in my dream, and it was a real noise, one I always liked, until recently. The television was full of a cartoon for children, of horrible flesh-armoured beings destroying each other; I reached for the remote control, digging into my back, and stubbed the television's rudimentary spectacle out. Janet came in, gave me a glance, and carried on into the kitchen.

'You're early, aren't you?' I said. 'What time is it?'

She didn't reply; the tap was running and my voice was hoarse from sleep.

'It's children's television time,' I answered myself, and looked at my watch; I had been sleeping on my arm, and my numb wrist was engraved with deep red angry lines from the upholstery. 'It's not five,' I said, getting up and following her into the kitchen. 'You're home early.'

Janet was drinking a glass of water; it was one of her things, how much water you needed to drink a day, and she rarely entered anywhere without immediately fetching a deep glass of tap water. 'Yes,' she said, finally, putting it down but not turning round. 'I'm home early.'

I picked up a glass and the plate which I'd eaten my lunch off, still on the kitchen table; I usually had such things washed by the time she came home. 'Nothing wrong?' I said. 'You're not ill or anything?'

'No,' she said. 'No, I just came home a bit early.'

'You never come home early,' I said.

'Today, I've come home early,' she said.

There seemed nothing more to say about it; there was something harsh and tensed in her voice. I put the plate and glass down again, and turned as if to go back into the sitting room. Something hurled past me, just missing my head, thumping down on the old blue armchair we kept in the corner of the kitchen, failing to smash. Someone – Janet – had thrown a heavy glass at me, meaning it to smash violently, and perhaps to smash against the back of my head. I turned incredulously, and there was Janet; not with a look of rage on her face, but a horrible wide unmeaning smile; she grotesquely curt-sied, and then, her hands fluttering, twirled round like a small girl showing off.

'Janet, Christ,' I said.

'Look, darling,' she said. 'Don't you notice anything special?'

'Anything special?' I said, cowering a little at this new wife of mine; all at once I seemed to have been thrown into a cartoon, a sitcom world, where husbands forgot anniversaries and birthdays, where they failed to notice their wives' new hairdos, new outfits, new lovers . . . 'You're wearing your pink suit,' I said eventually.

'Yes,' she said. 'Yes, I'm wearing my pink suit.'

'You don't often wear it,' I said.

'No,' she said. 'I've worn it four times, including today.'

'You can still get into it,' I said.

'Of course I can get into it,' she said. 'Are you saying I've put on weight?'

'I didn't notice when you put it on this morning,' I said.

'Between the moment I woke up and the moment I left the house this morning,' she said, 'you didn't look at me or speak to me. So, no, you didn't.'

'That can't be true,' I said. She shrugged. 'You ought to wear it more often,' I said. 'It suits you.'

'So everyone said,' Janet said. 'All day at the office, everyone kept saying, "Gosh, you look nice in that."'

'Well, you do,' I said.

'Well, now I'm going to take it off again,' Janet said. She walked past me, and went upstairs. I picked the glass up from where it lay, unbroken, on the cushion of the chair. I remembered that pink suit, buying it. I don't know why I hadn't seen it that day. It was the day before I woke up and found that she had gone. Or perhaps the day before that. It's hard to be sure.

9

By mid-afternoon, things had clearly got out of hand. I was sitting, cross-legged, in a heap of clothes. They were on the bed in our bedroom. The wardrobe doors were swinging loose and open. Inside, the shelves and rails had been stripped bare in my hunt, and shone at me like scavenged bones. The chest of drawers, too – that had been opened up and emptied. The heap of clothes on the bed; me, like a pasha, on top of them all, rooting. The clothes were all my wife's.

Somewhere at the bottom of this pile were the contents of the filing cabinet where she kept any papers which might prove important. That search had yielded nothing, though it had taken two hours. Nothing but the papers I would have known about. That was no good. I was rooting, excavating, through my wife's life as I turned out her pockets and her cabinets, but I didn't know exactly what I was looking for. Her scrimped-for, saved-up, best-treat, cared-for wardrobe had gone through my jealous fumbling hands. I hadn't understood that I had been jealous. If you had asked me before lunch how I felt about my wife having left me, I would have said that I was absorbing the fact steadily. I would have said that, thinking that I was being honest.

I would have been wrong. I had, after all, been walking round the fact incredulously, not knowing how to start in on it. In the morning, you can walk down a leafy suburban street, with a song in your heart and hiccups in your gut, with no sorrow bigger than a single magpie. You've managed to tell yourself that you are dealing with the idea that your wife has left you. And by the afternoon, you are a wreck, sitting on a pile of your wife's clothes, going through her pockets, not knowing what you are trying to find, not exactly. It is a sort of metamorphosis. This – I had discovered – is what the magician does to work such a transformation. She says to you, over the telephone, from a great distance, this sentence: 'Go and look in your wardrobe. You'll find the reason in there.'

Once I saw a film, a private home movie from the 1960s, of a celebrity house party. It was made to amuse a few glamorous people, but it involved two famous figures. So in the end it was on television and even I got to see it. There is a Chinese screen on a country-house lawn somewhere in England. The actor Peter Sellers walks into shot, rubbing his hands ingratiatingly, and says in an old-fashioned music-hall voice, 'Ladies and gentlemen. I will now perform my world-famous Princess Margaret impersonation. Quiet, if you please.' He dashes behind the screen, to Ealing-comedy chase music; a lot of clothes are flung in the air; and then from the other side emerges an immaculate Princess Margaret, graciously smiling and waving. It really is her.

But what I thought was this: what had happened to the man who went behind the screen? What was left of him? What remains, after a man has been violently transformed into Princess Margaret?

I bought clothes swiftly, alone, knowing exactly what I wanted. Janet had bought these clothes slowly, uncertainly, and always asking for advice and a second opinion. She had gone round shops before Christmas, making notes, so as to have a good idea of what might be in the sales. She knew which shops lowered prices a day or two before the sale officially began. She took care of her clothes, as I did; she knew what suited her, and, realistically, what fitted her; and yet she was always looking for something new, something different. She was not a woman for whom a dress size was an item of faith; a rare virtue. They were kept in clear zipped bags, between layers of tissue, with mothballs. I had taken them all out, and crumpled them up. They should have reproached me for it, but they didn't. Boss, the servile cheeky jackets hailed me; Next, they usefully suggested when I had finished with each of them; Principles, they reminded me when I seemed to be flagging. I was finding nothing; zilch, zip, nada, Prada.

In the ruin of Janet's wardrobe I looked for confirmation. There must be something somewhere to be found. She thought I had found it. Now I had to find it, to understand what I was jealous about; what I had to be jealous about.

10

Four hours earlier. When I had picked up the phone, back at home, Janet's voice had taken me by surprise.

'Where are you?' I said, for something to say.

'Why?'

'I just wondered,' I said.

'What does it matter?'

'Well, you don't have to tell me if you don't want,' I said. 'But I don't know why you wouldn't want to tell me. !'

'What's that noise?'

'What noise?'

'Like you dropped –'

'!'

'– something. That noise.'

'It's just the hiccups.'

'You had the hiccups last time I called. You've got them again?'

'They never went away. I can't seem to get shot of them.'

There was a sort of reversing noise at the end of the phone, an actress's sigh designed to be heard at the back of the stalls, a sigh an absconding wife would send halfway across Europe.

'You really are hopeless,' she said.

'I've tried everything,' I said.

'Have you been to the doctor?' she said.

'I'd feel a fool,' I said. 'Do you think people go to the doctor with the hiccups?'

'You *are* a fool,' she said. She couldn't help it, the affection; she'd slipped into it, and corrected herself. 'You. Are a *fool*.' She made that reversing noise again. For a moment there was nothing but crackle and impatience between us, and the nations of Europe, wherever she was. 'I don't know why, but you're really annoying me now. I'm going to put the phone down. Goodbye.'

'Go on, then, hang up. Goodbye,' I said, untroubled.

It is so curious, the way we don't say what we mean and the way we can't be truthful. My wife was on her mobile phone. Probably for years and years to come, people are still going to say 'I'm going to hang up' or 'I'm going to put the phone down now' rather than 'I'm going to press the off button now.' Put two small boys in a room with a bad smell, and watch them; they will peg their noses and pull an imaginary chain. Have they ever seen a lavatory with a chain to tug? Go on, say something; listen to yourself lying. So of course I knew that Janet didn't mean what she was saying. She hadn't finished with me at all. People all over the world, when they say these things, when they say 'You're really annoying me, I'm going to ring off', they mean the same thing. They mean that when they phoned, they were about to tell you what you needed to know. The plan was that in five minutes they'd be saying 'Seventhly', and you'd be putty in their hands.

Infuriatingly, Janet had found herself giving me advice about hiccups. This, as I say, happens to people all over the world; or perhaps mainly to my wife. I wouldn't really know. But it was quite plain to me that she hadn't finished with me. I was in the kitchen at the time, two glasses into another bottle of champagne. (It wasn't working, either, but it had its consolations.) I sat and watched the telephone on the wall as a zoo-bred seal watches a fondly dangled herring at the canapé hour. It took seven minutes, and then it rang.

'Look,' Janet said. 'It doesn't matter where I am, but if I tell you where I am, I'm just telling you where I am, you know what I mean? You're not to get on a plane and come and find me, that's all I'm saying.'

'No, I wasn't going to do that,' I said. It hadn't occurred to me. 'It hadn't occurred to me,' I said.

'No romantic gestures, OK?' she said.

'I don't know if I could run to all that chocolate,' I said. (I won't explain. It was just a joke that we had between us for as long as we could remember. I don't know what it was about or who first said it or why it was funny in the first place. But about once a week one of us said to the other, 'I don't know if I could run to all that chocolate.' That's what marriage is like, or what ours was like; a joke not worth explaining to anyone else. It just slipped out. I wasn't trying to break her heart or anything.)

'Oh, you,' Janet said.

'Double you,' I said, optimistically.

'Ex,' she reminded me.

'Why?' I wondered.

'Zed,' she concluded. 'Anyway, by the time you got here, I'd have gone on somewhere else, so you'd be wasting your time.'

'Ooh, no,' I said. 'Mustn't be wasting our times, can't be doing with a waste of time.'

'Tell me about it,' she said, not accusingly, but still with that fond private music in her voice; I could see her face, her eyes, the opening smile I used to like so much to see on her waking face on the pillow, shining out at the morning. 'OK, I'm in Budapest.'

'Is it nice?'

'Do you remember that time –'

'What time?'

'That time we went to that Hungarian restaurant that looked like a railway carriage with all that red velvet on the walls?'

'It was my birthday. In Soho.'

'And you had a pile of goose.'

'Oh, that restaurant.'

'Well, it's not much like that.'

'But is it nice?' I said.

'Oh, it's nice enough,' she said, impatient again, as if I were missing the point. I might have asked a terminal cancer patient if the wallpaper in the room at the hospice was nice. 'Don't you think we need to talk?'

'Where are you going next?'

'Seriously?'

'OK, I promise, I won't go there either. I just wondered.'

'There really wouldn't be any point, you know – oh, all right, Istanbul. Look, I'm recharging the battery on the phone when I can, so you might not necessarily –'

'Istanbul?'

'What is this? Don't you think – listen, words of one syllable – we need, OK, we need to talk.'

'OK.'

She meant she needed to talk. She began. I listened. It was no hardship. I always listened to Janet. That was what she most meant to me, the thing I first noticed about her. Or maybe the thing I noticed she did to me. Perhaps that. It was special. She was the woman I would listen to whatever she was saying. She could talk nonsense, she could say nothing in particular, she could repeat herself, tell the same story I'd heard twenty times, she could be embarrassing or silly or unfunny. Everyone is the same. Sometimes they talk sense, sometimes they don't. I wasn't so besotted with her not to see this. Everyone I had ever met had sometimes been interesting when they talked and sometimes boring, wrong and silly; when I talked, this was true of me, too. The thing about Janet which was so different was that I listened to her.

I had noticed this the first time we met. The listening had never gone away. My whole life, it had been as if I had been meeting nobody but geography teachers, and paying attention or not paying attention when they talked to me. They could be saying something new or something

predictable, it didn't matter. That was true about everyone
– my mother, father, sister, Franky, indexers, everyone.
Sometimes I heard them being shockingly dull; sometimes
they started to dredge up something painful, and, afterwards, I had no idea what they had found so hard to
confide. If my father, one Sunday afternoon, had told me
that he'd been sucking off the postman for the last twenty
years, I would have been perfectly capable of zoning out.
Surely conversation was always like that. I had been under
the impression that existence was one long afternoon of
geography revision. If I had imagined my marriage, I
would have envisaged a fat woman talking, and me saying
'Yes, dear' from time to time, and all the while, my mind
delving absently through the floral covers like a mole
through clover. The only thing I always invariably heard
was when people told me that they loved me. Sometimes
that was all I heard. But Janet interested me. She always
had. I listened to her now.

She roamed around, trying to find some reason for
what had happened, for what she had done. She didn't
know either, it seemed. She wanted to explain what she
didn't understand, why she'd gone, and quickly,
inevitably, she went on to why she'd come in the first
place. I couldn't help her; I couldn't explain why we
had got married. It wasn't something we had ever
discussed. Naturally, we'd got married. (I could have
pointed out that if either of you sees the alternative, you
probably ought to take that alternative. Of course we
were going to get married. The idea of anything else
would have been grotesque. Of course we were going

to get married. But I couldn't tell you why. It never needed discussing.)

She went on talking, and it embarrassed me a little. I'd seen the movies. To be honest, I'd probably seen more movies on the relevant subject than Janet had, since no one notices if an indexer, working at home, skives off for an hour or two and watches a crummy old movie in the afternoon. The thing I know, which Janet probably didn't, is what a wife, such as Janet, says to a husband, such as me, John, in this conversation. I listened with keen anticipation. Janet was a good girl. She followed the dialogue exactly.

'You must have seen,' she said.

'We just don't seem to be able to get through to each other,' she said.

'It's not you,' she said.

'I can't explain, not exactly.'

'It's not that I don't love you any more, you mustn't think that.'

Even when women are telling the truth, they talk like that. Not just in these circumstances, not just in the movies. It was terribly interesting. They talk about general feelings, they circle and sketch, they invoke abstractions. Their tragedies are gossip and hint. Men want to fix an engine; women want to be Mrs Siddons, sacrificing to the faceless Sybils. I am an indexer; my wife, as she talked, could not be boiled down, could not be indexed.

There was something helpless about these abstractions; something despairing about the way she went from one thing to another, not being able to explain, invoking just a feeling she had, citing looks and shrugs and tones of voice as if they were evidence. I listened for a while, and then helped her out.

'It's Mrs Grainger, isn't it?' I said.

'No, not just that –' she said. 'But I just thought – I mean, when I saw – no, it's more than that –' She meant yes.

This is what happened.

It was two weeks before, on a Saturday morning. Janet had gone downstairs to put the coffee on. Me, I was lazing in bed, scratching my balls like a cartoon husband. It is so nice, that marriage moment. The gormless stiffy you have, that warm farty wallowing on an idle morning, your chin rustling at the clean pillow, the cunty smell on your fingers, the smell, like burnt umber, of the coffee slowly Bistoing its way into your yawning stupor, and you knowing that you might fuck your wife or you might not get round to it, but you are definitely going to go to Sainsbury's sometime today. Triff. The letter box clattered – another cheerful sound to hear, confirming that the postman is up and about on his whistling rounds and someone, if only the gas company, has been thinking about you. I could hear Janet going to pick up the mail with her brisk padding tread, and then going back to the kitchen much more slowly. She was reading something, you could tell.

As it turned out it was a postcard from Mrs Grainger. Something quite trivial. She was merely writing to ask if I could 'do another "day"' that week. 'I have my "ladies" coming round on Wednesday. So sorry to spring this on you.' It had never occurred to me to tell her not to write or telephone. She simply never had. I turned up when I was supposed to, twice a week, and any change in her beetle-like, trundling routine was heralded many weeks or months in advance (that year, she'd gone to Salzburg for a week in August, and the arrangements had been firmed up in time for Thanksgiving the year before; Mountbatten had given less notice for the partitioning of India). There was never any need for her to talk to me outside my 'hours'. I hadn't seen this situation arising – not that I'd seen my days at Mrs Grainger's as secret, exactly. They were just a part of my life which Janet didn't know about. I mean, she didn't know that I watched terrible old movies about unhappy marriages in the afternoon. Of course, you don't say to your wife, 'I'll inform you about matters on a need-to-know basis,' but that is what it's like.

Janet certainly didn't know that for something over a year, her husband had been visiting an old lady twice a week, doing housework in her tasselled and fringed velvet and satin, pink and gilt and plush home; she had no idea, for instance, that I spent hours reading anything disgraceful or salacious from the *Daily Telegraph* out loud to her; phoning up tradesmen and (a favourite treat, this one, with Mrs Grainger) going along with her to John Lewis to return kitchen gadgets to 'Johnny Lew-Lew', as she called the department store, and standing there with a frown, for moral support.

None of this had seemed worth mentioning to Janet. Only when she was standing there at the end of the bed did I see how peculiar it might seem to her. The post-card (Labrador puppies) was in her hand, her face was crumpled with sleep and concern. Who, she was asking, with pain and concern, was Catherine Grainger, exactly?

I explained. I don't know why, but it did seem to me, as I talked, as if I had had a secret, and had shamefully kept it from Janet. I couldn't see how to put it any other way. At the end, Janet asked me if I really expected her to believe that. I was surprised. There was no particular reason why she should not believe what I said, and I said so. Janet raised the possibility that Mrs Grainger was, in reality, my tart, as she called her. I told her that she must be joking. She had not yet seen Mrs Grainger, of course, so I can't blame her for then saying that she was glad that one person in this room thought it was so fucking funny. On this point I stick to my guns. It was so fucking funny. If you were casting the role of a tart of mine in the movie of my life, you would not consider Mrs Grainger for very long. She would lack a certain necessary verisimilitude and plausibility.

The conversation went on for a while between two fixed positions, like a rally between two indefinitely fit lesbians at Wimbledon. After an hour or so, Janet got dressed and went out. 'I'm going out,' she said. When she returned, I was still in bed. She'd gone round to confront Mrs Grainger, to see her husband's tart with her own eyes. What she had seen was Mrs Grainger. She came back in baffled. The story made no sense, but it was true. She sat on the edge of the bed, in her best shoes and a suit – not a weekend suit, a banking suit, a suit to confront harlots in – and eyed me. I smiled, shrugged, did my best. She said nothing for a while; then, her voice almost breaking, as if with grief, with despair, she said what she would have said of a real scarlet harlot. 'How long has this been going on, exactly?' she said. I told her. She raised her hands; she raised her eyebrows; she slumped her shoulders. I had had to make my own coffee; I finished the cup in two long gulps, and smiled shyly.

That would do as well as anything to analyse over the phone. Certainly, it was only a couple of weeks after that odd morning that Janet disappeared and the hiccups turned up. It must have been pretty odd for Mrs Grainger, too. 'She wanted to know if I had any daughters,' Mrs Grainger said in her rasping voice when I turned up as arranged, the Tuesday after. 'I said I didn't. Well, I don't. I don't know whether I said the right thing. So that's your wife, then.' 'Yes,' I said. 'That's my wife.'

Janet, distant in Budapest, pondered this for a moment. 'Yes,' she said. 'Perhaps it is that. Normally, I'd say that was a small thing, it's stupid, forget it. But, you know, my God, everything else – yes, maybe that was the thing which makes you think, Christ, things are going wrong around here. You seem so strange these days.'

'Lots of people have two jobs,' I said.

'But a year you don't mention it, that is not lots of people, that is not normal, do you see the point? I'm not talking about your old lady, and let's be open, let's stop pretending, because we both know perfectly well what we're talking about when we're not talking about anything and avoiding the subject and going on like this, you not talking to me, you switching off.'

'Look,' I said. 'I still just have no idea why you should want to leave me. I just don't understand. Give me the reason. There must be a reason, surely.'

'All right,' she said. 'I'll give you the reason. Go and look at your wardrobe. The reason I left you, you'll find it there. Just you go and look at it. All right?'

'There's something in the wardrobe?' I said. 'You're telling me to go and look in the wardrobe?'

'That's just –' she said. 'If you can't – well, sorry, I've got to go now, the battery's low.'

The telephone clicked.

Up till then, I hadn't been jealous or anxious. At least, I hadn't thought so. But quite abruptly, I found I cared. My wife had shown me what reasons there might be. There might be directions and motives beneath what had seemed an instinctive and unshaped sequence of events, my life. More than that, she had flattered me by supposing that I had reasons to act as I did. My rudderless, absent, undirected benevolence had a cause, she had assumed; she believed that I brooded over intentions and plans like a murderer in Shakespeare. I wouldn't have thought this likely to be true. But perhaps I had been wrong. A sort of advanced clinical paranoia started to grip me as I sat there in the kitchen with my fourth glass of champagne, gazing at the silent telephone. The possibility that everything in my life was mysteriously connected in a sinister, beavering way seemed very real. Until that moment, there had been nothing planned, no conspiracy; no cause or effect; no consequences; no inevitable series of acts and responses; no control. My life had been a series of visitations and annunciations, and neither I nor anyone else had had any power over them. My life had been the sort of life which could have been lived in either direction, forwards or backwards. Sometimes a stranger arrived unannounced in your garden, and then went away again. There was no plan and no direction, and I was happy with that. A telephone call had shown how wrong I had been. My wife had left me because of something in the wardrobe. She had left me a clue, somewhere in her wardrobe, which would explain why she had run away. It seemed cowardly to me, being unable to tell me directly. The bottle was nearer empty than full, but there was too much in it for a single glass. I upturned it, glugging it down, two, three gulps. There were things to do. As I ran upstairs to the locked filing cabinet we kept by the wardrobe, a cabinet I knew to be full of papers, my drunken heart was pumping.

In the end it was there. I found it late that night. The house by then was destroyed, every one of the cupboards emptied, every object in the house lying in rude piles on the floor. She meant me to find it; she had wanted me to look for it first, destroying what was mine in the search. I sat and looked at the piece of paper. I read it over and over. It was a telephone number, no more than that. There was no name attached. It had been in one of her pockets, exactly where she would keep it to conceal it from me. I knew exactly whose telephone number it must be. It must be Gareth's.

Gareth? I thought. Gareth – ah, yes – the man who

paid for the house, who I'd never met. Gareth??? I shoutily thought. I was supposed to have found something – what, a note, a letter, a used condom filled to the brim with banker-flavoured spunk? Seven hundred and sixty-three thousand pounds a year, I thought, and that was years ago; Christ knows how much money he had accumulated in the years since Janet left him, years of pining and promotion. His bank account must be bulging and aching for a big spend, freighted and groaning like his unspent testicles.

From time to time I telephoned the number of her mobile phone. It was switched off, somewhere between Budapest and Istanbul. At two in the morning, I gave up trying. For hours I had been listening to the same voice. It was a man's voice, a recording from the telephone company under whose skies my wife was speeding like a bullet, speeding further and further away from me and my tears. The voice, it was telling me over and over again in Hungarian that this number was currently unavailable. I think it was Hungarian. I didn't understand the words, but you understand when a machine tells you that your wife is running away from you, that she is not there; that there is no knowing when her voice is next going to be there for you. You understand this, even when the message comes in one of the Finno-Ugric languages. Trust me on this one.

11

Franky had been dead now for seventeen years, and she was seventeen when she died. She died on a Friday night, with the whole weekend before her. She left the house at half past eight, and never came back. She was wearing clothes which she had bought that day. A friend of hers, a girl, called for her, and they went to the Anchor, not far from my parents' house. It is an old pub, which is still just as it was, a big empty barn which fills up on weekend nights and which no one would go into during the week. There were other friends of hers there, and they drank until closing time. After that, they walked half a mile to a nightclub, called Zooey's. There is still a night-club there, but it has changed name several times in the last seventeen years, and probably looks quite different inside. There were seven of them in the group, and they danced, and sat, and talked to each other. Sometime after one o'clock, everyone agreed afterwards, Franky, my sister, said that she felt like going home. Someone offered to walk home with her, but she refused, saying that she would be fine. She probably saw that the others were having a good time, and didn't want to cut their evening short. Anyway, she never got home. Her body was found, two days later, in a hole among a copse of trees. It is surprising that London has these odd dark corners, where no one goes, and everyone afterwards remarked that someone must have heard or seen something. I know that isn't necessarily true. Where my sister's body was found is surrounded by a circuit of busy roads, but the patch of common and trees and bushes is quite dark at night, and no one rushing by in a car would have heard any kind of human noise, or been listening for one. I have been to the pub, but never to the nightclub. I have never been to any kind of nightclub.

She was alive for seventeen years, and she has been dead for seventeen years, and the man who killed her has been in prison for nearly seventeen years. I know all the dates, including her birthday, but all that doesn't matter any more. Seventeen years ago, the timetable of my sister's Friday night out came to matter a lot. She left the house at eight thirty, because my mother remembered the television programme which was starting. She got to the pub around a quarter to nine. She left the pub after closing time. She left the club some time after one o'clock. After that, we don't really know what happened when, but my sister would have known; known how long it took from the time she came across the man who killed her to the time she died. I suppose the man knows that, too. That, I don't really want to know. I was only ten at the time. I sort of remember her, but my memory is all tied up with and directed by the photographs of her, the family photographs which got into the newspapers and which immediately became precious. The man who killed her must still be in prison. I suppose when he gets released, somebody would come and tell us first.

It was quite a famous case at the time. We still have the newspapers and everything. They all mention one thing, that her body was found naked, and they all call her Frances, which no one ever called her. But our family name is ordinary, and no one routinely connects us to that murder, even if they remember it. No journalist has come to photograph us since then, or to ask us how we feel about her murderer being released from prison. I don't know what I would say. I know his name, but I don't want to write it down. My family is not like other families. After that, I suppose, it never could be.

12

'Goodbye, goodbye,' I cried, standing on the pavement and waving. 'Have a happy –'

But my voice sounded high and unnatural to me, as uncomfortable as my new suit, cutting into my armpits.

'Have a happy and long honeymoon,' I settled for, finally. But I had taken so long over deciding what to call out that the car with my sister and her grinning new husband had moved off. My voice rang out with its embarrassing cheer, as the other guests turned back to each other.

My mother once said to me that I was one for changing horses in midstream. I didn't know what she meant then, of course, as we lived in Bromley, where there were no streams or horses. She was talking about my habit of watching the television for five minutes and then getting up to turn it over, and then five minutes after that getting up to turn it back.

She was right, I see that now. I was always someone who was setting off in one direction and then changing his mind for no good reason and then changing his mind again for no reason at all. So when I started on 'Have a happy –' I got caught short because I didn't know what happy thing I wanted them to have. *Have a happy marriage* would have been very odd, like saying *Have a nice life* when what you really mean is *I hope I never see you ever again*. So I settled for wishing them a happy honeymoon, only then I ruined it by saying happy and long. I suppose I was thinking of retirements. Only it just came out sounding smutty, and I was left standing alone in the wedding group outside the Chelsea registry office, with my blue arm still raised, waving at the Saturday-morning traffic.

Next to me was a girl, my age, or thereabouts. She was small and brown and Indian, with an expression which was not exactly a frown, but more concentrating. I had seen her earlier, waiting outside the registry office. She was wearing one of those Indian coats which are crusty with embroidery and gold. Then I had noticed her and thought that, if she had to be wearing something Indian, I was glad she was wearing that and not a sari which displays six inches of fat brown back and always makes me feel a little bit faint. At her feet was a huge satchel, bulging and full, like a suitcase in a cartoon.

'Bride or groom?' she said abruptly.

I did not think for one moment that she could be speaking to me, but then I saw there was no one else.

'Yes, you,' she said. I had said nothing. 'Bride or groom?'

'Bride,' I said. 'She's my – ! – sister, in fact.'

'Hip, hip, hurrah,' she said. 'He speaks. Can he speak and walk at the same time? Only time will tell.'

I did not know what to say to this. She had a curious quick drawling way of speaking, and as she spoke, she did not look at me, but at the road. So I said nothing.

'Why did you shout "Have a happy and long honeymoon"?' she said. 'Are you going, now?'

I would rather she hadn't remembered exactly the words I had used. 'I thought I ought – ! – to shout something,' I said. 'And I hope they do have a – ! – happy honeymoon.'

'But they aren't going on honeymoon now,' she said. Now she did turn, scrutinising me. 'They're going to the reception. Aren't you going to the reception?'

'Yes,' I said. 'Yes, I suppose I am.' Somehow I had got it into my head that that was it, though now I remembered that there was a party.

'I have no one to go with,' she said. 'I wonder if you would be so kind as to take me.'

'I don't have a car,' I said. I did have a car, but I hadn't brought it. I had worried about being able to park in Chelsea on a Saturday morning and had come in all the way by tube. On the District Line, my hand had kept going up to hide the flower in my buttonhole. For an amazing moment in my head I was riding the tube in a gold brocaded coat, and smiling with broad confidence when the people started to stare.

'Then we can share a taxi,' she said. She brought her two fingers up to her mouth, and whistled, a real old-fashioned barrow-boy whistle, though no taxi was in sight. The guests who were still loitering on the pavement looked round with astonishment, but she paid no attention. And in a moment a taxi did come, and she let me open the door for her.

'So kind – so very kind – of you,' she murmured as she stepped in. Her walk was like her way of talking; she stepped forward swiftly and precisely, but did not seem to get anywhere very quickly. I looked at her in amazement. It seemed to me incredible that she meant what she said.

I see I have forgotten to say what this girl's name was. She told me – she must have told me – at some point in this conversation, but I forgot to say at the time. Her name was Wasia.

I rarely took taxis in London. When I travelled about London, I generally preferred to take the Underground. I had a car, as I said, but usually it stayed where it was, in the garage. For me, London was an archipelago, each atoll of known territory around an Underground station. I connected them up uncertainly and, if I had to drive through the great expanse of the city, generally got lost, an *A to Z* on my knee. I preferred, for the same reason, not to take taxis; I felt they would see my uncertainty, and take me a roundabout way, to make money. When the driver took a side street I didn't recognise, I felt nervous, knowing that I was going to be rooked in some way, and sat trying to remember how much money I had in my pocket. Even if he had done it because he had seen a line of traffic ahead, or knew a clever short cut. And taxi drivers always want to talk to you, too.

I followed Wasia into the taxi, and before I was properly settled, I found that she had thrust her great bag on to my lap.

'Where are we going?' Wasia said. Her mouth was pursed, her expression grumpy and no longer grateful.

I leant forward and, instead of telling her, told the taxi driver the address. It was a private house; I wasn't entirely sure who it belonged to. In the course of the family discussions about the wedding arrangements, I had missed some crucial explanation and had never really worked it out. It seemed to belong to a woman called Georgina, who had offered to lend it, since she had a big garden and lived near the registry office. Sometimes it seemed to me that Georgina worked with my sister, sometimes that she was some kind of aunt of my new brother-in-law, and sometimes that she was a woman who owed money to my parents' friend Mr Tredinnick. The arrangements for the wedding had been so involved and so endlessly discussed that I hadn't quite managed to find out.

'Is that far?' Wasia said, like a small child, as the cab set off. She seemed displeased in some way, although up to now I had done everything she had told me to do. 'It sounds like Fulham.'

'It is in Fulham,' I said.

'You've got terrible hiccups,' Wasia said. 'Were you hiccupping all the way through?'

'I was trying to be quiet,' I said. 'You didn't hear me, did you?'

'Oh, at a wedding, you never notice anything apart from the people getting married,' Wasia said. 'I must have been lost in the sheer romanticism of the occasion.'

I looked at her, astonished. The night before, I had

been talking like someone in a film. But that was last night. I had not expected still to be listening to terrible lines from terrible films the next day. The film in which a girl says that she must have been lost in the sheer romanticism of the occasion was so terrible that it had never been made and never would be. Wasia looked back at me, as if challenging me to find anything wrong with the sentiment.

'I seldom go to weddings,' I offered. Seldom; the style seemed to be catching.

She seemed to digest this, and sat back. From somewhere in her coat, she produced a packet of cigarettes – an unusual make in a pastel-coloured packet, it looked like some industrial feminine mystery, like a pregnancy-testing kit – and quickly lit one. She didn't offer me one, and in fact, I don't smoke. After a moment, the driver, without turning, rapped heavily on the dividing glass, indicating the 'No Smoking' sign. Wasia ignored him.

'Will all your family be there?' she asked me.

'I think so,' I said. 'I think they were all there at the service.'

'The service?' she said, blowing out a thin stream of intensely feminine smoke. 'Is that the right word? I thought you only had services in church.'

'She was wearing a proper wedding dress, though,' I said.

'Yes, that's true,' Wasia said. 'Yes, she was, wasn't she?'

The driver slid back the glass partition.

'Can you cut that out, please?' he said. He was a little man, old and thin like a retired jockey.

'Cut what out?' Wasia said.

'Smoking like that,' he said. 'Can't you see the sign?'

'I thought that was a request,' Wasia said.

'It is a request,' he said. 'It's a request not to smoke in my cab.'

'And is it illegal to smoke a fag,' Wasia said, 'in your cab?' She put a terrible weight on the word *fag*, as if it was somehow ridiculous.

'If I say it is,' the driver said, 'that's the way it is.'

'There's no law that says you can't smoke in a black cab,' Wasia said. 'You can only ask people politely if they would refrain from doing so. And I want to have a cigarette.'

'And there's no law,' the driver said, 'that stops me from stopping and putting you out right now if you smoke. In my cab.'

'I'll wind the window down,' Wasia said, girlishly. 'Promise I will.'

'Just put it out, please,' the driver said. 'Now, please.'

'Oh, very well,' Wasia said, and took one last drag on her cigarette, before dropping it on the floor and grinding her foot on it. I noticed that she had finished anyway.

'Sorry about that,' I said quietly to the driver as we got out and Wasia left me to pay. But he said nothing. He just took care to give me the wrong change.

There was an explanation for the way my family was, but it wasn't an explanation I often produced. People were usually not interested enough in us, and too interested by the explanation. To me, we seemed different from other people's families. When we came together, as from time to time you have to, at Christmas or weddings, for instance, we seemed an odd and unlikely assortment of people, who were polite and sad to each other. Other families seemed to have had first choice, and we – my mum and my dad, my sister who was still alive and getting married, my aunt Dorothy and the unemployable cousins and my great-uncle Sam – seemed like the ones left at the end, after everyone else had been chosen and carried off. We stuck together like the last chocolates in a box.

The door of the big square brick house stood open, an unusual sight in London. My sister and her new husband stood just inside, still in their wedding clothes, smiling as if they had won something large and fluffy in a raffle and were determined not to be embarrassed about it. Next to my new brother-in-law was the woman whose house this was. Her name was Georgina. Her connection and authority, though unclear to me, seemed to entitle her to stand by the pair of them, shaking hands and welcoming people to her house. It was unsuccessful; she looked like the manageress, an impression not dispelled by the fact that she was disdainfully wearing the sort of suit professional women wear to the office, and nothing more obviously festive.

'Thank you for coming,' my sister said automatically as she shook a hand for the fifteenth time, and then she saw she was talking to her brother. Me, I mean. She turned to her husband and laughed. He looked at her with her mouth open, laughing, and then he looked at me, and smiled uncertainly.

'That's all right,' I said.

'*Your buttonhole,*' she hissed suddenly.

I looked at my flower. Something in the taxi had happened to it – perhaps Wasia's bag, which I had been holding close – and it was crushed and going brown at the edges. 'I'll get rid of it,' I said.

'Hello,' Wasia said. 'I'm Wasia. Congratulations. What a lovely day you are having for your wedding. The weather, I mean, of course.' She was speaking in a little-girl's voice, and her smile was broad and big and empty. This surprised me, as I had for some reason assumed that Wasia was my sister's friend, and not her husband's. Then Wasia introduced herself to Richard, my new brother-in-law, and I realised she knew neither of them. She moved off into the house confidently, hitching her huge handbag over her shoulder and taking a glass from a boy – probably a son of the house. My sister looked at me, puzzled for a moment, and then, to my surprise, clapped me on the shoulder. It is odd to have your back slapped by someone in a wedding dress. I don't know why.

'I'm sorry – ! – Janet couldn't come,' I said.

She clapped my back again, and started laughing heartily. 'I shouldn't laugh,' she said. 'But it's just – I mean, Janet taking off like that, it would be sad, but you don't waste –'

'Yes,' I said, bewildered. 'Janet left me – I didn't want to spoil –'

'You are a dark horse,' she said. I didn't know what she meant, and was going to say something, but my sister was no longer listening. Another taxi was drawing up on the pavement outside. I followed Wasia through the house and into the garden. The garden was somehow not quite like a proper garden; it had the air of being recently installed. I subsequently learnt from Mr Tredinnick that Georgina had paid a firm to come in and rip out all the weeds and put a lot of plants in. The lavishness of this was misleading; the expenditure of renovating her garden was somehow represented as her wedding present, and the wedding present of half a dozen of the other guests who had contributed to the costs. The plants all sat forlornly alone, islands in a sea of just-turned earth. It would look better in a year or two.

My plan was to go up to some of my sister's friends, who I had seen on the pavement outside the registry office, and introduce myself. But in the garden, there were only four or five little groups, and each of them seemed too small for me to go up to. Not for the first time, I felt ill at ease, not quite sure what my role was here. I needed a book of wedding etiquette, to tell me what the brother of the bride ought to do. At a wedding, the bride and groom have a sort of awesome isolation, the bride with her perfect hair and her impossible dress, installed in pomp and luxury at the head of the table like the figures on the cake; and on her family is conferred a degree of that isolation. It seemed to me that I was in a conspicuous sort of position for once, and ought to be preparing to make a speech. I don't mean that I was conspicuous because I was standing on my own at the top of the steps leading down into the garden, or because I was wretchedly hiccupping. I mean that I was the bride's brother, and people might expect me to introduce myself to them.

'Hello, son,' Mr Tredinnick said, coming up behind me, flushed and bald.

'Hello,' I said.

He cast a dispassionate eye down my clothes. 'You want to wear a tie to your sister's wedding,' he said. 'It doesn't look very respectful, now, son, does it?'

'I never wear a tie,' I said. 'I don't like it, having something round my neck like that.'

'It doesn't look good,' Mr Tredinnick said. 'And that's a funny sort of suit, too.'

'What's wrong with it?' I said. It was a perfectly good suit. Suits were one thing I did know about.

'You want to come to me to buy a suit,' Mr Tredinnick said. 'I could get you a good one, a good price. You got that in a shop, now, didn't you?'

'Well –,' I said. '!' I said.

'You don't want to do that,' Mr Tredinnick said.

Mr Tredinnick was always telling me about my wants. It seemed to me that he knew more about what I wanted than I knew myself. I did not know whether he was right, in this case, or not. He may have been; I bought my clothes myself, on my own, without advice. 'You want to stop hiccupping, and all,' he advised. 'It doesn't look good, you know.'

I acknowledged the truth of this.

'I thought you never touched the stuff,' he said, nodding at the glass of champagne I was holding. 'Mother's ruin, that stuff.'

'I thought that was gin,' I said.

'No, that's *champagne*,' Mr Tredinnick explained kindly. '*Champagne*. You have it at weddings. Might cure your hiccups.'

'That's why I'm drinking it,' I said.

Mr Tredinnick gave me a short, hostile survey, as if I were ridiculing him. He walked past me, muttering 'Come on, Jimmy, son,' and I followed him down into the garden. Jimmy is not my name. That was just what Mr Tredinnick had always decided to call me.

I see that I have not said who Mr Tredinnick was. He had been part of our lives for a very long time, but his relation to any of us was not very clear. He owned a café which was not far from where my mother and father lived, and when my sister was at school she had worked there for a short while. My sister who was just now getting married, I mean. He was a capable man, who seemed to have mastered something none of us had ever quite got the hang of. Whether we knew him before my sister worked at the café, I don't know. But before I quite understood it, he had got to know my mother and father, and was coming round to give them odd scraps of advice. 'We must ask Mr Tredinnick,' my father would say whenever any small difficulty arose, and he always did. He was Italian; he once told me he had been a prisoner of war in Cambridgeshire. 'I was just a kid, you know,' he pointed out. He had met a local girl and stayed in this country. After marrying her, of course. Mr Tredinnick had gone on to explain that he had taken his wife's name, wanting to seem English in all things. 'Or Cornish,' he always said, laughing and explaining that Tredinnick, of course, was an old Cornish name and his wife's family must originally have come from there. He was completely ageless, deplorable, astonishing as a film star.

A small hand took mine. For a moment I thought it must be Wasia's, but it was only one of Mr Tredinnick's children. He had four or five, who followed around in his opulent wake. He had divorced and married again, a much younger woman, rather late in life, and some of his children were very young to have quite an old father. He had kept his first wife's name after the divorce, explaining that it was more bother than it was worth to change it again, and his second wife had taken his first wife's name, without, it seemed, complaining about it. I couldn't remember the name of this child of his, who squinted up at me with an expression of dissatisfaction. I hoped I wasn't going to be looking after him all afternoon. I hunkered down beside him, having no one else to talk to.

'Do you want some cake?' I said.

He shook his head; it was just as well, since there was no cake yet.

'Shall we go and find Mummy?' I said. He considered this, and then, for no reason at all, started to cry silently. I stood up resolutely, and turned away from him. The people near us looked at me curiously, as if I had done or said something terrible to him. I often had this effect on children.

Wasia, by now, was talking to my mother. I went over. Her eyes were flickering up and down, taking in what my mother was wearing.

'What a lovely hat,' she said politely, in the same little-girl voice.

My mother looked helpless, and said nothing.

'I so love coming to weddings,' Wasia went on sociably. 'It gives one such a chance to dress up, and wear a lovely hat.'

This was an odd thing to say, as Wasia was not wearing a hat.

'Thank you so much for inviting me,' she went on. 'Does Samantha only have one brother?'

'Samantha?' my mother said, puzzled.

'Your daughter,' Wasia said. 'Your daughter Samantha.'

'Sarah,' my mother said.

'That's what I said,' Wasia said. 'Or I thought I did. Silly me! Saratha.'

She said Samantha again, or nearly; it seemed to me that she tried to alter the sound of the name, so as to make it seem as if she had really said Sarah, but in a strange foreign accent.

'Are there only the two of them?' Wasia said again.

'No,' my mother said. Her eyes were wandering about the garden, counting the flowers. My mother seemed to be looking around for an escape route. Then she came back and said what I knew she would say. 'No, I had another daughter, but she died.'

'Oh dear,' Wasia said. 'I am sorry.'

We all stood there for a moment and thought in our different ways about my dead sister. Then I saw that it was up to me to take Wasia away.

'How did you know that was my mother?' I said.

Wasia waved in a general way, and perhaps it hadn't been difficult to identify the nervous mother of the confident bride. She reached into her bag, and took out another cigarette from her pouch. I watched her light it, and all at once it struck me that none of my family smoked or had ever smoked. I wished Wasia had left it for another five minutes. My dead sister's name had come up – well, not her name, but the fact of her death – and Wasia was lighting a cigarette as if no one had said anything.

'This is such a lovely party,' she said. 'And Sarah makes such a lovely bride, doesn't she?'

Sarah was nowhere to be seen – still greeting the arrivals in her big dress, I expect – but I agreed.

'Poor you with your hiccups,' Wasia said.

'Do you think,' Wasia said, 'that anyone would mind very much if I took a couple of photographs? I think I brought my camera here, and I ought to use up the film.'

'No, of course not,' I said. That, I see now, was the beginning of all our troubles. Wasia reached again into her bag, and lugged out an enormous camera. She hung it around her neck, raised it to her eye and struck a peculiar posture, one leg back, as if preparing to run a race. I looked at what she was photographing, but it was only Mr Tredinnick, telling one of his many red-faced anecdotes to a politely listening group. I did not know any of his audience. Only Mr Tredinnick was laughing at his own story. It occurred to me that Wasia probably thought that Mr Tredinnick was my father, but I did not say anything. My real father was sitting on a bench, on his own, and probably would not have made such a good photograph. Wasia paused in her odd posture, and the machine made a heavy, solid noise, *ker-chunk*, and then twice more, *ker-chunk, ker-chunk*. The people near us looked round. Wasia lowered the camera and sighed, almost with pleasure.

A light spatter of applause started in the garden as my sister came out with her new husband. She stood at the top of the steps, her arm in his, smiling tightly. Wasia carried on taking photographs, but to my surprise she was not photographing my sister; she was photographing the people in the garden, applauding. I looked at her with surprise, and then she turned her camera on me, and before I could assemble a smile, she had photographed me, three times, quickly in succession.

The real photographer rushed up with his equipment. He was calling something out as he did so. I suppose he was trying to amass the family together, to take his photographs, but everyone just stood there with a drink in one hand and a plate in another, trying unsuccessfully to applaud.

'Bride and groom first,' he was calling. 'Bride and groom.' He was a very tall man, well over six foot, and awkwardly shaped. Sarah and her husband came forward, and struck an adoring pose; she sank, quite naturally, down six inches or so and put on a loving upward gaze into his face. By me, there was a big *ker-chunk* as Wasia took a photograph.

'There's no need,' I said. 'You'll see the photographs the professional photographer's taking, if you want.'

Wasia shook her head impatiently, and raised her

camera again. It seemed to me that from where we stood, she could hardly avoid including the professional photographer, bending down in a ridiculous posture, in her snap, but I said nothing.

'Parents of the bride and groom, please,' the photographer called, and the four of them moved in resolutely. Wasia carried on taking her snaps, rapidly, one after the other. You could see the proper photographer was becoming aware of her, and nervous; at one point, she darted forward and took a photograph which could only possibly be of him. He stopped, and stood up, and glared at her. 'Do you mind?' he said, but Wasia just took another photograph.

I wandered from group to group, laughing at the ends of people's jokes, defusing the hostile or questioning gaze of strangers with explanations of who I was. It was tiring after a while, and I went into the house. I stood in the hall, enjoying the quiet dark, hung with old pictures of buildings; and then, from a room which might have been the dining room, I heard a voice. It was one of the waiters, complaining to one of the caterers, who had set up shop there.

'I'll tell you something,' he was saying, 'I'm not going near that cow again.'

'Which cow?'

'That cow, the Indian one.'

'Oh, she's a cow.'

'You know what she's said to me? She goes Ooh, look what is it, yummy, putting it on, like. And then she goes to me, like when no one else can hear her, she goes Can't you go and get me something else because I'm not eating that. So I go It's very nice, madam. So she goes No it's not it's a pile of fucking shit. She says that. And she goes This is the worst fucking wedding I ever came to and your food is fucking shit and if you don't get me something I can eat I'm going to give you a kick up the arse.'

'The fuck.'

'So I go Well I don't have to take this. And she goes Yes you do you're a fucking waiter.'

'So.'

'So I walk off because I don't have to take that.'

'She must be on drugs or something.'

I turned and walked away, back into the garden. Wasia came up to me, still holding her camera. 'I do hope they come out,' she said. 'My piccies, I mean. Do you think you could find me a drink? I really must go in a minute or two.'

The party went its satisfyingly conventional way after Wasia's departure. 'Sorry about your wife. I could have told you, mind, because I never trusted her an inch,' Mr Tredinnick said, an hour or two later, coming up with one of his many children sleeping in his arms.

'Yes, she was horrible,' I said angrily.

'But that's a nice girl, your girlfriend,' Mr Tredinnick said, hardly noticing. 'Has she been here long?'

'All day,' I said rudely.

Mr Tredinnick tutted and threw his head back, his usual gesture of impatience with me. He shook his head with leisurely amusement. 'I've nothing against –' he said broad-mindedly, in the end, and turned and went off. I don't know what he had nothing against. It was obviously plain to Mr Tredinnick, however.

It was only afterwards, as I steamed off towards the Fulham Road, that an odd big idea occurred to me. Why had Wasia come to my sister's wedding when she didn't know Sarah, or her husband, or anyone else there? She had seen me, standing alone on the pavement, and decided there and then that she wanted to get to know me, even if it meant going to a reception she hadn't been invited to. I shook my head at her audacity. And then I thought that I would not see her again, because I had forgotten to give her any way of telephoning me.

13

The good weather continued for some days after Sarah's wedding, but it was difficult to know what to do with it. Even though I had not been very much involved with the preparations for the festivities, I now missed them. No one in my family had done or talked of anything else for weeks, if not months, and now it was all over and there was nothing else to talk about, unless we were now going to talk about whether they were going to have children, whether they were having a happy honeymoon, and when the wedding photographs would arrive. For some reason, I had told my employer that I would not be working for five days after the wedding. This had seemed to me the right thing to do. Perhaps at the back of my mind I was thinking of those Middle Ages celebrations where the wedding feast goes on for days and days (I used to imagine a very slow sort of feast, with the noblemen sleeping in their chairs and not reaching the sweet course until Tuesday).

What really happened was that I woke up the next morning and had nothing at all to do or think about. Sarah's departure was so huge and complete that it was hard to believe she was ever going to come back. I went for a walk and bought the newspaper I usually read, and came back and looked at the newspaper. I read a novel which I had been reading on and off for a while. Finally I phoned my mother, and she told me to come round and help finish off the food that was left after my sister's wedding.

'I wonder what they're doing now,' my mother said over the tea table.

We all talked about this for a while.

'Of course, it's a different time of day, now, in the Seychelles,' Mr Tredinnick said. He was there, of course, as he often was.

So then my father got up from the table and went to get the atlas from above the television, and found them on the map of the world. We had looked at the Seychelles many times before; they looked like a sprinkling of pepper on the ocean. We all counted up the time zones between London and there, and worked out the time difference.

'Are they ahead of us, or behind?' my mother said.

We tried to work it out. My father thought it would be about lunchtime, but Mr Tredinnick said it would be in the middle of the night. I preferred Mr Tredinnick's idea, and not just because it was Mr Tredinnick's; it seemed more thrilling to me that they would now be sleeping – that everyone in the Seychelles would be sleeping – when we in London were eating our dinner.

'Of course, they'll be suffering from jet lag,' Mr Tredinnick said sagely. 'It's always much worse, isn't it, when you travel from west to east.'

Jet lag! We all thought of that for a while. Only Sarah in my family had ever travelled so far. Once, as a surprise, for my parents' thirtieth wedding anniversary, my sister had booked a weekend break in New York for them. They had gone, but most of their photographs afterwards had been of the hotel or arriving at the airport, and most of their comments were of how kind the people in the hotel had been to them. I think they had been afraid of being mugged or getting lost if they went out into the streets, and they had stayed safely where they were in a hotel room for four days, having, as my mother afterwards said, the whale of a time.

'Have another canapé, Mr Tredinnick,' my mother said. 'They're still quite good.'

Mr Tredinnick took one dubiously; they did not look very nice now, since the asparagus was bleeding into the cream cheese, but they still tasted all right. 'It's said to be the most romantic place in the world,' Mr Tredinnick said, talking about the Seychelles. 'An ideal place for a young couple to take a honeymoon. Isn't that right, Jimmy?'

He grinned at me. I felt annoyed at what he had said, not knowing what it implied, and did not know what to say.

'That was lovely of your auntie to offer to throw the party,' Mr Tredinnick went on. 'Really generous. That's a lovely big house she's got, really de luxe. I'd say she's got a bob or two. And a lovely garden. I like a nice garden. It was like something out of a Sunday magazine. Some people – !' He tutted, affectionately. 'Well, your turn next,' he said, gesturing at me.

I thought he was talking about the food, so I leant forward and took another of the cream-cheese-and-asparagus rolls.

'John's married already, Mr Tredinnick,' my father said.

'So he is,' Mr Tredinnick said comfortably.

'It was a very quiet wedding, though, John's,' my mother said.

'He'll have met Janet, though, won't he?' my father said.

'Oh, I know Janet,' Mr Tredinnick said. Then he dropped into *sotto voce*; his wink, when it came, was appalling and inevitable, like a crash. With Mr Tredinnick, you always felt like an unwilling accomplice in his worst social offences. 'She's done a bunk, though, hasn't she, son?'

In the end, I went home before Mr Tredinnick did, leaving him sitting with my parents in front of the television. When I went, he was giving advice to the people competing in game shows. 'Good night, son,' he said, not taking his eyes off the television, and I went without anyone getting up. It seemed as if none of my family was ever going to discuss the fact that my wife had left me. They'd even stopped discussing my hiccups.

14

I was woken up by someone hammering on the front door. Amazingly, it turned out to be the same German who had tried to rent a room, a week or so before. He was without his rucksacks, but I still recognised him.

'Good morning,' he said politely. 'I hope I do not wake or disturb you?'

'!' I said.

'This perhaps will seem a little strange to you,' he said, smoothly entering. 'May I enter and I will explain? Perhaps a cup of coffee, yes? Thank you.'

'Go outside,' I said, gesturing at the garden.

'Please, allow me, I shall help,' he said, leading me firmly into my own kitchen. 'It is better that I make the coffee because in England always the coffee is like the consommé where you can see the plate through it, and I will show you how we make coffee in Germany, so, good.'

'Oh, do fuck off,' I said. But I had only just woken up. I should have remembered what happened when you said 'fuck off' to this man. Again, he seemed not to hear the instruction.

'You are surprised to see me, I think,' he began. 'I would like to explain because perhaps to me it is surprising, too. My name is Hans-Kleist Klugg.'

'Is what?'

'Is Hans-Kleist Klugg.'

'Is that two names or three?'

'That is two names. There is a band.'

'A band?'

'A link.'

'!'

'A hyphen, yes, that is the word. Between Hans and Kleist, not between Kleist and Klugg, that would be absurd. Of course, that was not my name when I was born. My name was Hans Klugg only. Hans is the name of my grandfather who now is dead and Klugg is a very typical name in Bavaria because I am Bavarian. The reason I call myself Hans-Kleist Klugg is this, which I will tell you. You know, I think, that there is a writer in Germany who is called Kleist who is a very great writer and he is my favourite writer, you know that.'

'No, never heard of him,' I said.

'No, I think you are joking,' he said. 'Everybody in the world knows Kleist, I think, even in England. No, you are joking, to say that you do not know a writer who is as Kleist. To not know a story so funny as the stories which are the Kleist stories, I think that is not possible. There is a story which is so funny, so, I shall tell you, and you will see.'

Time passed.

'Yes,' I said. 'Right. Yes, that is a very funny story. So.'

'So this is not the story, or the reason you have opened the door this morning and have found me here, but only the story of why I am called as I am called, which is that I call myself after Kleist because it is my idea that when that is my name, I will hear his name every day as long as I live. And that will I think be a good thing.'

'My name's John,' I said.

'Yes, and that is a good name, too, I think,' the German continued. Anyone would have thought we were the oldest of friends. 'But it is not so good a name as Hans-Kleist Klugg because there are many people called John, but if I hear in the street that someone shouts Hans-Kleist, I know that they are shouting for me. I am,' the man said, slowing disconcertingly, his voice deepening into some kind of announcement, 'an artist. Not the sort of artist who puts oil paints down with a brush and gives you a picture of a hill or a tree or a house in the country, no, not that, because that is old and that is over, and I am not someone who takes a piece of stone, of marble, yes, marble, and then hits it and hits it until there is a head of someone because that is old and that is shit, you know, but I am an artist and I am making art because I am in England. OK, I explain. I am telling you this, now, that I am a homosexual. That is not a problem for you. So I am explaining my work of art which is a homosexual-theoretical work of art which I am making in England while I am travelling, because,' he paused, seriously, and engaged my expression directly, 'I am in the habit of having sex with many different men who I meet.'

'!' I said.

'You understand that the work of art which I am doing is the sex which I have with the many different men, that is the real work of art. But that is not the work of art which you can put in a gallery and which people can come and look at because that is not possible.'

'You'd find it tiring after a bit, I expect,' I said helpfully.

'Yes, that is so,' Hans-Kleist said. 'So the art which I show when I go back to Germany is a part of that, and it is this. It is the photographs which I take after I have had sex with a man, and the thing which I photograph is always the same thing, which is the condom which the man has used when he has fucked me and when he has finished with fucking me, but only that. You understand, yes? And that is the work of art which I do and many important and serious people in Germany have said some very polite things about the work which I do, as for instance that I am important like Michelangelo which is what one critic has said. I think you are ill.'

'No,' I said. 'I just can't seem to stop hiccupping. Go on, it's terribly interesting.'

'No, that is all, that is my work of art, and I have explained it,' Hans-Kleist said. 'But you are saying to yourself why is Hans-Kleist returning here and explaining this to me?'

I assented, in a general sort of way.

'This is the thing which I am explaining. Because for the last days I am continuing with my work of art, and I have invited six different men to fuck me for this reason, but all the time I do not concentrate on my work. My heart,' he said emphatically, 'is not in it.'

'Excellent,' I said, and meant it; I could see so clearly the intolerable Bavarian schoolboy, committing the English idiom to memory in a sunny Bavarian classroom. 'Your heart was not in it. Could you enjoy it anyway? I mean, if you thought of it just as, you know, fucking, rather than a work of art?'

'No, that is not possible,' Hans-Kleist said brusquely. 'I am not thinking of my work because when I am working, I am thinking in the last days, what was that that happened? I come and I ask to see a room, and the house, it is not a hotel, it is a house, and then I ask and the man says it is five hundred pounds, and the telephone rings and I explain to an Englishwoman that if she is wanting to be travelling then Germany is a good place, and then I go away, because all that seems not quite normal to me.'

'That's probably because you thought this was a hotel,' I said.

'Yes, that is true.'

'And it's not. It used to be, but it's not now.'

'But the five hundred pounds, please, explain.'

'I wanted to get rid of you.'

He looked at me, astonished, baffled. They are so extraordinary, truthful explanations. They always are.

'So this is funny, you were being funny with me, please?'

'!' I said.

He got up and paced, intently, concentrating, round the lawn. Every five yards or so, he paused; he attempted a laugh. It wasn't working for either of us. He laughed four times, circling the garden. He sat down. He looked at me, beseeching, baffled, helpless. I could have been a father who had just explained, in detail, how babies are made. He could have been my son. You could see the thoughts bubbling away in his poor German head like the baths at the baked-bean factory.

'You are interested in my artwork,' he said in the end.

'It sounds interesting, yes,' I said.

'So perhaps you can be part of it, if that is not a problem?'

'Part of –'

'The artwork, so, perhaps, if you like, you can fuck me, and then when you are finished, because I have here the camera, so now is a good time.'

'I'd rather not, if you don't mind,' I said.

'OK, so that is not a problem,' he said sunnily. 'But there is one thing I have to tell you which is a strange thing I think for you to hear.'

'What is that, then?' I said.

'I am here to tell you that I think I am in love with you.'

'Oh yes,' I said. '!' I said.

He left soon after that.

15

'But of course,' Miss Johnson was saying as I came into the office, 'she has been married three times before. One always forgets the second marriage, since it lasted so brief a time, and it is so seldom mentioned these days.'

I took my coat off slowly, hanging it on the hatstand. It was mid-morning in the office of *Indexes and Indexing*, and the two of them were having a break for coffee, or, in Mr Roy's case, hot water in a cup. There were three desks in the room; the two Mr Roy and Miss Johnson habitually used were facing each other in an almost gladiatorial way at either end of the office. In theory, both of them only worked for a day and a half each week for the magazine. The rest of the time, like me, they produced commissioned indexes for any passing trade. In practice, they seemed to come into the office every day. I don't know why they didn't work at home. There was really no need for the magazine to have an office at all, but the founder of the magazine, years before, had held down a teaching job in a university college in Bloomsbury. He had persuaded the college to give him a room to edit the magazine in. Since then, the governing body of the college had somehow failed to notice that Miss Johnson and Mr Roy, people with no connection whatever to the university, had the use of a decent-sized office rent-free in the middle of Bloomsbury. I suppose everyone at the university assumed it must be someone else's business.

Mr Roy was sitting on a stool in the middle of the office, one of those office chairs with five wheels, in front of Miss Johnson's desk. He looked effortlessly rapt, like a nervous candidate at a job interview.

'And George is her son?' he said, sipping at his cup of hot water.

'No, not quite,' Miss Johnson said. 'You see – it was really most unfortunate – Henrietta married Ian Platt, who was the landlord of the "pub", and in the course of their honeymoon in Derbyshire, he lost his footing on some slippery rocks and fell into a crevasse, the weather being poor, and he died before he could be got to hospital. One often feels that he, really, was the man she truly loved, poor woman.'

'But I don't understand about George,' Mr Roy said.

'Well, that was a surprise all round,' Miss Johnson said. 'One knew nothing of this. To add to the difficulties of the situation, a stranger, a young black man, appeared at the funeral, and announced that he was Ian's son from a previous marriage. Henrietta knew nothing of Ian's previous marriage to a woman from Nigeria, let alone of a grown-up son, so you may imagine the complications which ensued. That was George, who has been in the village ever since.'

'I see,' Mr Roy said, ruminating. 'But, to be strictly accurate, you must admit that Henrietta is not quite right to refer to George as her own son's half-brother, as she does. There appears to be no connection at all.'

'Oh, if it is a matter of the strictest accuracy –' Miss Johnson said. The two of them seemed to notice my quiet entry for the first time. 'Good morning, Mr Carrington. What a pleasant surprise.'

Mr Roy gave a sour little nod. I greeted them, putting my papers down on the third desk, among all the other detritus which seemed to be dumped there by the two of them, as well as by the other more occasional users of the office. I wasn't there often enough to claim a desk of my own, as the other two had. I resented this without wanting to do or say anything concrete about it.

Miss Johnson had reached the end of her story. Mr Roy, taking that or my entry as a signal, gracefully manoeuvred himself back behind his desk without actually getting up; ruddering himself backwards in the wheeled chair with his heels. When I had first met them, I had thought for a while that they were more intimate than they actually were. Very regularly, Miss Johnson would embark on a confiding, sensational story of this sort. Anyone would have thought that her friends and acquaintances lived unusually dramatic lives; Mr Roy gave the impression of caring a great deal, listening raptly as he did to them. Even the direst tribulations of our best friends' friends tend to grow dull quickly, and I thought it was good of him to keep listening with what seemed his full attention. The only thing which puzzled me was why Miss Johnson would retail all this intimate misery and shame in front of me, without any restraint.

It was some time before the penny dropped. What sounded like a richer and more sensational social life than you could expect so beadily tweeded an indexer to lead was, in fact, the steadily elaborating footnotes to a radio soap opera to which Miss Johnson and Mr Roy were addicted. After listening to several of her bewildering stories – 'Alas,' Miss Johnson would sigh over her morning coffee, set off by nothing at all, 'I rather fear that Saskia's crack habit is all too likely to lead her into casual prostitution' – it was clear that she was not only so profound a devotee of the village doings as not to have any powers of imagining a life, like mine, without it, but considered herself an unbeatable expert on the plot-so-far. For her, you would naturally know who she was talking about; you would also, naturally, not know as much as she did. She had listened to it for decades, and could tease out the most obscure allusion, slapping down any nervous rivalry from Mr Roy without hesitation. That was why she always seemed to be talking about her friends, and Mr Roy about people with whom he had a passing acquaintance. Whether either of them actually had any friends, I don't know, although 'my mother' and 'my friend Janice' were occasional characters in her narratives and his respectively. They had once gone out for a drink together, the Christmas before last, and were still mentioning it as an adventure in March.

'Had you arrived a little earlier,' Miss Johnson said to me in a full, satisfied tone, 'or had either of us known you were planning to come in today, you could have had your "morning coffee" with us. Alas, we are quite finished, now.'

'Young men always prefer to take their morning coffee in an "espresso bar",' Mr Roy said gleefully. 'We can hardly expect Mr Carrington to rush in order to take an "instant" coffee with two old fogeys, as he no doubt regards us.'

'Ah yes,' Miss Johnson observed. 'Cappuccino, no doubt.'

'That would be the height of sophistication,' Mr Roy said.

'Perhaps for us,' Miss Johnson spun on. 'One understands, interestingly, that Italians regard the practice of drinking cappuccino after a meal as the utmost barbarism. My mother and I, on a coach tour through the gardens of northern Italy, had to be told this by a retired Anglican vicar who sat in the seat across the aisle from mine, Mother naturally having the window seat. I believe, in fact, that no Italian worth his salt would stoop to drinking a cappuccino after eleven in the morning.'

'Well, it is only ten minutes past eleven at the moment,' Mr Roy said. 'So Mr Carrington was quite within the letter of the Italic law.'

Mr Roy, I don't know why, thought that 'italic' was the word for anything relating to Italy. One day I was going to make his sour old Hindu face crumple up in tears when I corrected him.

'I haven't had a cup of coffee at all, actually,' I said, switching the computer on. As always, I felt as if I were in danger of turning into a fantasy figure in their lives, and my existence of losing any substance. Their frequent habit, even when I was in the room, of beginning a sentence 'No doubt Mr Carrington would think . . .' unnerved me in exactly this way. God knows what richly deranged webs of fantasy they wove about me when I wasn't there.

'No coffee?' Miss Johnson said. 'You must be feeling in urgent need of a cup. Of course, should you ever want one, I shall be most happy to lend you a spoonful from my jar and a splash of milk, although I fear we cannot rise to the heights of the *cappuccino* you are accustomed to.'

'That's quite all right,' I said; the offer seemed, as usual, to relate to an undefined future of unbounded festivity rather than, say, now. 'I really came in to do some work for an hour or two, and then I have to be off.'

'Ah, "work",' Mr Roy said, in exactly the relieved tone he used when remembering the name of an old character in *Buncombe Parva*. 'We shall disturb you no more.'

I got out the fat mattress of the manuscript I was working on, held together with two rubber bands. I picked up the computer disk, which had fallen to the floor, and slid it into the computer.

'Did you have a pleasant weekend?' Miss Johnson said without raising her eyes from the index of a new history of Byzantium.

'Yes, very nice,' I said absently. 'My sister got married.'

'How odd,' Miss Johnson said. 'We were just speaking of weddings when . . .' She trailed off, perhaps remembering that I had overheard some of the conversation, and might not think a wedding in an instalment of *Buncombe Parva* twenty years ago as important as my own sister's wedding. 'White, I hope?'

'Yes, her husband's white,' I said, not altogether paying attention.

The thought had come to me on the train from Wandsworth that morning. It's an appealing time and place to think. By ten, the herded commuters have dispersed to their offices, and the train trundles in, one-third full at most. With no one but a few hooded wastrels and a handful of women, heading up for their own purposes, I liked to stretch my legs out and watch the snailing London streets wind themselves up into urban knots under a blue sky spattered with clean clouds. An idyllic view, the sort of day which reminds you of the Ladybird books of your childhood.

The train went from stop to stop; a kindly train, taking notice of places other trains snootily overlooked. From time to time someone got on, someone got off. That London morning, I realised what I ought to be doing, what I could achieve. Indexing was my job, and if it was at the heart of my life, it was also at the heart of any intelligent thought. That was what I had realised. It seemed to me so wrong that the labours I put into my work should go unnoticed, unrecognised, unless an unusual author should happen to think about it, and write half a sentence in his acknowledgements, thanking Mr J. Carrington for compiling the index. The problem had been weighing on my mind for a long time, but all at once, I saw exactly what I ought to do, and this was it.

I should publish a book myself.

It is always a dazzling thought, future celebrity. It seemed to hit my head from behind like a brick wrapped in velvet. I saw the book, all at once. I was not going to change professions in writing it; I was not going to turn myself from an indexer into an indexee; rather, the book I would write would turn the dowdy and overlooked understudy of literature into a great limelit diva. Books – every book anyone had ever written – were at root worthy only of contempt. They were imperfect, but mine would not be imperfect. It would be a book consisting of nothing but an index, a gigantic index; an index to a book which could never be written because there would be nothing to add to such an index. In front of my eyes swam a phantom volume, with my name on the cover, and a marvellous title: *Index To A History Of The World*. Everything which had happened, ever, in the world, would be beautifully removed from its slather and mud, from cause and effect, from one thing leading haplessly to another, and everything related by pure concept. What historians tried to do was to separate the trivial from the significant; when an indexer came along and did exactly the same job of separation to the book they had written, it proved to what degree they had failed. There would be nothing to add to such an index but ephemera. Headings and sub-headings, sub-headings to sub-headings. Everything would make perfect sense, and, if anyone began to read it imagining a book which did not exist, a book to which this might be appended, they would finish it knowing that there was no more need ever to think about such a book. The index would be enough.

At Waterloo I sat, alone in the train, entranced by my own vision. I did not retreat back into the real world until passengers started to get on, looking at me warily, wanting to be taken back to where I had come from. I got up. That was what I had to work on, at the offices of *Indexes and Indexing*; not the beautiful index to the idiotic book, not what I had been commissioned to finish by the end of the month. But somehow, between Waterloo and Bloomsbury, the dream seemed to evaporate; I walked into the office; I sat down; I started to go on with the index to the book, what I had been commissioned to produce.

'What is that extraordinary noise?' Miss Johnson suddenly said. 'It's been going on for twenty minutes now – almost like a balloon popping in the next room, although I hardly think *they* can be holding a party of any sort.' She raised her head like a whistled-for dog, examining the four corners of the ceiling suspiciously.

'It's me,' I said. 'I have the hiccups.'

'That will come from drinking your morning cappuccino too swiftly,' Mr Roy said gleefully.

'Just so,' Miss Johnson said.

16

Someone says that human happiness resides in the ability to sit quietly, alone in a room. After about an hour of the Johnson and Roy treatment, my knees and my brain were as taut as rubber bands, and I had to go. My lost vision of indexing was gone for ever. I excused myself, saying that I had only dropped in and now I had to meet a friend for lunch – their expressions said *exactly*, and for ever now in their eyes I would be the cappuccino drinker, the indexer with lunchable friends. Actually, there was no friend and there was no lunch; I was simply finding it impossible to sit in a room quietly, alone or not.

The restlessness, too, was fuelled by two ostinatos, chiming away regularly. They were there all the time; one in my head, the other from my mouth. I had timed the hiccups, and had found that they were occurring at intervals which ranged from every seven seconds to every minute and a half. They were slower in the evening, for some reason. The slowest were the cruel ones; you would think that it had quite stopped, for a minute of peace and calm, the muscles in your stomach would start to relax, and then – ! But in my mind, too, a sort of hiccup. People say that men think about sex every seven seconds, or every fourteen seconds, or every thirty-one seconds – it differs according to whose account you read, and also, I suppose, according to what man we are talking about here. I must have screwed up the statistics being kept by that particular government office – the Ministry of Desire, perhaps. I only seemed to think about sex once every six weeks. The thing which was in my mind once a minute or so, was hardly a thought; just a name. It was much more like the gormless ecstasy of a gospel choir, all swaying and warbling their blessed name: *Gareth*. It seemed to me that this constant accompaniment to my waking hours must be as loud to those about me as my hiccups.

London gets more difficult as you travel further eastwards. The streets do not run squarely, but converge, forming triangles and pyramids until you hardly know where or what direction you are going in. The City was not my territory, and as I walked eastwards, driven by my ambition and my ticcing, both inwards and outwards, I knew less and less where I was or where I was going. At lunchtime, the streets were busy with the City's denizens; rich saunterers – some even pinstriped and cigar-wielding, like a Marxist cartoon – pale hungry young men in packs, stilettoed secretaries with umbrellas, powerful women in Chanel and Reeboks. I was wearing a suit, like them, but no tie; the lack made me feel like a tramp. I did not belong here. I looked in the faces of the men, but none of them were Gareth, a man I had never met or seen. The index in my mind flowed on, spurting up from time to time with that gospel taunt, *Gareth*; and I don't know how I did it, but all at once I was in front of the building where Janet had worked when she met him.

It had been a solid old building, but in order to show that such a thing could be done, the bank had ripped out the first three floors of the façade and replaced it with a wall of glass. The lobby was vast and bare; behind a chrome-and-marble desk, half the length of a train, there were four immaculate receptionists talking into the floating black bubbles of their earpieces, lavishly distant from each other. Behind the security guards with their metal-detecting booths, there was an astonishing thing: in the biggest vessel I had ever seen, a full-grown oak tree. The vast window of the entrance had been created simply to show this vast waste. There was no reason to do such a thing, except to show that they had the money to have a lobby forty feet high, and could afford to have the huge window cleaned once a week. Perhaps cleaned perpetually, night and day, since there was a window cleaner at work on it now. He was perched on an elaborately engineered arrangement of ladders and cradles, completely unlike the properties used by window cleaners anywhere else. As I stood indecisively outside the bank, the people of the City swarming about me, the window cleaner looked down as if he had sensed an unlicensed intruder here. He looked faintly amused, even contemptuous, and with astonishment I saw that he was wearing a uniform: a set of overalls amusingly decorated to resemble a pinstriped suit and tie, and on his back was a corporate logo. I went into the bank.

Neither the security guard nor his electronic tollbooth made any objection to me, or to my claim that I was here to see someone. Once through, I wasn't quite sure what I was doing there. I approached the long silvery desk, the receptionists looking at me with some curiosity. The four of them all seemed to be talking into their telephone apparatus; I didn't know which of them to approach. In the end, I went and stood in front of the second from the left, waiting. But this proved a mistake; her neighbour, ten feet away, finished her call and beckoned me over.

'I've come to see Gareth,' I said.

'Yes,' she said. From outside she, like her sisters, had seemed formidably adult, but now I could see that she was very young; she had the artificial, sandy coating promoted as beauty by those orange women who lurk in their white coats by the doors of department stores, but beneath it her skin rippled with pimples like risotto. 'And that would be Gareth –?'

'Yes, Gareth,' I said.

'No,' she said. 'There are 746 people who work in this building, any or all of whom may be called Gareth. His surname, please.'

'I don't know,' I said. 'He used to work with my wife. She doesn't work here any more. I know her name.'

'That will be a great help,' she said. To her left, one of the other receptionists was imperceptibly gliding by inches towards us, having spotted the entertainment for the afternoon. 'And your name is –?'

'John Carrington,' I said.

'You aren't on the list,' she said, producing a clipboard

abruptly, like a Colt from a cowboy's holster. 'Do you have an appointment with your Gareth?'

'No,' I said. 'I just wanted to see him. You see – oh, it doesn't matter.'

'It's quite all right,' another voice said. It was the receptionist who had been oiling over. She looked unexpectedly sympathetic. 'I don't know if we can help, but why don't you explain the situation?'

'Do you know Gareth?' I said.

'No,' she said. 'I can't say that I do, but what is it about, exactly?'

So I told them the whole story.

'That's awful,' the first said.

'Yes, I'll put you through – poor you –' the second said.

I told them some more of the story: it must have looked very odd to any passer-by, the receptionists clustered round me, entranced by my narrative.

'But where is she now?' the third said, who had wheeled herself over as well.

'You should try drinking water out of a glass backwards,' the first said.

'I think I remember her,' the third said. 'But you're sure she's not with Gareth?'

'I wish there was something we could do,' the fourth said, who had now joined us. 'Shouldn't someone get that?'

'If you were my husband –' the second said.

'That's just so sad,' the fourth said, and they all nodded vigorously, the ignored telephones singing away like tinnitus.

'That's it,' I said. 'I thought he might know something.'

'I wish we could help,' the first said.

'!' I said. I shrugged and turned away, almost tripping over the two security guards, who had abandoned their posts to listen to the story as well. I was almost tearful as I left. I couldn't have been more moved if it had been someone else's story. I slid heart-rendingly across the marble floor and, satisfyingly, I could see myself as I went like the closing scenes of a French movie. As I reached the revolving doors, I heard a cry behind me; I think it was the youngest and spottiest of the receptionists. Poor girl, she couldn't help it.

'I love you!' she called.

I turned and smiled and hiccupped. 'Thank you,' I said.

An outpouring and melting like that does not make you feel that you belong in the City. Rather, it makes you feel that nobody does. Nobody nice, that is; because if those orange girls and Janet and me were on one side, puzzling Gareth and his £763,000 a year was surely on the other. Confirmation of this followed. Standing on the street outside, I saw a figure who, like me, certainly did not belong here. It was hard to define exactly what it was, to specify what of several things about her – it was a woman – conspicuously set her apart from the other people walking in the same direction. Her clothes were respectable, but not like theirs; her walk was a little slower, the walk of someone with her own purpose, like a swimmer whose direction for the moment is that of a darting school of fish. It was probably the way she held her head; everyone else, I saw, held their neck stiffly, whether they were briskly inspecting the pavement as they walked or confidently holding their heads up, surveying their familiar territory. She was holding her head loosely and vaguely, like me, looking around with interest, letting things take her attention. Then her head turned fully towards me, or probably towards the glass wall of the bank, and I realised that her head was, indeed, very much like mine. It was my mother.

'Hello,' I said. 'What are you doing here?'

'Oh, I felt like it,' she said. 'I sometimes do.'

'It's not a crime,' I said.

We started to walk in the same direction. I noticed now how her walk, and mine, had some kind of family resemblance, some comfortable family pace.

'Sometimes,' my mother said, 'I pretend that I'm a tourist, and I come up on the train, and look at all sorts of things. It's interesting, the City.'

'I never knew,' I said.

'Knew that I come up here? Oh, you wouldn't,' she said.

'So what do you come and look at?' I said.

'The churches are interesting,' she said. 'Of course I don't really know much about them, but I like to go in them and have a good poke around.'

'Where have you been today?' I said, wondering a little.

'The one I like best is the Welsh church,' she said. 'Most people don't know about it. It's an old church, and they've built roads all around it now, but the church is still there. There's not much to see, but it's nice to go in and sit down, and have a think.'

'What do you think about?' I said. I felt remote, bewildered, but safe, listening to my mother like this. I don't know why she had started to tell me these things, to talk in an unfamiliar way, like an unfamiliar person; we had never walked down this street together before, and perhaps I seemed changed by the surroundings too, turned into someone she might talk to.

'Oh, lots of things,' she said.

'Do you talk to God, or what?' I said.

'No, not really,' she said. 'I wouldn't know what to say to God. It's more like talking than thinking, though, that's right.'

'Who do you talk to?'

'No one who's there.'

'Do you ever talk to Franky?' I said.

My mother stopped, abruptly, and turned to me. Her eyes shone like hard wet stone. 'No,' she said. 'I don't talk to Franky. She's dead, dead, dead.'

'I know,' I said. It was a foolish thing I had asked her. I should have known the answer; I didn't talk to my dead sister either. I had heard people say that they did talk to their dead relatives. I didn't. 'Janet left me,' I said.

'I know,' my mother said. 'She came and told me she was going to.'

Somehow, this didn't surprise me, though my wife and my mother had never been conspicuously close.

'I didn't know whether to tell you,' she went on. 'There didn't seem a lot of point to it. She was going to leave you whatever.'

It didn't surprise me, either, that my mother hadn't

commented on it, or wanted to talk to me about it. I hadn't tried to talk to her about it, either. It wouldn't seem strange, in our family.

'I don't know why she left me,' I said.

'No, she didn't tell me,' my mother said.

We walked on a while, in silence.

'Why don't you read what she says in her letter?' she said. 'She did leave you a letter, didn't she?'

'Yes,' I said. It was an extraordinary suggestion. I had read the letter. It was of no interest. But I knew that look in my mother's eyes, and I knew that tone of certainty in her voice. She doesn't come up very much in this story; I sometimes felt that she didn't come up much in anyone's story. Her kindness and her conversation I had always known, and always thought that it was simply Mother, like any other mother, as if her existence was a matter of duty and role, and not of her choice. But, quiet as she was, and unnoticed as her kindness was, she had always been able to take my attention with a particular look and a particular emphasis. Perhaps she had said to me, when I was too young not to cry when I felt like it, 'Why don't you go and look under your pillow?' And I would find a fifty pence, an exchange for the tooth which a wad of toffee had plucked out the night before. Or, 'Go and see if your sister's upstairs – she hasn't been down all day,' and I would find her crying, and without knowing that I had it in me to do such a thing, could persuade her in ten minutes that there are other boys, that at fourteen there are other things to do than cry about not being loved. My mother knew that, but I didn't. Or – but she had done it, many times, over good things as well. That day, she looked at me and told me to go and read the letter again, and without asking how she knew I should, I did what she suggested.

The house was in disorder by now. The kitchen was strewn with unfamiliar empty bottles and the remains of the meals I had irregularly been concocting out of what I could find on the shelves of Mr Patel's newsagent's shop. My hunt for anything to do with Gareth had left a dense layer of papers and clothes everywhere; I hadn't really done anything about it. But the letter Janet had left for me, that I had put down in a safe place, and it was still there, at the front of the letter rack in the hall. I pulled it out. I had read it, of course. But now I read it again.

Now that it's all a bit too late [it said], I can't help thinking about you. I keep seeing you as you were the first time I saw you. It was amazing, an amazing thing to see, you coming into the room in that house, and looking around, wondering what you were doing there. I thought straight away – I've never seen anyone like that before. And I hadn't. But there was nothing wrong with the way you looked, the way you stood, the way you dressed. That was what was so amazing; there was absolutely nothing wrong. I wondered how anyone could get to perfection like that. You struck me as someone who had looked in the mirror so many times to make adjustments and improvements that you'd forgotten who it was you were looking at.

OK, maybe I didn't think that straight away. There's

been plenty of time since then to see what you're like about your clothes. But I can promise you, you looked completely different from everyone else in the room. Everyone else had done their best to look nice for the party. You just knew how to do it. I looked you up and down, and wherever I stopped, it was perfect; the way your shoes shone, the little break of your trouser crease, the exact length of your jacket, everything simple, nothing you could comment on, nothing wrong. You just looked better than everyone else; better than me.

It's taken me years to start to wonder about someone who has perfect clothes always, every day. I thought you were beautiful by accident. You wanted to make yourself perfect. Perfect on the outside. You don't know that you do, but you do. The only reason I didn't realise that you'd decided to be perfect is that you succeeded. If you'd failed, if you'd tried to be beautiful and perfectly dressed and you'd not managed it, I'd have seen that it's a horrible, pathetic thing to do. You got it right, but you were wrong to want it. I don't know why you did.

I saw you and I wanted to marry you. I wanted to marry a man because he was perfect. I should have wondered what the hell I was going to do with a man if he was perfect. Go figure.

But you know what kind of letter this is, you know what you're reading. Go figure again, really. I've got to go. I've got your face in my head, the way I first saw it. I don't suppose you have that unless you're still in love with someone. I don't care either whether you still love me or not, because you don't save up your love to swap it for the same amount of love in return, you can still buy what you need with it even if you can't exchange it for someone else's little hoard. That's what I think. It's not that you're possesive, because you're not, and it's not that I don't feel possesive, because I do. But I've got to go.

It's just getting a bit strange round here and I don't understand it any more. I wouldn't mind it being strange so long as we both knew how strange it was. But you don't see how strange things are getting and I can't seem to explain that to you. Which is worrying. Listen, I've got to go, but don't start thinking I don't love you, I do. There are lots of imperfect things I haven't done and lots of imperfect places I haven't been and perhaps I'll come back, and perhaps I won't. The reason I'm going is that I think, without me, you can look at everything and see how wrong it all is, because it might be me that stops our life looking as strange as it is. This is really really hard.

But love anyway –

That's not how you spell possesive, is it?

I looked after my clothes; I always had. But that had always come from necessity, and Janet's letter made no sense to me. I had never been rich, and my small wardrobe had always had to be looked after carefully, to be good quality, to have no suggestion of eccentricity. I dressed well; I looked after my clothes; I spent time on it. Now, I always dressed in one of six grey suits with a white shirt;

I had five pairs of nearly identical black shoes, which I wore in strict rotation and cleaned every Saturday. Once a year, at the beginning of January, I threw away all my socks and underpants and bought fourteen new pairs of identical underpants, fourteen new pairs of identical socks. I dressed well. Janet's letter made absolutely no sense.

I had had, over the years, some clothes which meant a lot to me. That's true. The first one I remember was a sweater, a grey one. I must have been five or six, no older than that. It had a picture on the front, an appliquéd image of a red London bus, and red stripes round the collar and round the cuffs. I was crazily fond of it. The memory I have of it is a strange one, though. My mother had washed it, and hung it out on the line overnight. In the night, it suddenly snowed heavily, the temperature dropping below freezing. There it is, on the line, stiff as a pub sign, swinging in the wind, flat and hard with frost.

There are other treasured clothes I remember, but not that many. My clothes had never been a random, gaudy assortment, but always orderly and regular. I was still quite young, not long after Franky died, when I decided how I wanted to dress. My wardrobe was always uniform; I always had six of everything, all more or less the same, and rotated them carefully. I kept it all in good order. I looked how I wanted to look. If anyone had ever commented in anything but a general way on what I was wearing, on a particular garment, I would have felt that I had failed.

And yet it was true that I possessed, somehow, a pair of green velvet trousers and a crimson ruffled shirt. There was no denying that fact.

17

This really happened. Some time that month, this really happened, and it happened just like this. I don't know exactly when, though I know it was a weekday morning. It happened that hiccupping month.

We shopped in Putney rather than Wandsworth, usually. Janet thought the shops were better, and they were strung out along a single street, so – she said – you were more likely to bump into someone you knew. (She was terribly good at that sort of thing, the housewife natter about the price of peas; she could turn the idea of a cup of coffee into 'Shall we be wicked and play truant?' You'd never have guessed, really.)

On the way from our house to Putney High Street – the way we usually took, I mean – you passed an African church. London is full of churches for black people, and the churches are full; it's best not to think too hard about that, to imagine a life so grim that you would be reduced to asking God to do something about it. Most of these churches are exuberantly raucous scams, set up in hastily converted sheds. They have to trade under some barely rational name, all the good names, like the Church of England, having been taken long ago – the Church of Angelic Justice and the Holy Spirit, the Church for the Love of God. They are in a constant war of attrition with the noise-abatement people and, no doubt, the Revenue. Their congregations are kept going by two things: the certainty that no way are those fat godless bastards in the so-called Church of Faith over in Montpellier Street going to heaven, and by riding up and down the Northern Line with a Bible and a marker pen.

The African church you passed, though, was not quite like one of those; it was a proper church, and not a scam. It was not a shed, but a proper Victorian church, built for the Church of England. Of course, no one much goes to the Church of England these days. Some time ago, the church had given up on its regular punters – five old ladies and a grumpy couple who were only turning up because they were getting married there next month. I suppose the old ladies all died and went to heaven, anyway. Instead of that, it all at once became an Ethiopian church. You saw them, every Sunday, arriving from all over London; their fine-boned faces, the women handsome and devout under white headscarves; occasionally an unwilling Londonised daughter, embarrassed and refusing to cover her head until the last moment.

(You walk past, and you see Ethiopia, a country I've never seen; I see a church, an English Victorian church high on some high green mountains under a blue cloud-flecked sky, and those thin old matrons wrapped in their white shawls, walking ten happy miles to their Sunday service.

Of course, Ethiopia is not like this. Nowhere is. But that is what I saw.)

It seemed a great improvement to me, having this in Wandsworth, although I suppose there was not much to choose between one sort of nonsense and another.

The services happened at odd times. That morning, there was a small crowd coming out of the church. From inside, the sound of a voice deep in a chant; patient, ancient and hoarse, the sort of song which begins anywhere, circles round and round, and stops rather than finishes, as if it has drifted into your hearing and then drifts out to continue in some endless other place. I slowed, and then saw that it was a funeral. On the road, there was a hearse, its back door open. The undertaker stood by it in a frock coat and top hat, his hands clasped and his legs planted sturdily apart, like a soldier in the 'at ease' position. But you would have known it was a funeral without that, or without the coffin now being carried out. The crowd, thirty or forty of them, had it in the way they stood. You could see, this was a bad funeral; this was not the funeral of someone who had lived a long useful life to its end. I'd been to funerals, and people come out and start to talk, sombrely, decently, and they start to shake hands and even to smile and say 'Thank you for coming'. They were not doing that; they could hardly even look at each other. I wondered who this was; a son, a brother, a child. I had no hat to take off; I took out the gum I'd been chewing and stuffed it into the tissue in my pocket. I knew exactly the sort of funeral this was, because I'd been to Franky's, and I never

want to go to another one like it, I never want to see
another one like it.

The coffin was loaded into the hearse, and the
mourners moved towards the pavement. The chanting in
the church was still going on. The undertaker closed the
back door of the hearse, and walked, very slowly, round
it to the front in his top hat. The car started to move;
you didn't see the driver start the engine, and perhaps it
had been idling for a while. The undertaker started to
walk, directly in front of the car, and it moved forward
at the pace of his walking. It is not something you see
very often, that solemn pace, and it was good, it was well
done; the man in the top hat, the grief could have been
all his own.

This is why I remember it. This is what happened. This
is exactly what happened.

The church is on a busy road, a narrow one. All the
time I had been standing there, the normal traffic had
been driving past. The hearse had set off into a gap in the
traffic, but in a few seconds, behind it, the traffic was
slowed down to the same pace, the funereal pace – yes,
that's right, that's why you say that. There was, all at
once, a terrific noise; a car hooting. I thought, oh God,
they haven't seen, they don't know. Then it sounded
again, and again, and I looked. It was the car directly
behind the hearse, a new blue four-by-four. The driver
was a woman, a Sloaney blonde woman with an Alice
band and sleek dark hair. She was hooting. The traffic in
the other direction was heavy, and she could not over-
take for a moment. I could see her face, but she wasn't

looking at me. She was impatient, irritated, incredulous. Where was she coming from? Where was she going? In front of her, you knew where he was going; he was going where we all go. She wanted him to go there as fast as he could go.

There is no God and there is no praying but there on the pavement I started praying. I was praying to whatever it is that sends us a heart to feel anything for someone, anyone, for people we love and people we never knew, and there was no love in my thoughts; I prayed that there, at the end, when that woman died there would be no one there to say goodbye, not one mourner, no one to hire a man in a top hat to disrupt the traffic, that her children would have better things to do. I hated her too much to be silent.

'Fuck off!' a voice was shouting, and it was mine. 'Go on! Fuck off and don't fucking come back!'

It went on, hocketing over the chant in the church, but when it stopped, I saw a horrible thing. The mourners, in a crowd, their attention was on me. They didn't see a man who had thought and felt something. They saw someone who was shouting obscenities outside a funeral. They were good, decent people. Sometimes you see yourself from outside. It is never a good sight.

What Happened Before

Brenda had followed the two police officers out of the house, she found. She had said goodbye, had said thank you at the front door. Instead of closing the door and going back into the house, she had been drawn after them, as if they had the power to pull her into a different life. They turned; they were not surprised, but concerned. They waited for her to say what she had to say.

'I just wanted to know –' she said, faltering – and how should she know what that was, until she found herself asking it? – 'I just wanted to know – how did she die?'

The two police officers, a middle-aged man and a younger woman, exchanged no glances.

'It's probably for the best that you don't know the exact details,' the man said.

'We took a decision that it was not necessary for you both to see the body for identification purposes,' the woman said. The body; that was a shock. Brenda's daughter had been nothing but Franky in life, ever since she could talk and could name herself, but in death she had undergone a series of swift onomastic changes, reverting to Frances on the lips of policemen and the wet pages of the cheap newspapers now piling up, unread and unreadable, in the hall, and now into The Body. There was something reproachful about these renamings, as if her parents had irresponsibly misnamed her from the start. Under the official gaze, she was reverting to what an efficient mother should have christened her in the first place, Body. There was no need for her to see Body. The policewoman had said so. No need, whether for the purposes of identification or any other purpose.

They waited, and this was true. Brenda recalled now that a week before, when Franky's body had been found and the police had made their earlier visit – two different police officers, as if the facts could be channelled through anyone who happened to be on duty – the conversation had finished with this bleak but apparently insignificant declaration. It had not been necessary for her to see the body of her daughter for identification purposes. Then, a week before, the dry splash of shock had been such that she had hardly heard the sentence. But it had, it seemed, made some impact on her. With this reminder, she heard the sentence as if for the first time, and she saw that this small thing, this task which she need not carry out, would over time grow and root itself until, like the elm under which Franky's body had been found, it would shadow the fact itself. There had been no need to identify her daughter's body, and if Brenda had seen, once, years before, her daughter's body when it was lacy with her womb's mucus, her mouth yawning incredulously in the cold hospital air for her first shout into life, she would never now see her broken dead body, and the story for her had no ending.

These police officers, the man and the woman, had come to tell her something else, that the man who had killed her daughter had, they believed, been found. She waited there on the path, neatly planted tulips in a lucid line to either side of them. Her question hung in the air: how did Franky die. The name of the man who killed her, that she should know, but it now proved, as she had known, of no satisfaction or interest to her. What she needed to know, she found, was the manner of Franky's death, since, perhaps through selfishness, she needed to end the way her mind, for a week now, had been visiting death after death on her daughter, murdering her in so many dozens of ways, with knives, ropes, hands, boot heels, and listening to the many different sounds a girl could conceivably make in her last seconds. The deaths of Franky were so many, blooming and dividing out of the soil of her ignorance, and the one death she had endured would be bad, single and final.

But the spark of energy which had drawn Brenda out of the house and given her the question she needed to ask quickly faded, and she let them tell her, for whatever reason, the exact circumstances of the crime with an encroaching dullness. She listened carefully to the explanation, stumbling and unsure as it was, and it did not add to her pain at that moment; she filed it away, knowing that it could come to hurt her later, and certainly would. He explained that Franky had been raped, before she died, her hands tied together with a length of rope and her mouth sealed with tape – these details, the policeman said, clearly indicated that there was nothing spontaneous about the crime, but carried out with premeditation and planning. Afterwards, her throat had been cut, and deeply cut. There were some small jabs and wounds elsewhere on her body – on her arms and on her breasts, he specified, seeing that she needed, she wanted, the information – which suggested that before he had killed her, he had tried to subdue her, prodding with a knife to let her know what he was capable of. Perhaps he had not known what he was capable of; perhaps he had bluffed, and then stopped bluffing.

She learnt all this, nodding, and somehow grateful, and then all at once – one of those unnerving lapses and elisions of time which had so characterised the last week – she found that she was back inside her house without, apparently, having thanked or said goodbye to the officers. She had been told by one of her official visitors that she should expect to feel numb at first, that this was quite normal, but numbness was not an apt description. Rather, she felt acutely observant and aware of a world which had in an instant been eroded or dulled by the removal of a single, universal fact; as if the colour red had gone from the world, as if the London sparrow had overnight become extinct, as if a letter had gone from the alphabet, and all memory of such things gone, too.

The house she stood in was hers, she knew that, and nothing had changed. In the sitting room, she could hear her husband's voice, trying out one tentative sentence, asking the children something, and then the child answered, declining whatever it was that had been offered. The house had been hers, and it still was hers; one voice had gone from it, but that was all; there was no worldly benefit lost, no problem compensation could solve. But it did not feel like that; she felt the weight of the room upstairs, that room now so painfully full and painfully empty at once; full of possessions, ownerless. It seemed to her that with Franky's death she had lost her sense of the house as being hers. Rather, it seemed as if from now on they lived there at the whim of a rich absent landlord, now never seen, as if they must henceforth keep it tidy and clean at all times, in case that landlord should ever return without warning, claim what was hers. From now on, they would be living there, living their lives, on sufferance.

The days passed through her. She did not share what she had learnt from the policeman, and they did not talk about anything. There were four of them in her family; she counted her children. One, two. As if to demonstrate that their lives had been changed, they were prevented from returning to their daily business. Well, that was how it seemed; the children's school, her employer, her husband's employer, none of whom knew anything of the others, separately wrote to insist that the four of them were not needed, and should return only when they wanted to. The letters caused each of them disquiet, as they arrived, but only David, Brenda's husband, acted on his disquiet and telephoned his employer to clarify matters. The telephone was kept in the hallway, and Brenda sat on the topmost stair, her elbows on her knees and her chin in her hands, to listen to the conversation.

He had been exploring a subject for two nights with her now, and though she had had nothing to say, she still felt she should listen and discover the outcome. It seemed odd that David's disquiet should have settled so exactly on one question; was that the extent of it, or did he hold it up against the unconstrained blaze of the rage beyond? David was exact, uncertain, suspicious, and watched and warned, in case *they* – a vast, sinister chain of people above him – should do you down. He was the manager of an electronics shop, one of a large chain. His daughter's death had come to this, and Brenda listened.

'It's very good of you,' he said.

'Am I going to go on being paid?' he said.

'In full?' he said.

'Thank you. But when will you be expecting me back?'

'I see,' he said. 'Yes, that's what the letter says. But you must be expecting me back sometime. I mean, you won't be very happy if I don't come back to work for a year.'

'No,' he said. 'No, probably not a year. Not even a –'

'Well, the other thing,' he said. 'It's that I don't know what you mean by in full. Because this week I was supposed to be doing overtime and I don't know whether –'

'I see,' he said. 'No, I didn't expect it exactly. It's as well to be clear about these things from the start, because we don't want any unpleasantnesses to arise in the future. So for the immediate future – I'm just saying this so that we're both clear, both clear in our minds – you'll be paying me on the basic scale, just that, and I'll return when, when –'

'Yes,' he said. 'Yes, we got the flowers. Thank you very much.'

Brenda was not precisely embarrassed, but she could see and hear the woman he was speaking to as if she were in the house; her nervous incredulity, going into details she knew but had not expected having to explain. 'You'll never believe it,' the woman was saying to a colleague, now that David had put down the telephone; they were exactly alike, those two colleagues, women with untidy hair and red lipstick, women in grey suits and black shoes, women five feet four inches tall, women whose children were all still alive ... We don't want any unpleasantnesses to arise in the future, Brenda thought as her characters faded and David looked up at her. Not then, not in the future.

She understood him in a way. It was something like her feeling about the house. Without knowing it, she had always been keeping it in trust, and not considering what she was hoarding until the eventual recipient had walked, one night, into a moonless park and away. David was watchful about money, he always had been, and now there was more reason than ever to know exactly what he was storing. They looked at each other; they were helpless, with a whole staircase of unpleasantnesses between them.

The kindness of their employers, of the children's school, grew hard to bear. They did not intrude; you could hear them not intruding; but after a few maundering days behind their windows, the boy brought that to an end. The journalists had all gone; the policemen, even, had gone; but they did not go out; they walked around inside, skirting each other with their different-sized bodies, all of them, even the children, having acquired the politeness and consideration of near strangers. The civility, the painful lack of anything to do and anything to say exhausted them all, but the boy broke first. The stairs had become, for all of them, a good place to be, a good place to sit, and, as she dismally washed some pots in the kitchen, she could hear his voice from that intermediate space. She stopped the tap to hear what he was saying – she knew, just from the emphatic singing rhythm of the phrases, that he was talking to himself. That psalm-chanting of children – no, of boys, because Franky, she never sounded like that – the way they sang through their own determination; she set down the pot in the sink, and walked quietly to the door of the kitchen, listening to him. 'I THINK I'm now all RIGHT, I REALLY am, because I was THINKING, only THINKING, that maybe SCHOOL might be thinking, and they MIGHT have WRITTEN because things DO get lost, so CAN I go back, perhaps TOMORROW, because –'

She had been drawn out of the kitchen by the way he talked, and he broke off on seeing her. He looked so frightened. She remembered what that was like, when you were that age; when all at once you found yourself with a marvellous argument, something even your mother would have to accept and you would get your own wonderful way. She had intruded on it, and he knew that his brilliant defence of what he wanted to do had been heard before it was quite ready. But she was kind, yes, Brenda was kind, and she knew how to help him.

'Your father was saying,' she said, 'I don't know whether you feel up to it, but perhaps tomorrow, if you wanted, perhaps you could go to school. Only if you felt up to it, mind.'

After that, they all started drifting back towards their lives; after John, his sister, and then David. Each morning, there was no announcement, but they went back to work. Brenda was the last to go. Her job was not, in any case, real to her. It was what she called 'pin money' and everything substantial about it had always had the capacity to surprise her; the arrival of a payslip, or a reprimand when once she had been an hour late for no reason. She worked for the fire service, and though at times in her life Brenda would display bravery equal to anything required of firemen, her job was not a heroic one; she typed the letters for the station commander and his deputy. The same sensation of mild surprise came to her when the letter arrived, similar in every way to the letters her husband's employers and her children's school had sent, expressing sympathy and assuring her that she could take as much leave as seemed necessary; it was equally implausible that the fire service should employ her and that they should miss her presence. It was pin money.

She returned, however, in time, after everyone else had resumed their normal lives. The two lives which presented themselves to her were both implausible, and she felt as detached and remote from her life of grief as from her occupation, but having no other life, she preferred not to be at home. Once David had gone back to his job, the children restarted their halting education, it seemed impossible to her to follow any other course. But her return was delayed by a consideration which might at any other time have seemed unimportant; once she had decided that, the others having resumed their previous lives, she should do the same, she found herself wondering what the proper, the respectful, day of the week would be to return to her job. It was a general, unanswerable question over her life at this time, and this issue gave it a specific and problematic form. How should a woman correctly behave, in the aftermath of her teenage daughter's murder? When should she weep, when should she speak, on what subjects should she discourse, and at what lapse of time was it proper to return to those occupations of shopping, cooking, working, sleeping? How soon after her daughter's murder may a mother use the cashpoint outside the bank in the high street? She had no answers. It seemed to her that, difficult as all these questions were, the decision, not of how soon she should return to work, but on what day of the week she might properly do so, was almost insuperable. The task of deciding on the day required respect in two directions: respect towards her employer, and the public respect she must direct towards her daughter's death. That public display of grieving struck her quickly as something necessary but separate from the unjointed heat of solitary grief, quite different from the waves of astonishment and clarity which, reminding her that she had one daughter less, would leave her alone and tottering and unobserved in the kitchen while a pan, perhaps, clattered on the floor. If the public display and the private grief had been the same, she would have returned to work immediately or never, on any day or none.

But the question, once raised, of what day to start work again, could not be answered. To return on a Monday would give the impression that she had taken advantage of the weekend; to turn up on Friday would suggest that the rhythms of the week of work now had no importance for her; they would give her no work to do. But no other day seemed right either, since to begin work on a day in the middle of the week would imply that her grief, so paralysing one day, had eased overnight. She could not invite incredulity on that score.

Such difficulties, so intricate and disabling, like webs she had spun herself, trapping her ankles whenever she tried to move forward, had become familiar to her in many different situations. She had discovered that it was impossible spontaneously to address a remark to a stranger, for instance, or to respond to one, however trivial the occasion might be. Before, it had been her habit to buy food not from a single supermarket, but from several shops in succession, believing that money might be saved and that the quality of the goods was higher in a greengrocer's, a butcher's, a fishmonger's, a cheese shop. But now she found herself drawn to the crowded aisles of Sainsbury's, since there, she found, everything you needed could be taken from the shelves in pre-wrapped quantities, could be placed in the trolley, could be passed through the till and paid for without any kind of requirement to speak or comment to anyone. In the devout entrancement of the supermarket, the slow snaking progress from fruit to wine of the lonely shoppers like a line of pilgrims, she found respect and isolation, and no need to speak. Once, she had enjoyed exchanges in shops; had enjoyed, too, the sensuous appeal of loose-piled food as it was offered up, the petrol-dappled shine of mackerel, the glossy voluptuous curve, satin and dark as a conker, of calves' liver, the novelty-soap appeal of avocado and figs, nestling in their straw. That seemed to have gone, and gone, too, the private delight in the street flavours; before, she could have been lured into a shop by a gust of roasting coffee, new bread, the high scent, like a beautiful rich clean woman, of lilies in banks outside a florist's. Before, she could have stood there ecstatically taking it in, head back, as if lost not in pleasure but in nostalgia, like an old man on a cricket pitch, transported by the perfume of a petrol mower and new-cut grass. Could she still smell? Perhaps; but now there was nothing in it, and she bought her coffee, meat, fruit, and even the sad occasional treat of scentless scrubby carnations well wrapped in cellophane, from Sainsbury's.

The task of speaking was beyond her; she felt that, and she found at length that she was right. 'I fancy some pork,' David had said the night before. 'We haven't had pork since I don't know when.' But the supermarket when she reached it – these days, it took her until four or five to leave the house at all – had no pork. She went on, as if in a trance, and found herself in the butcher's. Too soon, she was at the head of the queue.

'I'd like some pork,' she said. The young man was new

to her, and he did not know her; he was plump and pink and healthy as butchers are.

'What cut would you like?' he said.

She looked back, helplessly. 'It's for four,' she said, and that line she had practised, for her own sake.

He tried again, too; familiar, perhaps, with customers without any degree of the culinary knowledge of anatomy once so universal. 'Well, what were you going to do with it?'

But now, the question seemed to raise all kinds of possibilities, few of which had anything to do with cooking; she felt quite as capable of saying that she planned to bury it in the garden, to give it to the poor, to use it as a fireside ornament as of anything else, and it was with a conscious effort that she said, 'Perhaps for roasting.' The boy accepted this, and sold her what she needed. Once outside, she began uncontrollably to shake, almost in tears, at the astonishing difficulty of the simple exchange. She had done it, true, but it had been a task of gigantic proportions, and she hunched over with shame at what she had become, a woman incapable of asking for a joint of meat in a butcher's shop.

Such a woman, it should have been clear, could not carry out her previous occupation. This did not occur to her. In the end, she went back to the fire station on a Thursday. Her boss, the firemen were quiet about her, trying not to trouble her, but all that day, she did nothing but type a single letter, three paragraphs long; it took her four hours. From time to time the phone rang by her, but she did not, could not answer it, always contriving to be leaping up and going to the lavatory at the first ring. The next day she did not go back, nor on Monday. Tuesday and, perseveringly, Wednesday, she returned, and it was no better; and then she stayed at home. She tried only once more to go to work, goading, pushing, insulting herself in advance, but when she arrived, pale and resolute, the firemen sitting around looked at her in astonishment. It took some time for one of them to explain that it was a Sunday. She had not realised.

Of course, they eventually let her go, and she made no objection. She would have let herself go if she had been brave enough, sacked herself from her own existence. The story she told David was not quite accurate, and she led him to believe that she had resigned from her job, not being up to it at the moment, since his grief, if that is what it was, had taken the form of fretting and beetling over small practical details, over wrongs of the impersonal and financial variety. In possession of the facts, she had no doubt that he would take up a cause she herself had no interest in, and pursue the facts of the settlement until he had found some real or imagined injustice; would discuss it, so painfully, night after night with her, too. But she presented it to him as a matter of her emotions and capacities, and into those, as she knew from her own inabilities, he would not enquire.

It was then that Brenda realised she had a task to carry out, which was hers alone, a task to fill some of these empty days. She had to clear her daughter's bedroom of her daughter's possessions, to empty the wardrobe of her daughter's clothes, to take from the walls the images her daughter had placed there, to put in black bin bags the small and ugly objects which the years, the so few years of her daughter's life, had accumulated and arranged on the little-girl dressing table she had always had; small beady glass animals, china dolls, ruffled, pink and unspeaking objects now redolent of pain. The room had to be cleared, and cleared by her, if the room were not to become a shrine.

Brenda carried out this task over two weeks. Into the suffering of her mind in those two weeks we will not enter; at the darkest points in Brenda's long journey, we will not presume to light a torch. Through those days, she went alone. She goes alone.

If, afterwards, her memory of the trial itself remained vague and puzzling, she could always reconstruct, with no effort at all, the two weeks during which she disposed, having no choice, of her daughter's life into black bin bags.

When did you start to forget? And even now, mere months after Franky's death, Brenda could feel her shrinking in the memory. She could, if she chose, hear her voice again, but increasingly that voice was incapable of saying anything but a few characteristic phrases, could not enter as it once had into conversation. Sometimes, yes, she could see her face again or catch a little of her own whiff, the warm smell of her body, her clean hair pungent with the airy watermelon scent of the shampoo she had so liked; she had left a bottle half finished, and one day, David had unthinkingly used it on himself, but only once. Even Franky's face seemed to be receding from her, so that sometimes with a shock Brenda realised that having conjured up her dead daughter's features, what memory had supplied and what she had been contemplating was in fact the face of the other daughter. In the end, too soon, Franky's face had vanished, and the only way she could think of her was in the images preserved in the family photographs, like a celebrity Brenda had never seen or known. There was a painful consonance with the way Brenda considered Franky's murderer, who, though she had seen him and heard him levelly speak from the dock, could never afterwards be persuaded by contemplation to become anything but the celebrated picture which the newspapers printed and reprinted, and his name, which we will not repeat. The obscure figure gutturally gorging on Franky's pale body remained for Brenda faceless, empty, incredible, despite the unwelcome and extravagant efforts of her imagination, day after day.

In time, things returned. The first time she saw something, clearly and whole, as if the grey veil between her and the world had for a second been lifted, was three months after the event. They were eating dinner, the four of them, and she found herself looking at the boy, quizzing his existence and properties keenly. His blond hair quite abruptly struck her with a sharp pathos. It was unruly and unkempt, since no one had thought to take him to the barber's, but more than that, it bore the signs that he alone had attempted to deal with it, that no one else had been concerned about it. The front was smoothed down as best he could, she saw, but behind, where the mirror would not help him, he had not known to attend to it and it was knotted and scrubby as bindweed. No one had seen; and though the hair might now be attended to, she wondered what other neglects had been visited thoughtlessly upon him, what unseen consequences were now beginning to direct his life.

Franky grew no older, she never changed, in the years and decades which followed. Sometimes, in a dream or in an empty afternoon room, the face memory produced would be her face as it was before she died; sometimes, inexplicably, it would be the child's face, looking upwards. Brenda could see nothing, in the end, but the photographs. But if Franky's face never changed, an odder and more audacious series of changes took place in the remembered figure; she kept up with fashion. When Brenda thought of her, she saw her not in the clothes she had worn at the time and which she had been killed in – clothes which had been kept by the police until the trial and all appeals had been concluded, and burnt, surely, in a daze of relief soon afterwards. The white frilled shirt, the ballooning trousers flaring at the hip and jamming in door frames, the highwayman boots and the asymmetric pirate geometry of the hair, brushing one cheekbone – all that went over time, and the unageing Franky kept up with fashion, taking stilettos, to sharp black suits, to flat ballet dancer's shoes, to bulbous trainers, to leg warmers, big hair, bobs, slicked back hair, and a thousand outfits she would never know. Above the parade of fashion, her face retreated or advanced in time, but never quite succeeded in getting past seventeen.

These apparitions came and went, and over the years became less constant; a cause of gratitude and shame, that days and even weeks passed without her thinking of Franky. She kept no shrine in her mind, as she had kept none in her house, but the memories came forcefully and unbidden. Brenda knew, as the years and the decades passed and she grew older, that if anyone should ever ask her about Franky, she would say the conventional thing, that no day passed without her thinking of her, but it would not have been true. And nobody ever did ask. For the rest of her life, however, from time to time, a sentence overheard, a glimpse of a girl's face turning with a Franky smile in the street, the sight of a row of yellow tulips marshalled in municipal regularity could renew her grief and astonishment, unshareably.

There are too many of these moments to describe over the course of the decades, and it is improper and in-trusive that we should know what poor hiccupping John never knew about his own mother, but here is one, decades after Franky died. Brenda always had bad teeth and a dread of dentists; when she was a child, the mint humbugs probably sent her to the dentist and it was with a bag of mint humbugs that her stoic endurance of the dentist's drill was rewarded. It was uncharacteristic of her, one Christmas afternoon, so dashingly to attempt to crack a nut with her back teeth (the nutcracker having been commandeered, in the way he habitually commandeered the remote control for the television, by her husband) and she felt her soft sugary molar, softer than the nutshell, crack down some fault line. The crack seemed to her to

resound like gunfire, but in those intimate catastrophes
of the body, the senses are confused, and the abrupt assault
on the tooth could have been silent. She extracted the
nut, and said nothing; there was no pain, and she tried
to forget about it. Nevertheless, she knew with a throb-
bing dread itself like the toothache to come that the body's
powers of mending and curing do not extend to the teeth
and, in time, the dentist would have to be faced.

It was not until the beginning of February, however,
that the pain began with an Alpine ascent, doubling every
hour, and she found she had to tell her husband what had
happened. The next morning, having no choice, she was
in the dentist's waiting room.

Perhaps it was the pain which brought her mind closer
to Franky and Franky's end, without her having directly
thought of these sore facts. The spark of memory was
unforeseen and instant. If Brenda suffered under the
conviction that in many ways her thoughts and grief and
behaviour were eccentric and improper, unlike the ways
she ought to think and act, in reality she lived as she
might be expected to, and on this occasion, finding herself
in a dentist's waiting room, she picked up one of the old
magazines which are to be found in such places. She was
not and never had been a reader of magazines, and the
one she started to read, concerned with 'celebrities' of
the more abstruse variety, presented her with matters she
knew nothing whatever about. Nevertheless, she read on,
and in a moment her pain would be added to immeasur-
ably; because there, in the pages of a silly magazine, she
read a description of a woman who put on clothes for

money, who walked thirty feet in that direction and thirty feet back to where she had come from, who was photographed with her permission and without, a woman who came from Australia, a woman who was known to magazines like this one by the sobriquet 'The Body'. The Body, she read, and before she could breathe and gasp through her pain-racked mouth, it was as if the disguise of brightly coloured gloss, of weekly headlined silliness had fallen away from the messenger, as if the earth had crevassed just there where she sat, as if the regions of the dead had yawned and chundered with the name of her daughter, her last name, the name she had been given by the police officers at the very end. She could not cry, but as the earth shuddered beneath her feet, she trembled with it. And, like the aftershock of an earthquake, in five long seconds there came the face of Franky, floating as clear as a stain against the white wall of the room; but this time, she was dressed in black chiffon, her hair long, and she was laughing, her blue eyes dancing as if she were waiting for some beautiful punchline, and as she never had in life she was walking backwards, beckoning, fading, gone.

19

You've probably heard this one before, but these are the three worst lies. The first is this: 'People who need people are the luckiest people in the world.' Barbra, Barbra, what were you thinking of? Probably nothing much, since you're American and can't even spell your own name. The second is 'I'll only be a minute' – adapt this one to circumstances. The third, alas, is 'I love you'. Of course, sometimes people say one of these things, and it isn't a lie. Sometimes you tell someone you love that you love them. Sometimes someone says they'll be a minute, and sixty seconds later, there they are. It's even possible that one of those clingy bores Barbra likes so much could be lucky – I don't know, if he won the lottery or something. But in general, they sound like lies to me.

Janet was a terrible liar. She did it all the time, and she was very bad at it. But there's nothing special in that. I was a terrible liar. My mother was a terrible liar. Everyone I knew was a terrible liar. Even Franky was a terrible liar, and she certainly would have carried on being one. It is basically how people are. It is easier to tell a lie than to tell the truth. For instance, this is a truthful statement: 'People are morally the same, and intellectually different.' This, on the other hand, is a lie: 'No, that dress really suits you.' Which is easier to say? Which one have you said, or could you say? Janet, like everyone, was a terrible liar, having no alternative. Get a load of this.

'Where are you now?' I said.

'India, by now,' she said.

'Is it nice, then, India-by-now?'

'It's amazing. I'm having a fantastic time.'

'I'm glad.'

'I think we need to talk about stuff.'

'I don't, to tell you the truth.'

'I think you need to accept that we've split up, and I'm not coming back.'

'I've accepted that.'

'I'm glad.'

'I've accepted it to the point that I've met someone else.'

'What did you say?'

'Is this a bad line?'

'No.'

'I said I'd met someone else.'

'Good, I'm happy for you.'

'We're having sex together.'

'Oh yes.'

'I fuck her up her cunt when she asks me to, and I fuck her up her bum, when she asks me to.'

'And she asks you to.'

'Yes, she asks me to.'

'Are you glad?'

'That she asks me to fuck her up her bum?'

'Actually, I meant are you glad more generally.'

'About my life from beginning to now?'

'Less generally.'

'Yes, I'm glad.'

'I'm glad too.'

'She's a nice girl.'

'She sounds fucking A.'

'She's tip-top and all my friends like her.'

'What friends? India's amazing.'

'I've always wanted to go.'

I don't know whether she heard that; as I was saying how much I'd always wanted to go to India, the line cut out altogether. I waited for a minute or two by the phone, but it didn't ring. Count the lies in that; or to save time, try and find anything truthful that Janet said to me, or that I said to her. It's easy; there wasn't anything.

All that summer, I was hearing a song. I never went looking for music. It always crept up on me, like a drifting fart. Some people would hunt it down with their credit cards; would spend evenings in concert halls, opera houses, nightclubs, rock arenas, and to justify their expenditure, could tell you all about it. Music, it was something I liked well enough, but I never investigated it. All it ever got from me was an 'Oh yes, I know that'.

Some people know about it, and can tell you how it was made and when and what, or who, you happen to be listening to. I either knew a song or I didn't know it.

But how did I know those few minutes of music? It seems to creep up on you. In a shop, in a taxi, at a party, there is music playing which you hardly notice; and then, I suppose, you hear it again, still not noticing. At some point, it comes to your attention, and you learn what it is, but by that time you know it perfectly well. Everyone knows Beethoven's Fifth Symphony, for instance, the way it doomily falls downstairs. By the time anyone tells you that it is a symphony, it is by Beethoven, it has a number, it is already fairly familiar to you by some unobserved process.

There was a song that summer which had been circling me like this. In the end, I got to know it, got to know the words and the title, the performer and the record label, but by that time I could sing it from beginning to end. You heard it in shops, you overheard it in taxis, you were startled by impromptu renditions in the south London streets as the kids turned out of school. Alone and hiccupping, my mind turned to its twists and riffs, the languorous black funk of its insistent dance. It was a good tune, a good song, and I sang it without knowing what it was.

> *A face on a page*
> *A glimpse on a street*
> *A smile for the goat-fuck*
> *Those shoes on her feet*
> *They cost a million dollars*
> *A million dollars*
> *So smile.*

It's called celebrity.
Welcome to my lovely home
My marriage is just fine
I've dealt with all my demons
But now you've had your time
So off you go
It's called celebrity.
I don't know you
But you know me
That's why it's called
Celebrity.

It seemed a sad song to me. Its sadness was only partly in its subject, though it made me see how sad it would be to be famous. Nor was it altogether in the music, although the more I heard it, the more I thought that whatever the unrelenting energy of the cholesterol heartbeat, the way it turned and deepened and lengthened on the word million was mournful and regretful. The word million, the saddest word in the world; I had learnt that truth from Gareth, the saddest man I never met. The sadness was in the way it seemed to give me a glimpse of myself in old age. It seemed already freighted with nostalgia, and it was easier to imagine it as a song one had heard forty years before than a current favourite. That, I can't explain, but the more I heard it, the more I seemed to see myself in old age, in forty years' time, overhearing the dance hit of 2002 and saying, 'Goodness, do you remember this?'

It was like Marmite.

I love Marmite. Not everyone does, but I do. It was years ago, when I was still quite small, that Marmite made me realise that I was going to grow old and the world was going to change. I can't place this memory, but it's an exact one, filed away. My mother is standing there, in a sunny kitchen, the kitchen in Bromley, and watching me spread a slice of toast with Marmite. One of many slices of toast I'll be making and eating from one end of my childhood to the other, but this one, she's watching. She gives a fond little smile when I glance over at her.

'You love your Marmite, don't you?' she says.

'It's all right,' I say.

(You could probably date this memory from that line. You start saying 'It's all right' in that dismissive way when puberty strikes, and go on saying it for a couple of years, when you realise that you can go back to talking.)

'It's a good job you can live on it,' she says. 'At least you must be able to live on it. You're not dead yet, are you?'

'Living proof,' I say.

Then I put the slice of toast in my mouth, sideways, tear it in half between jaw and fist. It gets eaten in two chomps.

'Honestly,' she says.

'I love Marmite, me,' I say. For some reason I say this in a Birmingham accent.

'I can see that,' she says.

'Mummy,' I say. And this is ironic but not ironic, because I am still a little boy. 'What was your favourite thing to eat? I mean when you were a kid.'

'Oh, sweetheart,' she says, beaming as mothers do when it turns out, after all, that their kids still love them, when they feel like it. 'Oh, you ask some funny things. What did I like best when I was your age. Well, you couldn't get what you can get these days. There wasn't the choice. I remember the first time I saw a banana I must have been ten. The girl who lived next door to your grandparents, she was called Sally, she got given one, after the war. We went down to the bottom of the garden and we couldn't work out what to do with it.'

'Bananas?' I say.

'No, that's not what I liked best,' my mother says. She always knows what you mean. 'I was just giving an example. I know what I liked best. Jap – they were called Jap something. Like Japanese, I suppose. I couldn't get enough of them when I was your age. I loved them.'

'Jap –?' I say.

'No, you can't get them now,' she says. 'I don't know why. They just stopped making them. I haven't thought about them for years. Look what you've done, I'd sell my soul for a bag of them now. Easily pleased, that's me.'

I smile, and am embarrassed; because this is not a family where we talk much about love, even a love for sweets or Marmite, or about what we long for and what we miss. But underneath my embarrassment is a conviction that somewhere in the world there must still be a bag of her favourite sweets, and somehow I am going to find that bag for my mother, and give her a quarter-pound of her childhood back, one day.

'There'll come a time,' she says thoughtfully, 'when

you'll be asked what you liked best when you were little, and you won't have to think about it at all, will you?'

We don't talk much about love, and we don't, generally, smile at each other for no reason, cross a kitchen and kiss each other. I remember this. There is the thought, too, of my future self, and the day when I too will go into a shop and look for Marmite, and find that it is gone, that they've stopped making it, that the salty childhood taste, black as tears, now only exists in the memory of a few old men like me. I am ten; I am going to be an old man.

And the song was like that, throwing me forwards into a future of nostalgia. My pleasures were never simple. They always involved the sad conviction that they would be taken from me, that soon I would lose them and have nothing but effortful memory.

20

'Mrs Grainger's residence,' I said into the telephone.

There was a long silence.

'Mrs Grainger's residence,' I said again.

'Wasia,' the voice said. 'This is Wasia.'

I was surprised. I had been thinking about Wasia, on and off, for a few days. That morning was the first day I had worked since the wedding, and on my way to Mrs Grainger's house, I had stopped at a newsagent's and bought a packet of cigarettes. 'Twenty Marlboros, please,' I said, and cursed as I heard myself pronounce the cigarettes as the school is pronounced. But the man had taken my money and given me the packet as if there was nothing odd about my request. I put them in my pocket and walked out into the street. I planned to smoke my first cigarette when I was alone and unobserved, at Mrs Grainger's house, and afterwards, like Wasia but unlike my family, I would be a smoker. The reason was trivial, but I hung on to it because the other reason to start smoking seemed too ambitious, and it would be embarrassing if it didn't work. The other reason was that I wondered whether it might not put an end to the hiccups, which now had been going on for ten days continuously. The champagne had seemed like a good idea, and I had taken care to drink a bottle or two every day. But perhaps something else was needed.

Mrs Grainger was sitting down in the drawing room with one of her cronies when the phone rang. She had a little court of old ladies who came to call at odd, old-lady times. She entertained between meals, had what my mother would have referred to as 'morning coffee' and 'afternoon tea', although she, being snobbish, did not use these hotelier's terms. The prospect of lunch and, as the light waned in the late afternoon, the offer of a glass of sherry were her usual ways of dispatching her friends. Mrs Grainger ate alone, if you don't count me as company, and, since she could polish off a chop in the shameless time it took me to pick up my knife and fork, I guess she didn't count me.

'You won't be going anywhere, will you?' she used to say, and her tone was satisfied, not worried. She was a greedy and selfish old woman – it wasn't just her gleaming breezy way when presented with a pork pie, a knife and a fork, but other, less satiable greeds. She could suck you dry, if you let her. I sort of admired her; I felt that her existence was one any rational person should aspire to. If there is no Heaven and Hell and Judgment, if there is only one Thing left, only death left out of those Four Last Things, then anyone should hope, in the end, to be a rich, greedy, selfish, clever, amusing old woman surrounded by beaters diligently smoothing her path in life.

She said she could not look after her big old house any more. Or did not want to; she was perfectly fit and healthy, for her age, of course, and I think she just preferred to pay me to do the things which bored her. I washed her clothes, and ironed them, I shopped for food and cooked a hot plain lunch for her and a plain dinner which she could eat, cold, in the evening after I had gone. I watched television programmes with her during the day; programmes which seemed to bore her, but which she liked to watch anyway. I drove her wherever she wanted to go, and waited in the car outside her friends' houses while she drank a cup of tea with them, or played gin rummy for small stakes. (She must have been good at it; in her pink and velvet lounge, there was a whole shelf of small china animals which she had won off her friends.) Quite often, I was supposed to go with her into the dusty old shops where she bought her clothes and to express a preference for one sturdy tweed suit over another. She ignored my advice on these subjects, but she liked to hear it anyway.

She had been deeply occupied in the drawing room with her friend and a tiny task. If you led a life where any demands were ever made of you, then such a task would not need doing at all. Mrs Grainger could stretch these things out to fill a morning, until they were so substantial they needed assistance, paid and unpaid. In this case, she was 'sorting through', as she said, some old family photographs. The family photographs were never definitively sorted through; they were ordered, for the benefit of company, and then shuffled like a pack at poker and, a month later, inflicted on a different visiting old lady, in a different order. There is no reason to go into the particular old lady that day; she was a lesser courtier, who visited Mrs Grainger but was not visited in return (perhaps her house smelt of wee; perhaps her husband was still alive, and Mrs Grainger would make anyone think that it becomes rather vulgar, after a certain age, not to be a widow). She was called whatever she was called; she was grateful to Mrs Grainger and, to my humiliation, mildly in awe of me, an awe not diminished by the fact that I was hiccupping twice a minute like a yokel on a spree.

I was wandering in and out. The television was on, as it quite often was, half attended to. I had poured myself a cup of coffee, and they had cups of coffee and a choco-late biscuit; that, I did not take, making some sort of gesture to my status as a servant. It was an Australian programme they were watching, which had been going on for ever, five days a week. At that moment, two people, one old and one young, were building up to an argument and the end of the programme for today.

'How could you do that,' the elder of the two said. 'How could you behave like that – to your own – *half-brother . . .*'

The other actor looked suitably shocked.

'How,' said Mrs Grainger in her slow bored voice, 'is he Barry's half-brother?'

'Well,' the old lady said after a moment, 'I don't really look at –'

But in fact I was merely leaving a bored pause before answering. Remembering the details of Australian soap operas was just one of the things I did for Mrs Grainger, and she didn't acknowledge that her guest had said anything at all.

'Shane had a wife in Melbourne who died in an accident with an outboard motor, and she was carrying a child and there was a doctor on the beach who managed to deliver the baby and then offered to bring the child up, and afterwards Shane moved to another part of Australia and married Melanie and they had a child, who is Barry, before the owner of the café turned out to be Shane's first son in disguise,' I said. '!'

'Who is Melanie?' Mrs Grainger said. Sometimes I thought she paid no attention to the television programme at all, although she watched it every day, as, indeed, did I. I watched it because I thought she liked it.

'The thin woman with red hair. That one, there.'

'Do you look at this, Mary?' she asked her guest.

'I haven't until now, I must confess,' the old lady – whose name must have been Mary – offered bravely. 'But I must make the effort.'

'It's awful rubbish,' Mrs Grainger said. 'I can't imagine who watches it at all.' Then she smiled, forgivingly.

I said nothing, though it seemed impressive to me that Mrs Grainger had managed magnanimously to overlook her friend's low addiction to a show which, in fact, she had never had inflicted on her, rather than own up to watching it religiously, her vagueness about the plot, despite this assiduity, deriving from general slackness and, I suppose, the fact that I could always tell her about their lurid doings. Practising for Alzheimer's, her opulent laziness had produced a goldfish-like memory, reliably stretching about fifteen hours into the past. I was paid to supplement it.

Then the credits started and the telephone rang. I got up and lifted the telephone cover. When I answered the telephone, Mrs Grainger preferred me to stand up like a butler. Particularly if there were friends of hers there.

'This is Wasia,' the voice on the end of the telephone said.

'Were you watching *Barker's Pool*?' I said, for something to say. I thought this because the telephone had rung so promptly at the end of the half-hour programme.

'No,' she said. 'What is Barker's pool?'

'It's a television programme,' I said. Then I didn't know what else to say.

'Look,' she said impatiently. 'Look, I need to see you. I wondered if you were doing anything tonight.'

'Yes,' I said. Mrs Grainger had started fussily rearranging her skirt, and poking ineffectively at the television with her walking stick, to turn it off; she refused to use a remote control, and told me twice a week that they issued radioactive rays, which would make any man infertile, given time.

'Yes what?' Wasia said.

'It appears to be a friend of John's,' Mrs Grainger started explaining loudly to her friend Mary, who had shifted her slightly worried attention from the television to my conversation, as if I were merely another dramatic episode provided to get her through the day. 'I can't think why they're telephoning him here. I shall certainly have a word with him about it if he ever gets off the line.'

'What's that old woman saying?' Wasia said.

'Nothing,' I said. *Sorry*, I mouthed at Mrs Grainger.

'What's he saying?' Mary said to Mrs Grainger.

'I don't know,' Mrs Grainger said. 'It looked rather like *Bog off* to me. I shall certainly have a word with him.'

'I should jolly well hope so,' Mary said.

'Or it could be tomorrow,' Wasia said.

'No,' I said. 'No, I meant, you know, yes, !, tonight would be all right. I'm not doing anything tonight.'

'Well, you should say what you mean,' Wasia said, and she had put on her little-girl's voice again. Mrs Grainger was hitting her cushion impatiently. I tried to spread my hands apologetically, but I was holding the telephone and the gesture came out wrong. 'Well, I have to go. So I'll see you at Camden Town Underground station at half past seven o'clock.'

'Yes,' I said again. There was a long pause, as if Wasia was about to say something, but she said nothing, and then put the telephone down.

Mrs Grainger finished rearranging herself as I went to turn the television off. She was pulling one of her faces. Mary, the friend, settled back with a mild happy sigh, as if this was her favourite scene in a familiar play. I started to hurry out of the room before she could say anything, but she was too quick.

'I don't know that I quite like you receiving telephone calls from your friends here,' she said, hitting the floor with her stick to emphasise her points, *like, friends*.

'I'm sorry, Mrs Grainger,' I said. 'I don't give anyone

the telephone number here. ! I don't know how she had it.'

'She?' Mrs Grainger said. There was an awkward pause. 'Well, you must have given it to someone, I suppose.'

'I'm sorry, Mrs Grainger,' I said, picking up the empty coffee cups. 'I'll tell her not to telephone here again.'

'The thing is,' she said, 'what would happen if one of your friends telephoned here when I was alone, and I came hurrying down the stairs to answer it, and I tripped and fell, and broke a leg, and was lying here all on my own, all night, with a broken leg, and it was running downstairs to answer the telephone for a friend of yours? Have you thought of that? Of course,' she went on, turning to her friend, 'John's had a lot of problems recently, his wife, you know, one doesn't want to be a tartar –'

She gave that last word a peculiar emphasis all her own, the two syllables absolutely the same, tar, tar, like a mad music mistress.

'I promise it won't happen again,' I said, leaving the room. 'Not – ! – the wife – ! – the phone calls. ! ! !' It wouldn't be so much fun if I weren't there.

I went into the kitchen, and put the cups in the sink. Then I decided to smoke a cigarette. I got the packet out of my bag, and went to the back door. The cigarettes were as neatly packed as bricks, and I pulled one out. It was only then that I realised that I did not actually have a lighter. I could hear Mrs Grainger grumbling about in the sitting room. I lit a ring on the stove, and held the cigarette to it, and when it seemed to have caught fire, I took it reverently in my hand to the back door. You will think it odd that I had never smoked a cigarette before, but the situation had never arisen. I put it carefully in my mouth, and sucked. A warm gust of smoke came into my mouth. I held it there in the pouches of my cheeks for a moment. It felt like a warm small animal, solid and alive. Another hiccup burst out, and took the smoke out with it. I tried again, and this time it worked. I puffed it out again in a stream before the next hiccup. It seemed easy, and I wondered what it looked like, but there was no mirror in the kitchen. I did it again, and although the smoke was bitter, and like smoke, it was not entirely unpleasant. But of course I was not learning to smoke because it was agreeable, or because it was what I wanted to do, any more than I had taken to drinking champagne. I had taken it up because of the hiccups, which it did not seem to be affecting.

'What are you doing?' Mrs Grainger called querulously.

'Talk to your friend,' I called back rudely. It occurred to me that smokers actually inhaled the smoke, and did not merely hold it in their mouths for a moment. That might be it. I sucked again at the cigarette, and tried to swallow. A moment later, I was coughing furiously, holding on to the kitchen table as my body rebelled against this new and unpleasant sensation with a blurt of coughing and hiccupping and retching. It was the most unpleasant thing I could have imagined. I came round in north London, and Mrs Grainger was there, looking at me curiously. I offered her a cigarette wordlessly, and she took it. She lit it herself, using a box of matches which had been sitting on the kitchen surface all the time. I wondered how long it would take me to get to the end of the Marlboros. I imagined myself finishing the last of them, in a year's time, and giving a party to celebrate.

'My father,' Mrs Grainger said thoughtfully, 'he used to suffer most terribly from indigestion.'

I acknowledged this to be the case.

'It must be most distressing,' she said.

'I suppose it must,' I said.

'Surely, there must be something you could do about it,' she said, turning to me. 'I mean, to be perfectly honest, it's hardly very pleasant for everyone else, now, is it? I don't suppose you've thought of that, now, have you? It stands to reason, if it's nasty for us to listen to, it can't be very agreeable for you, now, can it?'

I realised she was talking about the hiccups, which she hadn't commented on before now. Selfish and not terribly curious, she hadn't thought it worth her concern, or so I had assumed.

'And then there's your wife,' she went on, as if she might as well carry on, having started. 'I mean, that's hardly satisfactory, that situation, now, is it? Stands to reason.'

'Mrs Grainger,' I said, 'it's not something –!'

'Well, where is she now?'

'I don't exactly know,' I said.

'You must know, roughly speaking, surely? It all seems most unsatisfactory. You don't seem to be putting a great deal of effort into persuading her to come back, as far as I can see.'

'That might be –' I started; I was going to say that I

wasn't sure that I wanted her back, but my voice, for some reason, was tentative; there was no frog in my throat, but the sentence would not quite form.

'It stands to reason, you can't do without her, she'll be waiting for you to go after her. And what about the children? Your children, you know, they need a mother and a father, but perhaps you hadn't considered that.'

'Mrs Grainger, we don't have any children,' I said. She was probably mildly confused after *Barker's Pool*, and certainly she was talking to me in much the same hectoring, gleeful tone with which she offered advice to those glowing apparitions with their complicated lives.

'Well, all I can say is it all seems perfect piffle and tosh to me,' she said triumphantly. 'Now, what were you planning for – where are we – lunch? Have I had lunch?'

Easy as it was to dismiss and ignore Mrs Grainger's dashing forays into my life, since her hussar-like decisiveness came from no particular interest or accurate recollection of anything she knew about the situation, I found myself rattling the pots around the stove and banging the plates about to a resentful, defensive rhythm. I did not care whether Janet came back. I had told myself that. As far as I cared, she could go on travelling further and further away from me until she found herself at the edge of the right-hand page in the atlas of the world, and, like Reepicheep, fell off that edge, never to be seen again. The fact is that you do not stomp and bash and scowl and deliberately oversalt someone's lunch if they have just got the wrong end of the stick. You do it when they are right, and you know they're right.

Mrs Grainger gave a sage nod, her arms crossed where her belly and collapsed heavy bosom made a vast floral mound, and trotted off to carve me up for the benefit of her guest. She made brisk work of it, and ten minutes later, she called to me to fetch Mary's coat.

'It's in the cloakroom,' I called back. 'Oh, very well –'

'Did I mention,' Mary said, changing the subject laboriously, 'what a stroke of luck I had? I won the lottery. Did I mention it?'

'The lottery?' Mrs Grainger said, as if she didn't know what it was.

'The lottery, you know, the lottery, every week, you buy a ticket and you choose your numbers and –'

'Oh, the *lottery*,' Mrs Grainger said.

'Well, it was quite a stroke of luck, because my numbers came up, so –'

'What, all of them?' I said, helping her on emphatically with her dim coat, the texture of dog hair and the colour of dog shit, as if this alone disproved the claim, though I don't suppose it would necessarily occur to a dim old lady with newly acquired millions to dash down to Gucci.

'Well, no, not all of them, but some,' she said. 'Three of them, actually. I was rather thrilled. I won ten pounds. Quite an excitement, though, heaven knows, these days, ten pounds, it doesn't go far, does it –'

Mrs Grainger was shooting me warning looks, but it was unnecessary. I had realised exactly how I was going to get Janet to come back to me. The odd thing is that I did not realise that I wanted her to come back until I understood how it would happen.

Pink Suit Three

For a long time after we married, Janet used to ask me in the mornings what she should wear for work. Not always, but from time to time. It wasn't a serious question; whenever I gave her an answer, she would always either promptly agree or disagree.

'What about that one, the brown one with the leather buttons?'

'No, of course not – I know –'

Because what she really wanted was to know what she'd already decided on. Sometimes she didn't know until she had me to agree or disagree with.

From time to time, asked this question, I'd tell her that she ought to rethink her whole approach to a wardrobe. Why have a wardrobe filled with twelve different things, all of which you liked moderately? Why not take some time to think of an outfit that really suited you, and then buy six identical versions of it to wear all the time? Why not have a wardrobe, in short –

'Like you, you mean?'

'Yes, I suppose I do mean that.'

– where there were no decisions to be made, where you liked everything because everything was the same. This, I was told, was an impossible and ludicrous suggestion –

'Well, that's just loony.'

– and if I couldn't see why a woman had to have a choice in the morning, and most men too, then one day, when it wouldn't make her late for work, she'd sit me down and explain exactly why.

It was a conversation we had reasonably often; not every day. Mostly she managed to dress herself. One day I was downstairs in my dressing gown and slippers, making breakfast, when she came down in something unexpected. She was wearing her pink suit.

'You're wearing your pink suit,' I said.

'Yes, I know,' she said.

'But you never wear your pink suit,' I said.

'No, not for work,' she said. 'It's not that I don't like it.'

'No, I know that,' I said. 'But you don't wear it for work.'

'Well, I got married in it,' she said. 'It would be a bit peculiar.'

'You can still get into your wedding dress,' I said.

'It's not a wedding dress,' she said. 'But I still have my girlish figure.'

'She kept her girlish figure,' I said.

'I didn't mean to,' she said.

'It does the job, doesn't it?' I said. 'The suit. I don't half fancy you, sometimes.'

'You and all,' she said with that brief shorthand

rendering of devotion which marriage teaches you. 'No, I cocked up – there's nothing else clean. I was going to go to the dry-cleaner's, but I just kept forgetting and now there's nothing which doesn't have chocolate on it.'

'You should have said,' I said. 'I've got nothing to do all day but pay people to get chocolate off your clothes.'

'Well, that's your job for today, then,' she said.

'They'll say it can't be done,' I said. 'All that chocolate.'

'Mmmm, chocolate –'

'Go on, lick my lapels, it's Lindt –'

'You really don't mind?'

'No, no,' I said. 'I was going to go to Putney anyway.'

'Really?'

'Well, no, but I don't mind.'

'Ta.'

'You know, you've got nice legs for an old married woman.'

'I knew it,' she said. 'It's too short, this skirt, isn't it?'

'Not from here,' I said, advancing on her.

'No, no,' Janet said. 'Get your hands off my arse, I'll be late, I'm late as it is –'

'They'll forgive you,' I said, molesting her appallingly.

'No, really, I can't be late –'

'But when we're old and grey and sitting by the fire and reminiscing, we're not going to be saying, Do you remember that day when you were bang on time for work –'

'And your point is, exactly? – mind, careful, they're new, these tights, don't ladder them –'

'– whereas we might well sit and say, Do you remember

that day when we had that terrific shag which made you late for work –'

'On the kitchen table –'

'On the kitchen table – oh, go on then –'

'And I'll say –'

'You'll say –'

'Which day in particular?'

Because we did this all the time, in fact.

'But best not, if you're in a hurry.'

'Fuck off. Over here. Quick one.'

'Quick one.'

It goes into the vocabulary; the vocabulary of your marriage; a language which might be dying, a language spoken only by two people on earth; like poor Dolly Pentreath, when, at the end, there was only her brother she could speak to in Cornish; how happy their conversations must have been; and after that, Janet could say to me, 'What shall I wear?' and I'd say, 'The pink suit?' and she'd say, 'I don't have a lot of time, you know,' and I'd say, 'I'll do my best not to keep you,' and that would be that. You wouldn't even need to get the pink suit out of the wardrobe. Marriage; an audience to it would need footnotes, an index or at least a very considerately informative programme. But there never is an audience, even though, when a marriage is good, you feel that you could provide a cloakroom, tickets and popcorn for the appreciative multitudes.

22

There are supposed to be two hundred pubs in Camden Town. Pubs and bars – there is a difference, though it wouldn't be an easy difference to explain to someone who didn't understand. Two hundred places where you can get a drink, all selling enough to carry on in business, full of people drinking, all the time. Of course no one would want to go into all of them. Some of them are full of elegant young people and are shiny with chrome and polished wood floors. Others seem to keep going serving pints of Guinness to dirty old ladies, each of them sitting alone in a nest of much used plastic bags, bulging and splitting like big dirty fruit. There are bars specifically for homosexuals and for Irish people, for Hell's Angels and for hippies. Some of them are illegal, and you have to know about them and claim to be a friend of Terry's before they will let you in. Others are said to lock the door at eleven o'clock and carry on serving alcohol until their customers all go home, or fall over. In some pubs you can play darts, in others pool, in others backgammon, and in one or two, I heard once, you can ask for the game of Monopoly which is kept behind the bar. On this basis, each pub seems to have something of its own character. The whole of Camden Town, full of people drinking, all day long and all night long, in the two hundred pubs. Perhaps it was three hundred; that was only something somebody had told me once. I had probably been into four of them.

The nice weather was continuing, and I walked to Camden Town from Mrs Grainger's house. I knew the way. You turned left at the end of her road, and walked down the hill, through Belsize Park, Chalk Farm and straight on until you reached the Sunday market on the left and then the tube station. To my surprise, I met Mr Tredinnick on the street, halfway between Belsize Park and Chalk Farm. He was standing, quite still, outside an antique shop, gazing into space, as if thinking deeply. He had a knack of turning up at odd times and in odd places, but I was still surprised to see him there like that.

'Hello, son,' he said, addressing me. Then he became alert, all at once. 'I'm on a job,' he said. 'Look. Can you spare half an hour?'

'Now?' I said. I had never known how to refuse Mr Tredinnick anything.

'I didn't mean –' he thought hard – 'yesterday, did I? Yes, now.'

'I don't know,' I said.

Mr Tredinnick scowled and tutted; I scowled and hiccupped. 'I need you to do us a favour,' he said. 'Won't take a minute.'

'I can't,' I said firmly. He looked at me in amazement.

'Well,' he said ruminatively. 'If you can't, you can't.'

'I can't,' I said again. I was impressed with myself.

'Don't shout, son,' he said.

Then I relented and told him that any other time would be fine. He told me to meet him at that corner the next day, at the same time. He was dressed very formally, even for him, with a fresh flower in his button-hole and a tie and a handkerchief which matched each other. Where he got his brown pinstriped suits from, I do not know; he may even have been carrying a cane.

Wasia was already waiting for me. I said hello to her, but she did not seem to see or hear me for a moment. Then she turned to me and tipped her head back, closing her eyes. I remembered to kiss her on both cheeks.

'I've just seen Mr Tredinnick,' I said.

'Who?' she said.

'He was at the wedding,' I said. 'I thought you met him.'

'I don't remember,' she said.

'You took a photograph of him,' I said.

'Did I?' she said.

'He's nearly seventy,' I said. 'Or maybe more. He doesn't look so old. He's Italian.'

'I don't remember meeting anyone,' she said. Then her voice changed again and she said, 'I only remember meeting you.'

'I just met him, standing on the street,' I said. 'It was very strange. He asked me to do him a favour. I don't know what he was doing up here.'

'Why are you telling me all this?' she said, slipping back into her normal voice. Then a tramp came up and we both refused to give him twenty-six pee, which was the curious sum of money he asked us for. He went away and we watched him go.

'Look,' she said. 'Are we going to stand here like a bunch of carrots all evening?'

'No,' I said. We stood there for a moment. Wasia was wearing more normal clothes today. She looked even smaller in them, but slightly less cross. At her feet there was the same bag she had brought to Sarah's wedding.

'There's a bar I know,' she said. 'It's just round the corner. Unless you had somewhere in mind. I don't want to go anywhere too noisy. I feel like talking.'

I followed her. It was not a bar I had been to before. The name of it I can't remember now. It was in a quiet street behind the main Camden Town drag. I went to go in, and was through the door before I realised that Wasia had stopped outside. I went back out.

'I don't want to go inside,' she said. 'I want to sit outside. Can you get me a drink?'

'What would you like?'

'A glass of dry white wine,' she said. 'Get a bottle and two glasses.'

I hadn't thought of what I wanted to drink, but I did what she told me. We settled down with the white wine. There was no one else sitting outside the bar, and I felt self-conscious as people walked by. I thought of lighting a cigarette, but did not trust myself not to cough and splutter. It would be better not to.

'Mr Tredinnick thought you were my girlfriend,' I said for something to say. 'Now that my wife's gone, you know.'

'Did he now,' she said. 'I wish you'd tell me who Mr Tredinnick is. You've talked about no one else since you finally turned up.'

This was unfair, since I had not been late, and I had only met Wasia five minutes before, but it was best to let it go. I started explaining to her again who Mr Tredinnick was.

She interrupted me. 'What happened to your sister?'

'She's in the Seychelles,' I said.

'I didn't mean her,' Wasia said. 'I meant your other sister. Your mother said she died.'

'Yes, that's right,' I said. 'She died.'

'That's what your mother said. She said you had a sister who died.'

'It was quite a long time ago now,' I said.

'You mean she died when she was born,' Wasia said.

'No,' I said. 'No, it was later than that.'

'How old was she?' Wasia said.

'She was a number of different ages,' I said.

'How old was she when she died,' Wasia said.

'She was almost grown up,' I said.

'Do you remember her?' Wasia said.

'Yes,' I said. 'I remember her, even if I'm not asked to remember her.'

Wasia drew her chair slightly forward, put her face on her chin, her elbow on the table. She looked into my face.

'You don't need to talk about her if you don't want to talk about her,' she said.

'No,' I said. 'No, I know I don't.'

But then I told Wasia the story of how Franky died.

In a way, once it was told, it was good to have told her. It wasn't secret. But it wasn't something I always wanted to tell people, even if they asked. Mostly, they didn't know how to ask. In fact, in the course of my life, I hadn't told the whole story like that all that often. Some people knew about it, and some people didn't. For instance, Mr Tredinnick knew the story in every detail: Mrs Grainger, on the other hand, had no idea how many sisters I had or had had. The people who knew never talked about it either, because it was a long time ago and we knew everything there was to know about it. So it rarely came up in conversation. It took about five minutes to tell the whole story, Wasia sipping her glass of wine quite steadily, like a child with a mug of milk, her eyes big and completely fixed on me. There was something steady about the way she listened. It was like a teacher listening to a pupil, or someone politely listening to a joke they already knew, so as not to offend. She listened with all her attention, drinking it all in, but it was as if she were measuring up my rendition against something in her head. I got to the end and stopped.

'That's a very sad story,' she said finally. 'I'm sorry, I didn't know. I wouldn't have asked if I'd known. I mean I wouldn't have asked your mother. I wouldn't have upset her for the world. I don't mind asking you. I hope we're going to be great friends. I don't know why, but I'm always right when I have that feeling that I'm going to be great friends with someone. Can't you stop hiccupping?'

'I hope so, too,' I said, not answering her last question. I reached forward and refilled her glass. Mine was still full.

'What a sad story,' she said again.

'Yes, it is,' I agreed. It was now that Wasia surprised me a great deal. She reached in the bag on her lap and swiftly took out the camera. So quickly that I could not react in any other way but instinctively, she took a photograph of me, and then another. I did not know what to say. She must have ended up with a photograph of me looking far from attractive or prepared for my portrait to be taken.

We drank our wine in silence for a while.

'I don't have a job,' Wasia said.

I didn't know what to say to that. In the end, I said, 'Is that so?'

'No,' she said. 'No, I don't need to work.'

'I'm an indexer,' I said.

'I don't know what that is,' Wasia said.

'I'm sure you do really,' I said.

'No, how should I know?'

'Well, you know what an index is, at the end of a book?' I said.

'So you're saying you're something at the end of a book, are you making sense to yourself even?'

'No,' I said. 'What I mean is – well, I work for an old lady in Hampstead, too, some days a week.'

'What?'

I repeated what I'd said.

'So you're not something in a book, you work for an old lady?'

'Yes.'

'Look, there's Hope,' Wasia said. I didn't understand what she meant at all. I thought she might be making some kind of metaphysical point, unconnected with the tall and yet slapdash woman who was now standing by our table with a bag over her elaborately draped arm. But that was who she meant, this slightly hairy but apparently expensively dressed woman. Wasia had made no gesture of acknowledgement, had not said that anyone would be joining us. But then Hope sat down and I understood, too late, what Wasia had been saying.

'Hello, Hope,' I said. 'That's a charming name.'

The girl looked at me with, it seemed, murderous intent, as if I were mocking her. I could understand that most people she met would quickly be tempted by mocking her; although she was exceptionally plain, moustachioed and dressed well beyond her deserts, she did not invite pity. Not only did her eyebrows meet in the middle, they melted into the general area of her hairline on either side. She said nothing to me, but I observed that nothing in the world conveys itself more readily and with less effort than naked hostility.

'Are you going anywhere special?' I tried again, guessing that her extraordinary outfit, contrived as if to make it fall off at any moment, had been much considered, and possibly even the work of some celebrated designer.

'Well, we're going out clubbing, aren't we?' she said. Her London voice, her slack mouth hanging open, made it sound like a challenge, as if I should know what she and her friends had been planning for the evening. 'Here's that bastard Ben.' She raised herself halfway from the chair, and shouted across the street. 'Yer late.'

The shaven-headed man ambling towards us in his turn, weaving through the traffic, shrugging as he came, didn't seem to mind this. He just pulled up another chair without looking at any of us, and reached for the bottle of wine. Then it seemed to occur to him that he didn't have a glass. He held it tightly in his fist, not knowing what to do. Then he put it between his thighs for safety, gripping it tightly.

'Traffic,' he said. 'Would have. Skunk. Yeah.'

'This is John,' Wasia said pleasantly. 'Don't mind Ben, he's just stoned.'

'Stoned,' Ben said. 'John.'

'He's not bringing any of his *friends*, is he?' Wasia asked Hope, in much the same tones as a medieval prince of Muscovy learning that their new acquaintance Attila was proposing to drop in for dinner. A waiter arrived with two glasses for them, and half-heartedly tried to pluck the bottle from between Ben's thighs. He quickly gave up; Ben was protected by an awesome reek, smelling, frankly, as if he had slept in his clothes and bathed, on rising, in lager.

'Don't worry about that,' Hope said. 'Just bring us another one.'

'Yeah,' Ben said, and triumphantly brought the half-full bottle to his mouth and emptied it in three large gulps.

'We can't be having this,' the waiter bravely said.

'You're already having it,' Hope said. 'Do you know who we are?'

For the first time in the history of the world, this sentence seemed to have its intended effect: the waiter

went for another bottle, and then left us alone. I wasn't
so sure about any of this. I had thought I was having a
drink with Wasia, but now it seemed that I was being
introduced to her friends. I tried to look on the bright
side – not conceivably very prominent – of an evening
with Hope and Ben. It ought to be a good thing that she
wanted them to meet me. The only reason it did not
strike me as a good thing was that they were extremely
nasty.

'What do you do?' I said sociably.

'What?' Hope said.

'!' I said.

She looked at me furiously, as if at another insult.

'What do I do?'

'Er –'

'Everything,' she said confidently. 'I do everything.
You get to know me, you'll see, there's nothing I don't
do. That's me, there's nothing in the world –'

'She's at college with me,' Wasia said.

'Oh yeah,' Hope said. 'That's what he meant. Only
when he said what do you do –'

'What?' Ben said, looking around him with a sort of
wildness.

'Him as well,' Wasia said.

'Him as well what,' Hope said.

'He's at college with me, too,' Wasia said. She was
enjoying this in some way.

'I never said he wasn't,' Hope said. 'Here, why do you
keep making that noise?'

I explained about the hiccups.

'It's horrible,' she said. 'It's freaking me out, can't you stop it?'

I explained again.

'But it's freaking me out,' Hope said, her voice rising. 'You've got to stop it, it's horrible.'

Then we all drank whatever we had in our glasses, all at the same time. Nasty as they were, I felt a kind of sympathy for Hope, and particularly for Ben, stinking and twitching in his chair, rubbing away with grimly onanistic elbow grease at the bottle of wine between his thighs, quite unaware of what he looked like. For both of them this was as frightful as it was for me. Wasia, on the other hand, was enjoying herself.

'Tell John about your project,' Wasia said. 'Hope, tell John about your project.'

'Why don't you tell him about yours?' Hope said. 'I'm not the paid entertainment or nothing.'

'Yours is more interesting,' Wasia said, smiling. 'Go on, tell him, it's interesting.'

'You don't give a shit,' Hope said. 'No one gives a shit about anything I do.'

'No, I'd like to hear,' I said. Then I hiccupped again.

'You're taking the piss,' she said. But then she subsided and told us. It must have been quite hard work, being Hope. 'You see, it's about them critics, I hate them critics. They think they know everything, like they're definitely right, like what they think, it's in stone, carved in stone, you know, whereas they couldn't do what I do, see? So the project, right, is that I get some critic or something to write some stupid review of a show, saying it's crap and all that, and it's printed in like a newspaper, right, only the thing is that there isn't a show, never was, it's like a review of something which never happened only he's pretending that it did and it was crap and that. So then once it's been printed I go, me, the artist, right, I take this review and I get someone to carve, like, the whole review on slabs of stone, because critics, you know, they think, like, what they think, it's written on stone, so he carves it, the stonemason, on slabs of stone, or maybe gravestones, I thought about that too only maybe that's a bit, you know, I don't know, and then all these stones, I install them, or I get someone to install them in a gallery, and that's like the work, the project. The End, My Project, By Hope.'

'Wow,' Wasia said.

'Sounds terrific,' I said. 'And then the critics review it again.'

'Yeah, they'd better,' Hope said.

'But what happens if they say it's a masterpiece?' I said.

'Well, they'd be right there because it's going to be, it's going to be a fucking masterpiece, too right,' Hope said.

'But then you might start thinking that critics aren't so bad after all and if they say that you're a genius then there's nothing wrong with that,' I said.

'Yeah, they'd be right,' Hope said, more doubtfully.

'But then the exhibition would look a bit stupid,' I said.

'Here, you, fuck off,' Hope said.

'Because if they say it works then it doesn't work and if they all think it doesn't work then it still doesn't work,' I said.

'I think John's saying,' Wasia said, 'that you've grasped a seductive paradox here.'

'Yeah, conceptual, it's all paradox, it's like ideas that you can't get your head round,' Hope said, mollified.

'Art, it's all shit,' Ben offered.

'Shit,' Hope said.

I lit a cigarette, shakily.

An hour or two later, after glassily passing through two more pubs, the four of us were sitting round a table in a Chinese restaurant in Gerrard Street. There were sixteen bowls of food clustered in the middle of the table: after placing the order, we had been moved to a bigger table. Wasia and I were eating – in my case rather self-consciously. Hope had a chopstick in each hand: from time to time, she reached out with one and prodded dubiously at one dish or another, like a junior surgeon on his first heart transplant. Ben, who had strangely ordered all this food, had swum back into something like consciousness and was telling us about his day. He talked with immense care, placing one foot in front of the other, fearing to slip and fall; it turned out that he had a faint Yorkshire accent.

'I wasn't going to,' he said. 'I was going down the studio. But before that I went down to the corner for some tabs. But before that I got up and I was going to have a bath and I got as far as the kitchen. And then I thought fuck that. So I was going to go back to bed because last night we'd been caning it. But then you think that's no good, is it? And then I went to have a look and I was in luck –'

'In look?'

'No, in luck, because there was maybe half a gram which we'd not got round to the night before. So I had a snort or two so that I wouldn't feel like going back to bed and then I goes off to the corner shop for the tabs. But then the phone goes and it's Archie saying that they're sitting in the garden and the sun's shining and there's a bag of skunk so then I say . . .'

I went on eating, morosely, as the saga unwound. Though they had been asked to meet me, or so it seemed, no one was interested in discovering anything about my life. Drunkenly pitying myself, I promised that they would not be told about my indexing, my house, my wife, my family, nothing. That'll serve them, I thought, listening to a malodorous bore murmuring in entrancement about his drug-fucked day, accounting for it, telling no story, indifferent to his listeners' suffering and in particular, I thought, mine. I would not have known I was there if it were not for the regular, flickering inspection of Wasia's shining-black eyes, like an animal watching for a reaction from its master.

'Who ordered all that food?' Hope said in the end.

'Christ knows,' Ben said.

'I'm skint,' Hope said.

'I'll get it,' Wasia said, with surprising good nature.

'I'll put something in,' I said.

'No, it's OK,' she said. 'Now what?'

'I thought we were going out,' Hope said. 'Wasn't that the idea? Oi, you, John, wasn't that the idea?'

'I don't know,' I said. 'It wasn't my idea.'

'Can you stop that?' she said. 'That noise, it's freaking me out. I want to go out.'

'There's this place I heard about . . .' Wasia said, tentatively, and as she spoke, she strangely reached her hand over to mine and stroked it gently.

'Yes, I heard about that place . . .' Hope said, her voice immediately changing, becoming more businesslike. She might have been given some kind of cue.

'Where is it again?' Ben said, and he, too, had lost his haziness, had sharpened up, had a contribution, it seemed, to make.

'It's in Streatham,' Wasia said. 'But I heard it was a great night. A club; everyone goes, it's the place to go.'

'I've never been to a nightclub,' I said.

'Oh, John,' Wasia said. 'You'll love it.'

'Yeah, I heard about that place,' Hope said. 'I heard it was the sort of place John would love, too.'

Wasia gave Hope a poisonous look.

'Yeah, I heard about that place, too,' Ben said. 'Come on, chum, it'll be fantastic, we'll have a great time.'

'I didn't say I didn't want to go,' I said.

They all paused.

'So you don't mind going to a nightclub?' Wasia said.

'No,' I said. 'It's just that I never have. I don't mind going.'

'Great,' Wasia said, but now she seemed a little doubtful. I couldn't understand the conversation at all, apart from the fact that it had been prepared earlier, like a pie on a programme.

I let Wasia pay, and followed the three of them out of

the restaurant. A sort of shame seemed to have come over them, and they weren't talking at all. I followed them, without speaking, into the back of a black cab, and heard Wasia ask the outraged driver to take us to Streatham. I settled back, not altogether enthusiastically, moving as best I could away from Ben's slumped body for the long stinking drive. London is flat, but as you move southwards, it can feel like a descent, spiralling downwards without brakes. My guides into the south London underworld were quiet with the obscure plans of their own, as if they had something to be ashamed of, and I let them lead me. The buildings of London shot away behind us to the noise of the driver's grumbling. I wondered why, unlike most people of my age, I had never ever been to a nightclub, and then something occurred to me. It was probably because I had been talking to Wasia about it earlier, but it might have been something to do with Franky's death. Every single account of her murder had specified that she had just left a nightclub: the word was reiterated and reiterated in newspaper articles, magazines, in the few sensational and horrible books. No, I didn't go to nightclubs. It wasn't so much an aversion as simply a conviction that the word had nothing to do with me, just as the manner of Franky's death had nothing whatever to do with her, and told you nothing whatever about her. The place we were going to was in no sense the background landscape to my sister's death. The geography of Franky's last night was meaningless for us, since we had never associated her with such places before. Not even the tree under which she was found caused us pain, and we had never avoided it. And perhaps I was wrong, because plenty of people never go to nightclubs. If I never went to nightclubs, it was because I would not have wanted to go to nightclubs, and not because they brought my sister to mind. In any case, it would have been selfish and dishonest of me to refuse to come along with Wasia and the others, and to use Franky as a selfish excuse: it would have made them feel terrible that they had even suggested such a thing. What in reality caused us pain and always had were the places and things which brought Franky to mind, the everyday things, the memories we had of her, the backcloths which seemed after her death to require what memory supplied, her face in repose, in front of them.

But all the same, with this descent came a memory. It was a helter-skelter. I must have been quite young. I don't know where it was, but the memory is firm. The wooden tower, brightly painted and lit; I go in with Franky my sister, holding her hand. My mother pays, pushes us forward gently, says, 'Go with your sister, you'll be all right,' and stays there. A man hands us two coarse mats to sit on as we slide down, like a prickly doormat. Franky my sister takes both of them, one for me. I go inside with Franky my sister, and there is a spiral staircase, a musty smell like moss and wet wood. (Sitting between Ben, who smelt like a wet beery forest, and Hope, who smelt of cat piss, maybe that was what brought it back.) We climb the stairs. There is no one else inside, and soon, my heart beating, we come out of a little hutch entrance at the top of a slide, slatted and wooden. You can see for miles: all over the fair, the thin screams floating across from mid-air Meccano cages, and beyond the trees, to the waste-land tracks of houses, row upon row upon row. I don't want to go first, but Franky my sister settles me on my mat, hugs my shoulders from behind and gives me a little push. Then I am sliding down, the gaps between each slatted square lining the slide making a noise, *cha-dong* like a slow train over the gaps in the rails, and I'm sliding down in a spiral, not too scarily, and seeing my mother at the bottom; then she is behind the tower, there she is again, and then all at once the itchy coconut mat under my bare legs gives way to the big doormat at the bottom, raw and scratchy. And that is it. I enjoyed it, I suddenly realise. I get up, smiling, go to my mother, and Franky my sister is already behind me. She has done what I did and she is taking my hand already.

My sister. You don't see helter-skelters any more. They were never exciting enough. I suppose they stopped being popular after the Manson murders. Helter-skelter: that was their slogan, wasn't it, whatever it meant? That would have been in 1969 or so. Well, then or not long after.

Hope was telling me about her last project. She seemed proud of it.

'So, right, I thought I'm a strong woman, so, like, for two years every time I went to bed with someone I said to them you're not coming to bed with me unless I can take a mould of your dick in plaster. So they all said yes or mostly all because sometimes they didn't want to and sometimes I couldn't be fucked. And then after two years I've got like two hundred dicks all moulded in plaster –'

'Two hundred?' I said.

'Two hundred, yeah, what you saying? You've got a problem with that? And these two hundred dicks I put them all on the floor of the gallery like this kind of forest only it's a forest of dicks. And if you want to get from one side of the room, right, you can't, not without knocking them over, the only person who's allowed to do that is me, so you see, it's about me being a strong woman because I'm allowed to knock over all these dicks if I like. And on the bottom I wrote their names only some of them I didn't know their names so I just made something up. You see, people say to me Hope, did he fuck you, like the next day or something, and you know what I say, I say No way, I fucked him, OK, because I'm a strong woman, and that was what the piece was about and it got in the papers, some of them.'

'Some of the – ! – dicks?'

'Some of the papers. You're freaking me out again.' She rearranged herself dismissively – it was an asymmetrical outfit, and the pocket from which she pulled out a tissue lay in a very unexpected place, almost between her visibly hairy breasts.

'Here, I know what'll stop that,' Ben said, perking up. 'Get some of this down you.'

He pulled something out of his pocket and rammed it quite violently up my nose. With the other hand, he pressed down hard on my other nostril; I tried to turn away, to Hope's face, malevolently grinning like a sacred monkey right in mine. I was startled and tried to pull back; but his hands were gripping my head, and I breathed in hard. Whatever it was – the device was rounded, plastic, I could feel that – shot raucously up my nose, stinging me. He held my head for a few seconds, then let go and slumped back, putting whatever it was back in his pocket.

'What was that?' I said when I had recovered. There was an unpleasant scrubbing sensation at the back of my nose and throat. I felt like sneezing, but could not.

'Oh, you'll like it,' Ben said.

'It'll stop him making that noise and all,' Hope said.

This might have been the funniest thing anyone had ever said. It was so funny that Wasia got out her camera and took a photograph of me amid all that hilarity. The flash was like a spurt of energy, there in the back of the cab.

'That's got shot of that noise you was making, hasn't it?' Hope said.

'!' I said dismally.

Outside the club, its name written over the door in looping purple neon, there was a man in a too-large dinner jacket, pretending to prepare for a queue. He looked like someone's younger brother. He watched us draw up and get out of the taxi with too much interest, as if far from sure that he would see many more before closing time; the steel barrier to control the expected queue was only three feet long. There were a few people inside, some even dancing, but it was not cool, even I could see that. The club was named after a famous fictional lover, whose love, too, was invented, and it seemed to me a room where everything had gone wrong. The walls and not the floor were densely carpeted. You could not see the colour in the thumping gloom, but I leant against those walls with my hand, and it was as raw as a doormat. It should have been on the floor, but the floor – the dance floor, I mean – was illuminated like a ceiling, and the few people were flailing on it. It was a wrong room, I felt; and the wrongest thing was that it had Wasia, Hope and Ben in it. No, still wronger, that I was in it. That was the wrongest thing of all.

'Isn't this great?' Wasia said after a time. The four of us were lined up against the bar with our four cans of beer, like skittles. The surface of the bar was a mirror, much ringed and splashed, its front again a wall of carpet.

'You're having a laugh,' Hope said, her solidarity with Wasia's purpose now, apparently gone. 'This is rubbish.'

'Yes, it's rubbish,' Wasia said, 'but it's so rubbish it's good.'

'That's rubbish,' Hope said. 'I don't buy that so-rubbish-it's-good thing no more. This is more like a so-rubbish-it's-rubbish thing going on.'

'Give it a chance,' Wasia said.

'Yeah, you've got to get your money's worth, haven't you,' Hope said. 'I mean, paying for the taxi and all, we can't have you wasting your money, so feel free to tell us that we're having a good time because it's like not allowed to say it's rubbish when it is because of all that money, you know what I mean, yeah?'

'That's not what I meant,' Wasia said. 'And in any case –'

'What do you do again?' I said to Ben sociably.

'This is doing me in,' he said. 'I've got to get out of here.'

'We've only just got here,' I said.

'Give it a rest,' he said, taking hold of the sleeve of my shirt. 'We've been here three hours. This is boring.'

He sounded in acute distress. I brought my left arm round and showed him my watch. He understood, reasonably quickly, what I meant, and looked for some time at the face, finally understanding, I think, that it was only eleven o'clock – perhaps an early time to find yourself in a nightclub, even one in the suburbs. At any event, he seemed satisfied with this and sunk back into his gloomy twitching.

'– a good time,' Wasia was insisting.

'Do you think they're having a good time, then, them on the dance floor?' Hope said. 'I've had better times at the dentist. It's not going on for no one, don't give me that.'

'It's only you who's not having fun,' Wasia said. 'John's having fun – and Ben's having fun – and I'm having fun – and those girls on the dance floor, they're certainly having fun.'

'You couldn't have a good time here,' Hope said. 'This is like the place where misery was born, like in that film, yeah? This is like – what's this place called? Bromley, yeah – this is like sad-people-land, right?'

Her smirk was like a violent facial curtsy, as if she had said something clever or witty.

'This isn't Bromley. This is Streatham. Bromley's where I come from,' I said cruelly.

But they all knew that.

'And Hope was born in Cricklewood,' Wasia said, almost singing the taunt.

'I want to dance,' Hope said.

'I thought this was rubbish?' I said.

'If we're not allowed to go then I want to dance,' Hope said.

'You want to dance with all those sad people from sad-people-land?' I said.

'I want to dance,' Hope said, hitting her little fists up and down on the mirrored surface of the bar.

'And I want some drugs,' Ben said, surfacing.

The barman, passing, gave us an unbelieving look of pity.

'Yeah, drugs,' Ben said, surfacing.

'I've not got any,' Hope said.

'The cupboard is bare,' Ben said sonorously.

'This is Bromley,' I said.

'No, it's Streatham,' Hope said, before taking the point and shutting up.

'There's only forty people in the whole club. No one's taking drugs here,' I said, optimistically.

'Go on, then,' Ben said, ignoring me. He let go of the bar, stood upright, bracing himself splendidly, and lumbered off into the spotlit gloom, weaving between dancers. At first he was conspicuous, but then, like an eye closing, he disappeared in this meagre crowd. They danced in a speculative way; although it was Friday night, only some of them had come out in appropriate or considered clothes. There was a girl and her ill-advised friend in tubular tops, thuggish and heavy cork mules anchoring them to the spot where they swayed like trees in the breeze. There was a boy in a black and tightly waisted shirt, moving through and assessing the dance floor, his eyes filing away and ordering the girls for future consideration. Their limbs and even hands seemed only loosely attached to their drifting torsos, executing wild or tentative flourishes of their own in the black air; here an arm would raise itself above the head, fist pumping at the ceiling; here elbows gripped close to the side, the hands straight out rippling like a jazz pianist; there a boy muscled forward with his shoulders in turn like a hard-faced old woman on the first day of the sale in china and glass. Some of them could dance – there was a man, total blank boredom on his face, whose body was entirely still except for the eight vertical inches between navel and thigh which bucked and writhed like a trapped python. Even those, however, appeared as odd to me as the much larger number who could not, bopping and loosely stretching with their arms, as if reaching for some object which probably wasn't there. I didn't see why you should do it, even if you could.

Someone was pressing something into my hand – the little plastic device or engine from the taxi – and, not really considering the matter, I took it and with my handkerchief around it, snorted from it without any help. The lights were prinking at me, too brilliantly, but all the same, I took it. Hope and Ben seemed no longer to dislike me, or were offering me these things despite disliking me, but the dumb explanation my mind offered was this: they've changed sides. I tried to pass the thing back, and, to my surprise, found myself giving it back to Wasia on my left.

'It's filling up,' I said for no reason.

'I want to dance,' Hope said.

'Why don't you, then?' Wasia said.

'I'm waiting for Ben,' Hope said. 'He's been gone ages.'

'Where is he?' I said. No one said anything. The flashes, randomly directed, of light over the dance floor were illuminating and freezing faces in unappealing, embarrassing gestures – a forced smile, a half-blink, the mouth falling open – like terrible party photographs. There was no one familiar here, no known faces lit in those half-seconds of focused light, only remarkable ones, ugly, needy, observing. The lives of such faces were unimaginable outside this place, outside, even, the lightning flashes of the spotlights. It was hot; my hair was plastered to my skull with sweat as if waxed down. For some reason I kept forgetting, then remembering again, that I was anything but alone; it was a shock to turn and see Wasia there, to remember that I knew her. It was almost like forgetting that I existed at all, being reminded of the fact, flashes of light illuminating me to myself.

What held me was the dance floor and the quick manifestations of its faces. In a second it produced something astonishing: a face quite devoid of any change in its appearance or expression. It had nothing but a general glossy benevolence, the skin stretched tight like a latex mask. But it was a face gone wrong. It must have been twice the size of a normal face, its individual features monstrously enlarged – eyes, chin, its vast circumference, all bulging obscenely. It was a grotesque carnival mask, but one made of flesh, a caricature of an attractive woman with its huge eyes and tiny mouth, set on a normal body.

As the spotlights followed it round, it showed itself no mask. You were looking not at a woman but at a medical condition, dancing under the lights. It was then, I think, that the song started – my song – and the woman who could only be famous, observed, watched wherever she walked the streets or showed her gross face in public danced to a song about celebrity.

And then Ben came back.

The four of us were still there dancing at the end, and the night had passed somehow. It had gone somewhere else entirely. If you hand over control of your time to near strangers, as I did, and you drink and swallow and sniff whatever you are offered – and each time it was offered not for pleasure but as a means to rid me of my attendant noise, still freaking Hope out at four in the morning – then you remember the time only in flashes between stretches of oblivion. Like the flashes of light going off in my face once the dancing had started, perhaps from the spotlights, perhaps not. Or strangers coming over and saying, 'I love you, mate, I fucking love you,' and even at the time making me realise that the world had stopped saying that to me, and now the world would only say that when the world was on drugs. Or the song came round again and a third time, and me insisting to Wasia, pulling her left hand and not the hand holding her camera, trying to make her dance with me to the tune of 'Celebrity', which seemed so true and sad and danceable. Or all my life, all of it that mattered, falling into these stretches of blank forgetting, wife, sister, existence, all packing themselves into the dark of padlocked luggage and consigned to some deep mental hold.

Only at the end, when I came out – the others had somehow gone, I don't know when or where – did everything clear decisively. I came out of the nightclub which had meant nothing to me, but outside was a yawning bouncer and four or five black men. They were hopeless frayed old men with their keys in their hands, offering rides and calling themselves taxis. Then for the first time I saw what I had been brought there to see: my sister leaving that place, or a place very like it, and going on her last short journey. Wasia had brought me there – if she had done it intentionally, I might have thought that she had wanted to see if I would cope. And I had coped. Now that I was not coping, she was not there to see it.

'You OK, man?' one of the men waiting said, apparently genuine in his concern. I wonder what I looked like.

I was OK. I was in London. I could go home. I wanted to go home. It was not that far, surely. A driver led me silently to his scrapyard wheels, courteously opened the rusty door; got in himself; turned enquiringly. I told him where I wanted to go.

'Man,' he said to himself. 'That's all I fucking need.'

Too true.

23

The favour I was to do Mr Tredinnick turned out to be to go with him and help him to buy a car, or a motor, as he called it. He explained this to me, seriously, standing at the street corner. I pointed out that I didn't know anything about cars, and couldn't be of much help to him, but he waved this objection away. Today, he was wearing a plain black suit with a white shirt and a black tie, as if he had just come from a funeral. He said that, when buying a motor, it always helped to take someone with you, since the seller would assume that the extra person was in some way an expert, and would therefore be less likely to hide the defects in the car. I took Mr Tredinnick's word for this, since he was usually right. But I had to tell him that I would find it difficult to say anything at all knowledgeable about cars, and he might find it better, in the end, to take a real expert with him.

'You won't have to say anything, son,' Mr Tredinnick said. 'In fact, it's better that you keep shtum. Just stand there and look critical, and stop making that noise, for Christ's sake.'

Privately, I doubted that I could even do this convincingly. But I agreed to do it. Mr Tredinnick looked at me curiously, and pointed out that I had already agreed to do him a favour, the day before, which I suppose was right.

Embarrassingly, the house of the owner of the car turned out to be exactly opposite Mrs Grainger's. Fortunately, he did not seem to recognise me. He was a middle-aged man with untidy ginger hair and a morose, hunched appearance. It was a black sports car, an old MG he was trying to sell to Mr Tredinnick, and I could imagine that his wife and children had ridiculed him into selling what was really a young man's car.

Mr Tredinnick went round the car, tapping it here and there, and then asked the owner to lift up the bonnet. He looked at the engine with concentrated disgust.

'Never had a day's problem with it,' the owner said nervously.

'Come here, son,' Mr Tredinnick said to me. I went over and looked at the engine. I shook my head and tutted. 'Well, I don't know,' Mr Tredinnick said. 'Might as well take it for a drive, though.'

This presented a problem, since there were only two seats. In the end, Mr Tredinnick and the owner sat in the front and I squeezed myself into the little space behind the seats. My face was pressed up against the side window and my neck crushed almost in half. Mr Tredinnick drove round and round for half an hour, alarming a few mothers by revving at traffic lights, while the owner tried to reassure him. Finally we got back, and I uncoiled myself painfully. I suppose you couldn't expect the owner to trust me and Mr Tredinnick with the car. We could have been anyone.

'What do you think of that, then, son?' Mr Tredinnick said.

'I don't know,' I said truthfully, shaking my head.

'All right,' Mr Tredinnick said to the owner. 'I'll have to think about it. But I'll tell you one thing. Two thousand quid? You're having a laugh.'

'It's in perfect condition,' the owner said. 'And this is a classic car, you know.'

'I'm going to think about it,' Mr Tredinnick said.

'Well, don't think about it too long,' the owner said bravely. 'I've got a list of potential buyers as long as my arm.'

'I bet,' Mr Tredinnick said scathingly. 'I'll be in touch, governor.'

We walked away.

'Pint,' Mr Tredinnick said. 'Nice motor that.'

'Very nice,' I agreed.

'Just the thing,' he said. 'See if he'd take fifteen hundred. We make a good team, you and me. Christ, you look rough. Not like you one bit.'

I followed Mr Tredinnick into a pub, and let him buy me a pint of bitter, which was what he was drinking.

'The thing about cars is,' he started.

'Is there a phone in here?' he finished, some minutes later. 'Best not to miss an opportunity like that. Fifteen hundred quid. A bargain.' He got up and went to look for a phone. I sat for a moment or two, marvelling at Mr

Tredinnick's ability to reconstruct the world in accordance with his wishes. No one would ever say 'You don't want to do that' to Mr Tredinnick. He knew what his wants were, and if at six o'clock the price of a car was two thousand pounds, and an hour later the price was five hundred pounds less, that was because that was what Mr Tredinnick wanted to pay for it. At the back of the pub, I could see him hunched over the telephone, talking very quietly and fast and distinctly. I watched him for a while.

Then all at once I got up and left the pub and I walked all the way home.

24

The next day I spoke to Wasia on the telephone. Then I spoke to my wife. Then I turned away two French girls, students, who believed that my house was a bed and breakfast: but they saw me, and glimpsed the state of the house over my shoulder as I opened the door, and clearly, they needed no turning away. A few days later, I went to my parents' house.

'This is the hotel we were staying in,' my sister said. 'This is the reception. This is the view from our room. Look, there's Richard, changing after we'd been to the beach.'

'Lovely room,' my father said, handing the photograph on. 'Lovely and light.'

By now, my sister and her new husband were back from the Seychelles, brown and smug and sated with two weeks of incessant sexual activity. We had all gone round there to hear about it.

'They specialise in honeymoons, this hotel,' my sister said. 'They make rather a point of it, in their brochures. This was the Caribbean night, the third night we were there. It was rather fun, and naturally, the food was perfectly delicious.'

'Lovely food, it looks,' Mr Tredinnick said, taking another photograph from her and adding it to the pile building up in his lap. 'It's not in the Caribbean, though, is it, the Seychelles?'

'Do pass the pictures to Mummy, Mr Tredinnick,' Sarah said. 'No, it's in quite the other direction. One turns left after Heathrow and keeps on going. This is the sun setting, from our window. As you see, we managed to take a panorama – let me put them together and you can see the whole effect. Two, three, four, there, five. Look, do you see?'

My sister put the five photographs in a special arrangement on the table and we all leant over and mewed appreciatively.

'And this is a beach we went to one day on another island; you had to take a little boat, so sweet. And do you know, as soon as my feet were on the sand, I said to Richard –'

'She said, I've been here before,' Richard said.

'That's exactly right,' Sarah said.

'And I thought, what's this, is she having a mystical experience?' said Richard. 'And frankly I thought, Christ, what have I married?'

The two of them laughed uproariously. 'He's a charming man, my husband, I must say,' Sarah said.

'But then, strangely enough, I thought exactly the same thing,' Richard said.

'You know about these things, Mr Tredinnick,' Sarah

said. 'Have a look, see what you think. Don't you recognise it? I recognised it immediately.'

We all looked at the photograph of the tropical beach, scattered with huge worn rocks, big and smooth as polystyrene, and leaning palm trees, and we all shook our heads.

'I've never been within a hundred miles of the Seychelles,' said Mr Tredinnick finally, as if this drastic underestimate would settle the matter.

'You'll kick yourselves when I tell you,' Sarah said. 'It's the beach where they filmed the Bounty advert. You know the Bounty advert?'

Sarah closed her eyes in ecstasy, tipped her head back and started singing the song.

'You know, that one for the chocolate bar,' she said when she was done. Richard was looking down at the floor, and I remembered what my mother had once said, that anyone would have thought he was marrying beneath him. 'Well, that turned out to be the place where it was filmed. They make quite a feature of it. There's a little shop, or rather a kiosk, where you can actually buy Bounty bars, there on the beach. There wasn't one before, but they perfectly sensibly decided to have one, because so many people started commenting on the fact. Absurd, but rather sweet, really.'

'A lovely place, it looks,' Mr Tredinnick said. 'Lovely and romantic.'

'Lovely,' my mother said. 'Did you have jet lag?'

'Oh,' Sarah said urbanely. 'Don't talk to me about jet lag. Going there and coming back.'

'There's a pill you can take,' Mr Tredinnick said.

'Nothing works,' Sarah assured him.

'A lovely spot, though,' my mother said, having done well to have come up with jet lag. 'There must be lots to do there.'

Sarah giggled, an ugly loud giggle which no one joined in with. 'Lots,' she said. 'Everyone disappeared after lunch. You could see them, hardly being able to wait to get it down. To get the food down, the food, I mean.'

'That's what it's there for, though, isn't it, a honeymoon?' Mr Tredinnick put in heartily. 'Young love.'

'Melatonin,' my father said. We all ignored him. He could have been talking about anything at all. 'Melatonin, it's called. You get it from computers, from the Internet.'

'We really had,' Sarah said, moving on and summing up like the chairman of the board, 'we really had a very happy and long honeymoon.'

Everyone looked at me expectantly, before they all burst out laughing. I didn't know that what I had called after them at the wedding had turned into a family joke. I tried to laugh with them, but it wouldn't come, and their merriment seemed to go on for some considerable time. Finally it died down, and there was only my father, chuckling away to himself.

'Happy –' you could hear him burbling, there in his chair – 'happy – and – and long –' He pulled himself together and said, 'Melatonin, that's right,' once more before shutting up again.

My sister sat back, her eyes shining with mirth. 'It turned into a big joke, you know, that. We couldn't stop laughing about it, and saying to each other over break-fast, was it happy and long for you, darling. And then we told the couple at the next table, an awfully nice couple, who by chance had got married on exactly the same day as we had, from Bradford, she was in marketing, frozen foods, imagine, we told them, and they started too, and by the end of the week practically everyone was saying it apart from naturally all the Germans. We've got a photo-graph of them, too. It's somewhere here in the pile.'

'I didn't mean to say it,' I said, as people all across the world, on tiny coral islands thousands of miles away leant back in their chairs and laughed at me without any restraint.

'Oh, never mind, Daisy,' my sister said spitefully.

'Daisy?' Richard said.

'It's just what I used to call him, when he was a little boy,' Sarah explained.

'Daisy?' Richard said again.

'Because of his middle name,' Sarah said. 'It's Michael, and we used to have those flowers in the garden, you know, Michaelmas daisies, and so he became Daisy. He loves it, really.'

'No, I don't,' I said. It was true. I never liked it.

'Yes, you do,' Sarah said.

'No, I don't,' I said. 'And in any case, it wasn't you who used to call me Daisy, not first, it was Franky.'

Even as I said it I knew that was an amazing thing to say in our house as my sister was handing around photo-graphs of her honeymoon, and I didn't care and I said it anyway. The doorbell rang.

'That's the door, Brenda,' my father said.

'The door?' my mother said. 'Who could that be?'

Now, I think I should have mentioned something a little earlier. I had asked Wasia to come round this evening and meet my parents and my sister. I asked her because I felt that she had included me in her life, however unappealingly, with the outing to the nightclub, and in return she could, as she had asked, meet my parents again. I didn't mention it, because I hadn't mentioned it to my parents. It is difficult for me to see why I hadn't, and it might even seem a little strange to ask someone to come round for dinner at your mother's house and not actually tell your mother that there is going to be someone there who will expect to be fed. When I say it now, it seems very strange indeed. But what had happened was that my invitation to Wasia, conveyed after our evening at the nightclub, had seemed to use up all my courage, and day after day went by without my being able to pick up the phone to tell my mother. The days had gone by: I had seen Wasia twice more, but still I had not said anything to my family. Now it was half past seven, the doorbell was ringing and still I had not mentioned it. Wasia had wanted to come later, on her own, though I had suggested that she might come with me.

'It's not Mrs Tredinnick, is it?' my mother said.

'No, of course not,' Mr Tredinnick said scornfully. 'She's safely at home where she ought to be.'

'Who?' my father said.

'Mrs Tredinnick,' my mother said. The doorbell rang again, longer.

'It's Wasia,' I said. 'It must be Wasia. I asked her to come round.'

'And who's Wasia when she's at home?' Richard said.

My sister gaped at me. 'The – girl who came to our wedding?'

'The immigrant?' Mr Tredinnick said.

'Yes,' I said. 'She's not an immigrant. She was born here. I thought it would be nice if she came round tonight.'

'I wish you'd said,' my mother murmured, but she got up and went to the door. You could hear Wasia's polite voice greeting my mother, and in a moment she came in, already smiling. Something happened when she came in. She just walked in, smiling, with her big bag, and the house was all at once much smaller. My mother stood behind her and spread her hands, wonderingly.

'Hello, Sarah,' Wasia cooed. 'How handsome and brown you are, and your *edible* husband.' She had forgotten his name, but Richard would never forget the word she had used, you could see that. 'And how lovely to see you again –' Mr Tredinnick half rising from his seat – 'and hello, and –' turning to me – 'hello, you.' She kissed me, kissed me properly, and my arms fell to my sides in the amazed amazing room.

'How kind of you,' Wasia said. 'To let me come tonight. I was thrilled.'

'You are a dark horse,' Mr Tredinnick said, looking not at me but at Wasia, and probably thinking of neither of us, but of Janet.

'Oh, you are a wit, I can see we are going to be great friends,' Wasia said. I was the dark horse, but Wasia was dark and Indian, and Mr Tredinnick blushed all at once, hugely.

'Would you like something to drink?' my mother said.

'I'd love a drink, Brenda,' Wasia said. Another little shock ran round the room. Richard had never called my mother Brenda. He called her *you*. 'Whatever you're having.' We were drinking tea: my mother went to open the bottle of white wine she was keeping for later. 'Oh, snaps, do show me.'

'They're of our honeymoon,' Sarah said ungraciously. 'We'd actually finished. It's awfully boring, looking at other people's holiday photographs.'

'Oh, I love them,' Wasia said. 'I could look at them all day.'

'Wasia likes to take photographs,' I said. 'She's a keen amateur photographer.'

'A keen amateur photographer,' Wasia said, smiling. 'Yes, that's right, that's what I am.'

She lit one of her feminine cigarettes and an awkward silence fell, broken by my mother coming back silently from the kitchen. Wasia took the glass of white wine from her, and half drained it in one go. It was up to me to do something.

'Did you buy the car, Mr Tredinnick?'

'I left an offer with him,' Mr Tredinnick said, still looking at what had come into the house. Then he pulled himself together and improved on his story. 'But then I thought better of it and told him that I didn't think it was worth what I'd offered even.'

'A new car?' my mother said. 'What's this?'

'I was going to buy a new car,' Mr Tredinnick said. 'Jimmy came to help. But I thought better of it.'

'I wasn't much help,' I said.

'Made all the difference,' Mr Tredinnick said with surprising loyalty. 'Or would have done, if I'd wanted to buy it in the end.'

'What was the car?' Richard said. Wasia was following all this keenly.

'An old MG,' Mr Tredinnick said. 'Pile of junk. What sort of camera do you use, Wossier?'

'Oh – me?' Wasia said. She delved into her bag and got out the huge one-eyed inspector.

'That looks like business,' Mr Tredinnick said.

'It's my daddy's old camera,' Wasia said. 'It's too complicated for me, really. I should get a little one, where you don't have to focus and you can just put it in your pocket.'

'That's right,' my father put in.

'This is too complicated,' Wasia said.

'What would you get instead?' Richard said.

'Something small, anyway,' Wasia said. 'This is too heavy. It would be useful to have something which went down below f/7 –'

She shut up, all at once, like a slamming door, and scowled intensely.

'An MG, though?' Richard said after a pause. 'How much was he asking?'

'I offered twelve hundred,' Mr Tredinnick said, lying. 'Which was more than it was worth. It was a classic motor, though. I'm after another one.'

'You had a narrow escape,' Richard said. 'It's the parts that are the thing. If anything goes, it costs a packet, any part at all.'

'Parts?' Mr Tredinnick said.

'You never know,' Richard said sagely.

'Where do you come from?' my mother said nervously to Wasia, but it was too late. Mr Tredinnick was in a fury in defence of the car he hadn't bought, or perhaps the one he hadn't found yet.

'The car I'll be getting, let me tell you, it'll be in tip-top nick,' he said. 'I know my onions where your classic car is concerned, it'll not need anything replacing, not for years. You think I'd buy some old banger? No way. Straight off the factory floor, that'll be the one for me, one old-lady driver, demonstration quality, demonstration quality. And if it needs a new screw or two – I'm not saying I'll walk away if it's not perfect, don't get me wrong, son – if it needs a new screw, I tell you what, I'll go out and I'll bleeding well buy one, because, because, it's not like I'm short of a bob or two, is it, now?'

Richard shrugged.

'And I don't know why you walked off like that,' Mr Tredinnick went on, turning to me. I'd been gritting my teeth for this for two hours. 'Take you out, teach you something about motors, do you a favour, buy you a drink, and I come back from the khazi and you've walked off, this was in the Prince George in Chalk Farm. Nice, that, very nice. I don't know what your mother would think of you.'

'I suddenly felt unwell,' I said. It sounded unconvincing. 'I had something I had to do, as well, I was already late.'

'Nice,' Mr Tredinnick growled, simmering back down into his usual state of semi-resentment, all the injuries of the world on his cross old face.

Ker-chunk.

We turned and looked at Wasia. She lowered her camera.

'Highgate,' she said.

'Highgate?' my mother said, confused.

'Highgate,' Wasia said. 'You asked where I come from.'

We didn't stay that long after dinner. My mother had cooked shepherd's pie and peas and made trifle too. It was Sarah's favourite meal, or it was the meal which was supposed to be her favourite meal. We all were supposed to have one. Mine was roast pork and ice cream afterwards. No one commented or noticed. Wasia politely refused, saying that she had already eaten. I say it was from politeness, but it would have been difficult to go on taking photographs while she was eating. My family and Mr Tredinnick just let her go on taking her photographs throughout dinner. The food on her plate, the pictures on the wall, me eating shepherd's pie, Richard telling us about his lost luggage which the airline actually brought to the hotel the next day, Mr Tredinnick glowering over his non-existent parts for his non-existent MG. Once, Wasia raised the camera in both hands directly in front of her at arm's length, frowned and took a photograph of herself. Nobody said anything; I'm sure we would have taken one of her if she'd asked. Perhaps Wasia seemed strange in other, bigger ways, Indian, tiny, smoking continuously, everything. It seemed to be the glassy expanse of her politeness they wondered at, and the amazing fact which she let slip, that she had come all the way from Highgate in a taxi.

'And he complained all the way, *sans cesse*, that he would never ever get a fare back from here and who did I think I was,' Wasia said. 'Terribly interesting question, normally, who do you think you are, but I don't think he meant it in a construction-of-the-self way, I think he was just being rude. So rude.'

'So rude,' Mr Tredinnick said, trying it out.

'Do you mind if I smoke?' I said.

'You don't *smoke*,' my sister said.

'I hate to see a lady smoke,' Richard said. '*Daisy.*' He started laughing; but he caught Wasia's eye, and fearing that he had been misunderstood, stopped short.

'You *don't* smoke,' Mr Tredinnick said.

'Yes, I do,' I said. To prove it, I got my cigarettes out. Wasia wordlessly offered me a light. I drew a big drag. Everyone was closely watching me. I might have been Sir Walter Raleigh at court, freshly returned with his carcinogenic discovery. I held the smoke in my throat for a moment, not coughing or choking or spluttering; I had not done so for days. I breathed it out, and the smoke was thin, as if it were food I had sucked all the goodness from. It was not smoke I was breathing, but a new sort of air. I tapped the cigarette on the edge of the pudding bowl, and took another drag. But then I coughed and choked and spluttered, all at the same time and everyone started talking, very busily, all at once.

We didn't stay very long after that. There was nothing to stay for. I unenthusiastically asked Sarah and Richard if they were coming too, but they looked at us, doubt-fully, and said they'd probably hang on a while longer. I was overpoweringly happy. I left with Wasia, and we walked to the bus stop. We didn't talk. We caught a bus to the train station, and the British Rail train took us to an Underground station. We didn't say anything at all, all the way. Wasia was following me, all the way to my house. She had never been there before. There was a wonderful rightness and inevitability about it all. The bus and the train and Underground train came at once for us, as if they were all waiting round the corner for us to turn up, to whisk us home. Tonight, the world was not going to inconvenience us.

There was nothing I wanted or needed to say to Wasia. I had never felt so much together with her. It seemed to me that I had left my family behind, that I hardly wanted my wife back, that I was in a new world, where the air was different and solid and nutritious, and we divinities would live without care, sucking goodness from fire. My mind raced on, thinking about the months, years ahead in the bluish light of public transport. Around me were Wasia, and Mrs Grainger maybe, and a great crowd of friends I didn't know yet, a great crowd of benevolent ghosts. Wasia had come into my family's house and made it small for me. I had left it behind, with its little old unspoken grief, and I was more happy than I could say.

We got home in less than an hour and a half. I opened my front door.

'What a fucking journey,' Wasia said.

I was surprised.

'Christ,' Wasia said, preceding me into the house. 'Do you live here?'

'Yes,' I said.

'You live like this?' Wasia said, picking her way through the debris in the hallway, into the debris in the sitting room. I followed her.

'Yes,' I said. 'It's not usually as bad as this. I've not had a lot of time for clearing up recently.'

She took out her camera, and started photographing again; the mess in the room.

'Don't do that,' I said. 'It's such a mess.'

She turned the beady eye of her camera on me, and – *ker-chunk* – there I was again, looking distressed. She carried on for almost five minutes.

'So,' she said, flopping down on to the sofa and pulling the cushions around her. 'So, she went to the Seychelles on her honeymoon, your sister.'

'Yes,' I said.

'God, how predictable and boring,' she said. I looked at her in astonishment. 'The most romantic place in the world. Can you imagine. God, the Seychelles, what a fucking hole. Imagine, your poor brother-in-law, shelling out for the whole once-in-a-lifetime thing, and getting to the most romantic place on earth and realising that he's expected to molest your boring old sister every single day after lunch.'

I hardly knew what to say to this.

'She's such a fucking snob,' Wasia said. 'She thinks she's so amazing and there are hundreds of women exactly like that, just in Bromley, wearing their Alice bands and being ashamed of their mums and remembering not to say *settee*. The way she winces when you all talk.'

You will be surprised, but it had not occurred to me that Wasia could be feeling anything but what I was feeling.

'She doesn't live in Bromley,' I said. 'She lives not far from here, actually.'

I stretched out my arm, and put it around her little shoulders, but she pulled away, almost angrily. I turned and looked at her. All her smiling face was gone, and she was black and scathing in her eyes.

'You take too much for granted,' she said.

'I'm sorry,' I said.

'Don't apologise,' she said. 'Only fools apologise.'

'I had a nice evening,' I said, as if it ought to have been contagious. I got up to make some coffee, or something. I still didn't understand. As I got up, a hiccup escaped me.

'And stop making that fucking noise,' Wasia said. 'It's driving me mental. I don't know where you're going – running off, scared, as usual, I suppose.'

I sat down again.

'So you had a nice evening,' she said. 'With Mummy and Daddy and Lucinda and Mr What's-his-name.'

'She's not called Lucinda,' I said.

'Don't think she wouldn't like to be,' Wasia said.

'I was pleased *you* came,' I said uncertainly.

'So you should be,' she said. 'Hours in a fucking taxi and hours coming back and now you only want one thing which you're not going to get, because if your sitting room looks like this I don't want to think what your sheets are like, and you don't care that I even had any kind of an evening, well, my evening was fucking horrible, fucking horrible, do you hear?'

'I didn't know,' I said.

'You're not interested,' she said. 'Anyway, I'm going to go now. I don't want to stay any longer with anyone as selfish and uninterested as you.'

'That's not fair,' I said. 'I'm not selfish.'

'You know,' Wasia said. It was as if I had said nothing at all. 'You've never asked me anything about myself at all. Do you know that? You've never asked me anything about my family, or what I do, or anything apart from *how are you* the moment we meet each other and then we're straight on to talk about John again. And if I told you how I was you wouldn't listen. You're the most selfish person I've ever met in my life. Go on, try and ask me something about myself. Just try.'

I sat, dumbfounded. 'Tell me all about yourself,' I said in the end, limply. I would have done better if she'd given me more warning.

'You're not interested,' she said, crossly, and hurled herself back into the sofa, clutching the cushions to her chest.

'I thought we were happy,' I said. 'I thought this was fun.'

'Maybe it was fun for you,' Wasia said. 'What do you mean, we? Did you think we were supposed to be having some kind of a relationship?'

'It'll be all right,' I said, not knowing what I should say. That was roughly what I thought, in fact.

'Well, if we were, it's all off. It's all too late, you fool,' she said. 'You – you're like someone proposing that we all ought to start rearranging the deckchairs on the *Titanic*. You want to give someone with lung cancer a sticking plaster. You want to give the kiss of life to a pork chop. You're someone, you're someone, who –'

'That's not true,' I said. She stopped, anyway.

We sat there in fuming silence. I was furious, too, by now. I felt anger shooting up inside me like a fountain. It struck me that Wasia, in some way, was enjoying this. It was utterly unfair: I was not a fool. I would not give the kiss of life to a pork chop. That was something I knew about myself.

'Maybe I don't need to see your family again,' she said. 'I've got to go.'

'When shall I see you again?' I said. 'Don't go. We've only just started talking.'

'I don't know when,' she said, gathering her things together. 'I'm very busy. I'm extremely busy, in fact. No, I think it would be best if we didn't see each other ever again.'

'I don't understand,' I said.

'Let me tell you one thing,' Wasia said. 'Hope and Ben, they didn't like you, not at all. They thought you were awful.'

'I worked that out,' I said. 'I couldn't stand them, either.'

'You're so fucking childish,' Wasia said. 'I really don't need people like you in my life. Goodbye.'

She got up and walked to the door. I followed her. I was so angry I couldn't think of anything to say at all.

I just hiccupped with rage. In the hallway, she stopped, but wouldn't look at me. She was waiting for something, but it wouldn't come. She seemed to know that there was something hidden in the air, which I was supposed to pluck out like a magician on stage. But I was no magician, and the moment passed. She opened the door and left. The double click of her departure, when the door shut, was like the neat noise of her camera lens's open and close, setting some moment down on paper, permanently. And in a moment, standing there, I heard from the other side of the door the real thing: Wasia photographing – what? – the garden, the closed front door? I expected nothing less of her.

I looked at the door in my face, and all at once I wanted to shout something. *Have a happy and long* – have a happy and long – but I did not know what I wished, nor whether I would have wished it for Wasia or for me. She had gone, that was clear. And now there was only one thing for it.

Pink Suit Two

'My mother's going to be furious,' I said to Janet. Once, long before.

'Just your mother?' she said. 'Not your father?'

'Perhaps him too,' I said. We were on a train, going to Bromley, to see my parents. A strange thing had happened; something my parents didn't yet know about. We had got married two weeks before, and had gone away together. Now we were back, and married; and we were going to tell them about it.

'She might be pleased,' Janet said. 'You never know.'

'On the phone –' I had called earlier – 'she didn't sound pleased. She was just upset that I'd disappeared off the face of the earth for two weeks.'

'You can't blame her,' Janet said.

'No,' I said. 'But you can't blame us, either. It seemed the best thing to do.'

'Of course she minds if one of her children just vanishes like that,' Janet said.

'Yes, I know,' I said. We were rattling along in this suburban train, the suburban suburbs rattling away behind us like party streamers. It was one of those trains which even then was rather on its last legs, the carriages divided into separate compartments with no corridor, so you got in and got out and in between stayed where you were: a train apparently designed by an Edwardian rapist. But we had got married two weeks before, and we were happy that we were alone in the carriage and no one would join us.

'What about yours?' I said.

'My what?' Janet said.

'Your mother,' I said. 'We didn't tell her, either. Is she furious?'

'No, she's not furious,' Janet said. 'As far as I know. She might be, when I get round to telling her.'

'You haven't told her?'

'I'll get round to it. I know what she'll say, though. She'll be horrified and outraged. She'll go –'

'T,' I clicked with my tongue, shaking my head. It was something we did together, making this noise and mocking Janet's mother. I had only met her once; she was a woman who crouched in the cleft of her armchair, her gaze flickering between the unextinguished television and this man who her daughter, she subsequently said, didn't deserve. If Janet hadn't made it clear afterwards how she felt about her envious mother, I would have been frightened of her and her malice. As it was, we mocked her, and made a T click with our tongues.

'She'll probably say –'

'How much?'

'How much?'

'Yes,' I said. 'It was worth it, though.'

'The wedding?'

'That wasn't expensive,' I said. 'I meant the suit, really. It's just beautiful. You're beautiful in it, I mean.'

'You don't think it's too much, do you?' Janet said.

'No,' I said, but it was; it was too much for the train, and to meet my parents in. I thought this, happily.

'Is that the suit I bought you?' Janet said.

'I don't know,' I said. 'It might be.'

'That's sad,' she said. 'You can't tell the difference between that suit and all the others.'

'But it's useful,' I said.

26

'And we're just coming up to Remember This at eleven o'clock,' the unctuous voice from the kitchen radio said, 'just after the news. That's just coming up. And now here's an old favourite from the Weather In The North –'

The voice, honeyed and breathy, as if speaking densely through mucus, continued from the radio. I was also listening to its manifestation a beat or so out of sync, on the telephone clapped firmly to my ear. I was perched on a kitchen stool. Another, perkier voice cut in over the Weather In The North as a switch was flicked in the radio studio.

'Still there, John?' the producer's voice said. 'Five minutes, OK? Don't go anywhere, just be relaxed, be yourself, if in doubt, keep talking, it doesn't matter what you say, and Mikie's going to be helping you along if you dry, OK?'

'That's fine,' I said. 'I'm not nervous, though –' but he had already flicked the switch before I had had a chance to answer or indeed confirm that I was still there. I was talking to the Weather In The North, and they weren't talking back.

This was my plan. It was called Remember This, a sickening radio slot of lost love and found love, hugely popular and once a week. It ran both on the radio show of this thoroughly chirpy Saturday-morning bloke and, transcribed, in a column of a newspaper. Miss Johnson used to tell me about this ghastly programme. It was the only thing she liked, apart from *Buncombe Parva*, and tears had sometimes formed in her eyes as she explained how it, and I Feel Your Body by Mel Master D, had reunited a vet from Bedford and his adulterous wife the Saturday before. It was just the thing. Both over the air and in print, it was terrifically popular; for my purposes, in the newspaper it would be read not just in this country but wherever English tourists went, anywhere in the world, sharing papers between themselves on beaches. There was no real reason to be sure that Janet would read my desperate plea, wherever she was. But I knew she would. I had no doubt whatever that this message in a bottle would reach her. And you could speak to your wife over the phone endlessly, saying the same thing, but if she read it in a newspaper, she would have no alternative. She would have to believe it, because there, she couldn't interrupt you or pick holes in what you were saying.

'One minute,' the perky producer was saying. 'Just finishing the weather – no, what am I saying? – the traffic.'

I sat and listened, my palm gripping the phone with cramp, and discovered, as if it were a suitable prelude to my heartbreaking story, that severe delays were occurring on the A3017 owing to a lorry shedding its load of cocoa powder over both carriageways. And then it was me.

'Remember this – your soft hand in my pocket?
Remember this – a two-pin plug, a three-pin socket?
Remember when we had that long hot weekend in Spain?
Remember the toilet where we fucked on the train?'

Or something.

'Welcome,' said the DJ, his chocolatey voice coming in over the sordid old Brown Sugar number, 'to Remember This, the time in the *Saturday Show* where YOU –' beat – 'tell us YOUR –' beat – 'stories. How you fell in love. How you faced those little difficulties everyone faces when you're in love –'

This part, presumably, I thought, was actually scripted.

'– and how maybe you split up and want to get back together again. And we'll be playing that special song in your relationship, just for you and the one you love, mixed male/female couples please only, folks, and also for the 4.2 million listeners at the last count to Britain's most tuned-in-to and straight-to-the-heart radio station verified by independent assessment. Today on the line we've got John from Putney in south London. Hello, John.'

'Hello, Mikie,' I said. 'It's more west London, really, though.'

'West London, I stand corrected. Now, John, you're here to tell us about your wife Janet, aren't you?'

'That's right, Mikie,' I said.

'Now, tell us how you met, mate,' he said.

'Well, we met at a party,' I said.

'Whoa, slow down, mate, when was this?' Mikie said.

'About eight years ago,' I said.

'Eight years, wow,' Mikie said. 'And you weren't sure about going to this party, were you?'

'That's right,' I said, as well I might, since Mikie was reading from a script which I'd contributed to earlier.

'You weren't sure that you really wanted to go, because you didn't think you'd know anyone there, is that right?'

'That's right, Mikie,' I said.

'But in the end,' Mikie said, his voice dropping seriously, 'you did go. And you're glad you did, aren't you?'

'That's right,' I said. 'Yes, I'm glad I did go, all things considered.'

'Why's that then, mate?'

'Well, it turned out to be quite a good party after all,' I said. I was about to explain about the hostess bursting into tears, which I'd enjoyed a great deal.

'That's not what I meant, though, not really,' Mikie said. 'You're glad you went because it was there that you met your wife Janet for the first time, isn't that right, mate?'

'Yes, that's right,' I said. '!'

'Now, John, mate, I know this is hard for you, but try to be strong for your old mate Mikie, OK, because we all want to hear your story, OK?'

'No, I'm not crying,' I said. 'I've got the hiccups.'

'OK, John, so you've got the hiccups on the radio, nice thing, could happen to anyone but it's happening to me.

So we were saying how you met your wife Janet for the first time, and would you say it was love at first sight?'

I opened my mouth, but then I couldn't quite say anything.

'John? Hello?'

'Yes,' I said eventually. 'Yes, that's right, in fact.'

'Thought we'd gone and lost you there,' Mikie said. 'Hiccups got the better of you. So it was love at first sight, even though Janet, that's the lovely lady who you fell in love with and married, she had a long-term boyfriend at the time, a very successful businessman, a tycoon you might say, called Gareth, and it's fair to say that you yourself, John, you haven't had a lot of success in life as far as that goes, yeah?'

'Well, I wouldn't say that,' I said. 'I'm a very good indexer of books.'

'So it must have been,' Mikie went on, ignoring my outrage on behalf of the indexing profession, 'true love on her part as well. And it turned out to be a whirlwind romance, isn't that right?'

'That's right, Mikie,' I said.

'And in fact no more than a month and a half after you first met, you were walking up the aisle together?'

'No, it was a year and a half,' I said. That, I thought, was probably not a whirlwind romance at all, but I stopped myself from pointing out that we would have walked down the aisle together having walked up it separately, and in any case there had been no aisle at the registry office where we had got married. It didn't seem romantic, and in any case, by now I was too helplessly absorbed in my own story to make any kind of rational objection to anything Mikie might say.

'Whirlwind, mate, whirlwind. So for eight years John and Janet couldn't have been happier together. There might be richer people in the world. There might even be more glamorous people in the world. But for eight years John and Janet had each other. They were happy and in love. And that's what counts in life. You're listening to Remember This on the BBC *Saturday Show*, the nation's best-loved radio show, and I've got John from Putney in London on the line telling us his own story in his own words, and don't worry, he's not sobbing, as I mistakingly thought a moment or two ago there, he's hiccupping. So, John, what's gone wrong?'

'Well, I don't really know – ! – how to put it,' I said.

'You wouldn't say that you'd grown apart, or that you stopped loving each other,' Mikie said.

'No,' I said. 'But there was this business with Mrs Grainger, I mean, this lady – ! – who I –'

'But as time goes on,' Mikie interrupted, nervously slipping back into his super-caring tones, 'you forget to tell each other how much you mean to each other, and then it's easy if one of you starts to think that the love has gone because you don't make every day special. Make every day special, people, remember that, you're listening to Remember This. And one day you woke up and Janet had gone.'

Awful as he was, Mikie's summary was more or less correct. I suppose it couldn't be avoided in the end.

'Yes,' I said. 'She's run off – ! – with Gareth. Her old

boyfriend, the one – ! – with all the money and I don't know where she is.'

'So,' Mikie said doubtfully – I hadn't mentioned her running off with Gareth to the researcher in advance – 'is there anything you'd like to say to Janet, now, on the *Saturday Show*?'

'!' I said.

'I expect you'd like to tell her that you love her very much and you want her to come home,' Mikie said. 'And how's about this very special song you'd like us to play for her that means so much to you and to her?'

I told him.

'Well, that's a bit of a strange request, since it only came out six weeks ago,' Mikie said.

'Look, it's what I want, so play it, all right?' I said.

'OK, OK, mate, if it's a special song for you and Janet, though I can't see how it can be, to be honest, but here's that special song for John and Janet from that precious two weeks before she ran off with someone else a month ago, and Janet, if you're out there listening, here it is.'

A face on a page
A glimpse on a street
A smile for the goat-fuck
Those shoes on her feet
They cost a million dollars
A million dollars
So smile.
It's called celebrity. Celebrity. Celebrity. Celebrity.
You're famous in my life

You don't know who I am
I'll paste you on my walls
I'll chase you to Japan
And yet you still won't know me
You still won't know my face in the crowd
Which pays a million dollars
A million dollars for you
Each day
So smile.
It's called celebrity.
Welcome to my lovely home
My marriage is just fine
I've dealt with all my demons
But now you've had your time
It's out on Tuesday
So off you go
It's called celebrity.
I don't know you
But you know me
That's why it's called
Celebrity and yes I'm
World-famous in Kansas yes I'm
World-famous in Kansas yes I'm
World-famous in Kansas and we're
Stuck in Kansas from now on in it's called
Celebrity.

And the day after next, it was in the papers, winging its way towards my wife, wherever she was. But it wasn't in the Remember This weekly column. It was on page

five. They called me Jilted John. They had talked to
Gareth and he said that he hadn't seen my wife in five
years, and in any case had got married himself two years
ago. He talked of suing me. I read this, and with a horrible
shudder I realised that the only reason I thought my wife
had run off with Gareth was that I had found a telephone
number in the pocket of one of her jackets, a number
which might have been anybody's. I went home and
phoned the number, which I had committed to memory.
The telephone spoke to me, and this is what it said: 'This
is the box office of the Odeon Leicester Square.' I put
the phone down. Oh God, I said. Please, don't let me go
mad, not that, not that. And all Janet had said was that
if I looked at my wardrobe, I might start to understand
why she'd left me. The papers, they didn't talk of suing
me; they didn't talk, either, about how much I loved and
missed my wife. They talked about my hiccups. If you
missed it the first time round, you could phone a premium-
line number and listen to it all over again. Mr Patel, handing
over the wrong paper, and Mrs Grainger, and Mr
Tredinnick, all of them, they looked at me and laughed
and shook their heads.

27

The next day it was Franky's birthday. It was the anniversary of Franky's birthday. I warned you it was going to be. That you don't need to know about and there is nothing to tell you about it. It was exactly like the same day every year. I did not see my family and they did not see each other. The telephone did not ring behind the drawn curtains. I kept that day for her. I did not drink or smoke or walk the streets, for her sake. At the end of the day I went to bed and I slept and I dreamt. I had a simple dream; I dreamt about something which you could always look at without pain or weariness. That is all you need to know. If you remembered the way your sister celebrated each of her so few birthdays before she died and became a celebrity, you would do exactly what I do. My parents do the same, and so does my sister, Sarah, the one who is still alive.

And then –

Janet's Journey

You could buy a ticket to the airport in exactly the same way you could buy one to any other place. The squarish ticket clerk at the Underground station would take your money and give you back a ticket with your change. He made a single efficient gesture out of it, like a dealer at poker. Perhaps he was hiding the fact, but she would have liked the beginnings of a response in his face, that was all, to her journey. But he dealt with her as the taxi driver had, as if she were only another transaction, and not someone who had left her husband now, and with the purchase of her ticket was starting a journey round the world. 'Don't hoot,' she had said to the taxi firm. 'Or ring the doorbell. I'll just be there.' That hadn't been interesting either, it seemed. As she walked away, she heard the woman who had been behind her ask for exactly the same thing, a ticket to Heathrow. Perhaps she too had left her husband, only an hour before. You never knew.

But something, after all, seemed to mark Janet out as a woman making a step, with her three leather cases and her suit for travelling in. The train arrived in a moment, and though it was a route used equally by commuters and more ambitious travellers, it was still early in the morning, and there was plenty of space. She sat down opposite a middle-aged woman on her own, whose clothes and hair had prematurely passed into a festive phase. Her candyfloss-pink blouse, strangely frilled, as if she had personally customised it with ribbons, the deckchair stripes of her full skirt and the plastic sandals embedded with glitter belonged to a slightly different person. Someone in Spain already, someone returning from their two weeks with skin the enraged shade of a bougainvillea flower. Janet regretted the vague thoughts of the Orient Express thundering through the tunnels of the night which had led her to put on a travelling suit. It was only her newest suit for work, anyway. She had seen herself reading in a first-class carriage, sending back dinners untasted, observing over cognac glasses and book how often that handsome young man had passed this way, as outside the Middle European night swept silently by. It was not very much like the Piccadilly Line. The suit had been a mistake. This woman, on the other hand, lit up the carriage.

'Off anywhere nice?' the woman said, leaning forward confidentially. Her voice was smooth and low and un-expectedly educated.

'Yes,' Janet said in a second. 'I'm going round the world.' This was not true; by now, it was not true. She was travelling, or about to travel, through the world only, and for the first time. But it was impossible to tell a stranger that, even at this point, she had no real idea where she was going to go. The only plan she had made was to go to the airport with her passport and leave. It was no plan at all.

'How lovely,' the woman said, losing interest slightly in the question as soon as it was answered. But it was the train pulling into a station which had made her vague. She smoothed down her randomly arranged outfit nervously, looking behind Janet's head. She was thinking of her luggage in a pile by the opening door, though the train was empty, and no one got in or out. The doors shut, and she started paying attention again. 'A round-the-world trip. How lovely. I've always longed to do something like that.'

'Me too,' Janet said weakly. 'Well, I've always wanted to do it, and here I am doing it.' For no particular reason, she felt she ought to talk to this stranger. Wherever she was going, she would know nobody, and ought to develop the habit, the knack of dropping into exchanges with strangers. Six years of marriage deprived you of that skill. 'I thought I'd do it sooner rather than later.'

'Where will you go –?' the woman began, but then the same thing happened, the doors opening, pausing, closing sweetly and taking her attention away as she peered in concern over Janet's shoulder.

'I don't know exactly,' Janet said patiently. She looked at the woman's hand to confirm something, and, yes, the woman had no wedding ring, and she was, surely, a woman who needed a marriage and a ring, if there had ever been one on offer. 'I'm flying out, just to some first stop, and then go on from there, I suppose – so you see –'

The woman's eyebrows were painted on to plucked raw skin; they would run with sweat in the holiday sun like mascara after weeping; now they raised in something like alarm. 'But you have to have a plan,' she said. 'I mean – what about hotels – and there are countries which ask you for a visa, aren't there? – and then – a girl alone –'

'Yes, I know,' Janet said, despite herself; though a plan wouldn't protect a girl alone, she hadn't thought of visas. 'Lions and tigers and bears, oh my.'

'Lions and –?' the woman said, puzzled and snubbed.

'It was something I wanted to do, I suppose, go round the world in one, in one go,' Janet went on weakly, regretting the snub. She would get nowhere, as she travelled round the world, as she travelled through the world, if she started like this.

'I like to go to an island every year for two weeks,' the woman offered, not exactly saying that she was going there now. 'I've been going there for years. They're almost like family now. I always book for the next year, the day I leave, and the owner and his family come out and they all say goodbye. Touching, really. I've seen his son grow up into – I've seen them grow up. "See you next year, Mary," they always say, except the grandmother, who can't speak much in the way of English, so she just puts a finger to her tear ducts, not actually crying, though, of course, they save that for funerals really.'

'Where is it, your island?' Janet said, not really able to comment on the happiness evidently brought by so ordinary a hotelier's sentiment. Though perhaps the woman was just finding a way to tell Janet her name.

'Oh, I'd honestly rather not say, not to be unfriendly,' the woman said, so complacently that she must have been asked this before, and responded in this same way. 'It's so unspoilt, you see, it hasn't changed in years, and that's so rare, I wouldn't want people knowing it in case they spoilt it.'

'Right,' Janet said, thinking that it was startlingly rude to suggest that Janet on her own could ruin an entire Mediterranean island. 'Menus in English, concrete hotels, yes, you're quite right, I suppose.'

'Nudist beaches, Australians with their rucksacks, yes, absolutely,' the woman continued enthusiastically, pronouncing the word 'noodist'; the man across the aisle, with his *Daily Telegraph* folded vertically, shot them a startled look.

'Absolutely,' Janet said. A beach full of well-knit naked Australians reeled pleasantly before her eyes; it seemed as likely to prove an agreeable destination as some port with embittered old fishermen bashing away at some octopus, but she weakly agreed. Her presence would, indeed, sour a place like piss in a bottle of milk. Perhaps this was true, because now that they were nearly at Heathrow, the gaudy woman was too lost in a detailed incantation of the beauties of the island, the beauties of her hosts, the son, yes, the son as well, an island Janet strongly suspected of being Minorca, too lost to take any notice of the accumulation of travellers in the train, tourists, Londoners, people getting in and out and perhaps seizing her now unobserved bags, and Janet thought that this was true, that she did not want to go to a place which contained her. She would sour the idyll by looking at it. She wondered what it would mean, to want to go to a place where you were not.

'But how long will you be away?' the woman asked.

'Three months,' Janet said. With an instinct that she would rather not have had, she remembered that people hang around in trains and airports simply to find out the addresses of empty houses. Though this woman was no cat burglar, there were others now around them. 'But my husband's staying at home all that time,' she said swiftly.

'You've left him behind?' Mary said. She crinkled up her nose, not seeming to believe in the husband. It was true that Janet's wedding ring was in her handbag and not on her finger.

'Yes, I've left him,' Janet said, not saying exactly the same thing. But it seemed as if, having offered this intimate detail, Janet had lost the power to interest the woman, who drew back sceptically. A husband – one to deter eavesdropping burglars, nothing more than that, she appeared to be thinking. The train was coming into Heathrow, and as they both stood up, Janet wished she could think of any civil way to let anyone around them know that the two of them did not belong together. Their conversation would not have suggested that they were friends, but anyone listening would have mistakenly thought that their situations were similar, and that now they might very well choose to go away together. They had nothing in common, but it wouldn't have looked like that. Janet could only trust in the gap between their clothes – her sober suit and the woman's carnival assortment – to do all that. Janet said goodbye politely in her black suit, like a hilltop monastery observing the departure of a funfair from its environs.

It was apparently harder to go anywhere – anywhere at all in the next two hours, it didn't matter, Janet explained reasonably – than to stay where you were, immobile, unloved. Well, of course it was. Everybody knew that. Janet had approached a ticket desk, waited behind a rope with her three leather valises on a trolley. The man in front of her in the queue was making some kind of scarlet fuss. How difficult people could be! The fey ticket clerk looked up sardonically from underneath a noticeably unsuccessful exercise in blond streaks, like a child who knows exactly where in the flower bed he has buried his father's wallet, and is waiting for the God-almighty posturing to blow itself out. He had seen it all before, you could tell that, and several times today, too. The terms of the quarrel were unclear, but she watched it in dumbshow. And then all at once, it was over, a ticket was being handed over, and the two of them parted, apparently on terms of great friendship, though without obviously having conceded an inch from their initial positions. It was so odd, being a traveller. She would have to practise a little.

'Next please,' the man called, smiling and shaking his head; she had been lost in one of the episodes of this rootless day, as the world around her took on an instantaneous and horrifying vividness for a moment. She tore herself away from the contemplation of the grey-lit low space, festooned with loose electrical wires from the ceiling, the panels all removed, and beneath them, what seemed just then joyless refugee hordes, their belongings heaped on trolleys as they began a dreadful pilgrimage . . . the horror she felt was ludicrous, meaningless, without basis, and all she was looking at with peculiar intensity was an airport departure lounge and a lot of perfectly ordinary people.

'Yes,' she said, and explained.

'Anywhere?' the man said.

'Yes, anywhere. Any seat you have, anywhere in the world, in the next couple of hours.'

'Oh, I like this sort of challenge,' the man said, and brought his hands down from his face to the desk. He typed something so flamboyantly, he might have been a child playing at offices. 'You've brightened my day, I can tell you.'

'We aim to please,' Janet said. 'It doesn't have to be any airline in particular.'

'Oh, now you're spoiling it,' the man said, inspecting his screen. 'And we were getting on so well. No, I can only sell you a seat on a BA flight, this is the BA desk. But you don't want to fly with anyone else anyway.'

'No, I wouldn't,' Janet said.

'And between you and me, I flew once on another airline, Lufthansa they call it, and never again, the stewardesses all *smelt*.'

'What did they smell of?'

'Poo,' the man said. 'So you've come to the right place. Right. You could go to Calcutta in an hour and a half.'

'I think I might need a visa for India,' Janet said expertly.

'Yes, you might well,' the man said. 'But anyway, you don't look the type to start caring about starving children. Or there's New York.'

'No.'

'I had a friend from New York once, nice boy he was, but no you say. Or there's Athens after that.'

'Athens.'

'Where East meets West, you know. I can do you quite a good deal for that. Of course you wouldn't be stopping in Athens. Do you mind me being cheeky and asking why you're organising your holiday like this? I'm just being nosy.'

Janet looked at him. That, after all, was the question, and though she would not explain it to a chatty stranger behind a desk, she had sooner or later to condense the vague feeling of looming catastrophe which had filled her last weeks into a single question. Last night's abrupt packing of the bags, the dawn departure had clearly provided an answer to that inchoate dilemma. What the terms of the question had been, she could not say. She gave him a casual answer; he said something flippant back; and there she was with a ticket to Athens in her hand, and the flight leaving in ninety minutes.

All the way in the plane, she thought of this, irritably turning away the reheated food in the little compartmented tray, like a model of a cramped and dark apartment in plastic. She rejected the offers of one drink after another, ignored the suggestion of the fat man by her that she should take her share of these things, and he should have them in addition to his own ration.

And then they were in Athens and she had no idea why. Janet followed the others out of the plane, down past the graciously satisfied farewells of the cabin staff and the grimmer assessments of the ground staff, one of whom, to her astonishment, was talking in a bubbling foreign language as she passed. Greek, she supposed; a sort of party trick. She went with the crowd down the tube, the extended and fragile grey plastic caterpillar, like a hot oven between the chill plane and the chill corridors and lobbies of the airport itself, looking very much like the airport she had just left.

It was an unusual crowd, and Janet noted their physical imperfections in vivid flashes. Half were pale holiday-makers, their clothes as yet uncommittedly festive, trying to accommodate a British and a Greek spring at once, with a pair of black socks and lace-ups beneath faded khaki shorts. But the Greeks were as curious, returning from some kind of business, dressed like the foreigners Janet in a previous life had presented with cups of tea and led to the offices of the bank's directors. Dressed like accountants, already talking into their mobile phones, you could not look at them without imagining them reaching their homes and, with relief, stripping off, dropping their suits on the floor in puddles, walking in their Greek skin into a hot shower. She ran her hands down her own dark suit. She went with their purposeful stride, thinking that it was not as warm as she had thought it would be; in her confusion the air conditioning seemed like the weather.

But she passed through the immigration control, her passport briefly glanced at – didn't they know what they were letting in – and in a trance through the hall where her bags were already circling the belted island in solitary magnificence. It was only then, with the brief 'oh my' as she walked through the lizard flicker of the customs official, found herself in normal, undirected life, the life of cities out of the realms of surveillance, that she realised that this was the wrong place.

For some reason, since Janet had bought the ticket, she had made no effort to direct her mind towards the place. She had not bought a guidebook to read on the plane, she had not thought about buying holiday insurance, she had not considered the question of how to find a hotel to stay in. She hadn't made any kind of imaginative effort, hadn't constructed an Athens in her head which the real Athens would subsequently bend into its own more brutal shape. If she had ever thought of Athens it had been with an image of men in togas, walking through groves of arthritically twisted night-green trees, exchanging profound thoughts in the dappled groves. The word *epistemology* floated incomprehensibly, horribly, into her mind. There was nothing else. She didn't know, yet, what she wanted from this place apart from the impossibility of a place without thoughts of John and a place without a Janet to think these thoughts. What she hadn't wanted was an airport and, at its exit at the portals of the city, men holding up tatty placards, misspelt names. Behind that, a city like any other, with traffic, neighbourhoods, gleaming new universities, a city where accountants could look down from their twelfth-floor accountancy offices to consider a girl, lost in the street, doing her best in the vast noise of a language she could not read or speak.

She sat down, her heavy hand on her luggage trolley, aghast. In the leaden movements of a nightmare, she watched a gaudy and ridiculous figure patter past her, all smiles, realising that it was inevitably, horribly, Mary, the woman from the train, going to her blissfully undiscovered island. Mary's gaze went over her, all happiness, but did not seem to recognise her. On she trotted, determined, ecstatically fulfilled even in the hall of Athens airport, trotting onwards out of Janet's life. Janet could not follow her to that island, into that ludicrous satisfaction; she didn't know how. From somewhere, she had acquired a man who was pushing her trolley with an expression very much like devotion. At that moment, Janet felt so helpless and lonely she was incapable of identifying a hired porter.

She had no idea where to go, or what to do next. She had not travelled, and had never developed the traveller's knack of worming out of any place some element of interest, of finding encounters with strangers in an ugly city enough to redeem an unwelcome problem, when transport dries up and you are stuck in a place you have no wish to be. Janet wanted everything to be perfect, at that moment, and it would have done no good to tell her about the many fascinations of Athens. There was no one to tell her any of that. She wouldn't, couldn't have listened.

After some time she raised her eyes. (There was a well-briefed German nun, passing just then in discreet mufti, on her way to the Parthenon; how Janet reminded her of

a Greuze virgin, imploring the martyring heavens!) Above
her was a row of screens, tilted and bolted like a fair-
ground car, all showing the same information; a screen
full of Greek. She looked away quickly, revolted and sick-
ened; not even *television* would help her here. But then
it did help her, because her eyes were drawn back to the
screens, and as if she had acquired the gift of tongues, it
seemed to her that she could read the screens as if the
information was in English before it cruelly reverted to
impenetrable Greek. It was a list of destinations. That
hadn't occurred to her. There was no reason for her
journey to finish here. She could take her luggage and
credit card, and continue her journey to another place
and perhaps even another, until she found where it was
she needed to be.

So it was that by the time she was settled in an
eighteen-seater plane bound for Paros, buffeted alarm-
ingly by every warm breeze, she had discovered with
some amusement that like sad Mary with her selfish
fulfilment she had started to think she must continue her
voyage to the end of the line. The plane was fragile and
antique, rattling, gulping, plummeting over a sea as blue
as an eye, the sea of your dreams. The pilots sat directly
in front of Janet, not troubling to close the curtain
between the cabin and the cockpit. They munched their
sandwiches unconcernedly. You could see the figures on
the dials quite clearly, registering who knew what, rising
and falling with the beat of the propellers, to Janet's wild
anxiety. She always knew she was going to die in a plane
crash – well, she hadn't always known that, but she knew

it now – and certainly in one where the bolts holding the propellers on had been tightened and checked after someone's very good lunch. But that was unfair, because as she looked down at the silky blue depths with its impasto of yacht trails, she found an idea of an island forming. Not Paros, because she would continue from Paros as far as you could go, to the end of the line. For her that could be the ends of the earth.

The airport was only a strip of land, surrounded by a fence and more brown dry earth. There was a small white building, fifteen paces long, under a bare blue sky. She waited impatiently for her bags, seeing all the while that impatience was one of the things she had to get away from. They came soon, and quickly she had commandeered the only taxi. She was driven to the port, not seeing the clusters of white-and-blue cubed buildings, the flashes of red and yellow poppies, the wild purple and white and pink outbursts by the road; sometimes, only, not knowing what it was, recognising but not identifying it, she breathed an ecstatic breath of oregano or hot sage, carried in through the window by the hot breeze. The clean smell of pine, behind it all, the blue smell of the sea, but she did not pause. She knew where she was going. So soon, there she was on a rumbling boat heading out to sea, going to the end of the line, the end of the line.

It was late afternoon. It was incredible to her that this could still be the day she had left her husband. The events had followed each other like a story told by a child, linked by nothing but And then, And then, And then, one thing after another, and no one in charge. The boat seemed old

and heavy – who first thought that iron, if there was
enough of it, could float on the sea? Beneath the thick
reflective paint, even the iron deck might have been made
out of coarse bolted sheets of thick iron, like girders. For
the first time the people around her were not travellers,
mostly. There was a group of four retired Swedes, fool-
ishly moustached, dressed in the dark, with florid
Hawaiian shirts topping swimming shorts in red and neon
lime, neat as schoolgirls in their terrible white socks saving
their white feet from spoiling. She stared at them. It was
the knots and bursts of the varicose veins, their legs like
Stilton, which drew her, but for the sake of her London
suit, they stared at her too and talked in the childish
yodels into which anything, she supposed, must be
crammed in Sweden. They were there but that was not
everybody. Now at the end of the hot day, builders
working on one island were travelling back to another,
where they lived and slept and brought up their children.
They were in shorts and boots, their skin absorbing and
reflecting the light of the sea like a fantasy handbag in a
window. Their thick ordinary boots and talking hands
were encrusted with dry cement like the creamy yellow
surface of fudge. She looked at them – how good it was
to feel lust again! – and all but the youngest, a glossy
handsome boy with the flecks and careless streaks of
white paint in his dense black hair, looked back with frank
curious pleasure. The youngest fixed his gaze on the deck,
and much as his friends nudged him and gurglingly incited
him, he would not look up at her. She had quite forgotten,
all day, what she looked like, her privilege, and had seen

no mirrors. *I could take a lover now*, she thought in a terrible, terrible way, knowing that she would not.

But then it seemed that this was it, the end of the line, as far as you could go, and as the boat twisted and curled in towards a long stone jetty, twenty or thirty people standing there expectantly, she looked at the place where she had come to. A line of houses, white and blue, scattered with bushy red bursts of flowers, piled up randomly in cubes like a child's abandoned game with building blocks, and across the harbour front, behind the blue-and-white fishing boats came a woman, all in black, riding a grey old donkey without any sense that here she was being a postcard, doing everything she could to show Janet what exactly it had been that the banality of her dreams had stretched towards. This was the end of the line. The boat idled across the clear blue water of the harbour into rest. This was the place from where Janet could go round the world. And then –

John's Dream

Sometimes, it doesn't matter if all you see is the white sail of a yacht with a red flag on its mast, scattering the floating ducks as it sails into the blue water of a summer harbour.

A House by the Sea

And then –

The boats came in, once or twice a day. The little harbour was all there was on the island, apart from the occasional house in its own land, further down the coast. They had been built to let to tourists, but few tourists came here – almost none for more than a few days. The houses ultimately tended to be colonised by the parents and children and cousins of the builders, who, in brief periods of speculative affluence, had put them up. The island was famous only for one thing: an immense cave at the southern tip. In it, a bishop had once celebrated a Mass. Thousands of credulous people from all over the archipelago had come. (It had been centuries ago.) The occasion had been splendid, candles dripping over the stalactites and stalagmites, a brocaded choir singing to the eerie echoes like supplicating owls. The bishop-prince had left his palace, far away, and come to this desolate place, these deformed works of the earth. It was Christmas, 1665. There was some thought that with the coming of the Year of the Beast, 1666, there might be no further opportunities to beg for divine mercy, so he came – why? – here.

The island watched the princes and holy men and pilgrims sail away into the same blue which Janet arrived from; they watched them as if they were carrying all that gratitude and guilt away with them. Then they went back to their steady occupation. They lived on whatever happened to come up in the nets, however odd-looking; they mended boats and net; they held water as a precious thing; they soon forgot about the Year of the Beast, which came and went without anything more apocalyptic than an outbreak of the blackleg among the island's goats, and that, the goats were prone to anyway. The church had its uses, of course. It christened and married and buried the islanders, and since it was the largest and most conspicuous building about the harbour, the islanders had taken to using it as a signal to the ferryman across the strait on Paros; they opened the door wide if they needed to summon him.

Such visits across the strait were not that common, limited to visiting cousins, selling or buying livestock, or to woo a wife. (The island's cheese was good, and had the incidental property of inclining wives who ate it extensively to give birth to boys; a blessing, but resulting in a superfluity of men, who had mostly to go to Paros to marry.) What happened elsewhere during that dread year, they never quite knew, but the world went on as before; nor did they ever know what the feelings of the bishop-prince had been when the year had passed, and he seemed to have undertaken the arduous voyage to the remotest desert for no purpose whatever, except to bring back an infestation of fleas which could not be got out of the palace linen. Perhaps he told himself that he had averted the catastrophe; but no one could find that entirely convincing.

What had seemed in 1665 a bare and repulsive desert had, thanks to drastic changes in aesthetic taste, come to look like an idyllic and even beautiful place by the time Janet arrived there. It was no more than five miles long, and at its widest about two miles, rising to one peak, about five hundred feet high, and a lower one just next to it, like an echo or a wave in the sea. Oddly, no one had ever climbed the higher of these two miniature mountains to the peak, not even goatherds, until 1923, although it presented no particular challenge; it was simply that no one had ever seen the point of doing so, and even the first person – an intrepid German traveller – who had made the ascent one spring morning never had any idea that he was walking where no one else had ever walked. But Greece was full of unconquered mountains of this sort and perhaps still is. The island was the smallest of three in a line stretching from west to east, the lowest peak of an underwater range, and the least important in every respect; it was dotted with creamily sandy beaches, sliding very slowly into the sea – something which no one ever thought of as adding to the island's merits until 1970 at least. It was largely bare of vegetation of any sort, and even olive trees struggled here. In later years, entrepreneurs persuaded palm trees to grow behind the beaches, but they had an embarrassed and alien air, like trees on holiday. Unlike the neighbouring and more fecund islands, here the bougainvillea grew only with encouragement, and the most obvious plantlife, apart from the low and desperately clinging heather and sage on the hills, were the searing colours in the villa gardens, gardens as bright and raucous as a Torquay landlady's. There was some fresh water; there were some goats; the resources were narrow.

The one town, a tiny one, was built about the shallow harbour. It was not disturbed by much traffic. There were two tavernas by the quayside, amicably next to each other and sharing customers easily. They lent supplies and even – if one was busier than the other for some reason – kitchen staff. They were much the same in what they served; one preferred to chop the onion in the *horiatike* more finely, and might have had slightly higher pretensions, but in the main the food which was put on the blue tablecloths was the same as that put on the red tablecloths. There was the blue-domed church with the conspicuous door, no longer used to signal to the ferry, which came on time twice a day, which was whitewashed like everything else. There were two hotels, both on the seafront, not much patronised even later in the season.

From time to time a party of Swedes arrived. It was always Swedes, Janet came to notice; they never stayed for more than three nights. She puzzled over the appeal of this island in particular to the Swedish nation, and exclusively, it seemed, to them. The mystery was solved when she fell into conversation with one of them, and in the course of hearing his life story, discovered that ten or more years ago this island had been picked on by a travel programme on Swedish television and recommended as an entirely undiscovered gem. That struck Janet as extremely funny;

to recommend an island for that reason in that way was obviously an absolutely reliable method of destroying the virtues you were praising it for, and in about two months, the island was no longer undiscovered in any way. The tide of Swedes, apparently, was only now subsiding. After a few weeks, she asked Marina about it.

'It was *ghorrible*,' Marina said, shuddering. 'Still they come and they get off the ferry boat and po-po-po they are disappointed. But now they not so many, nobody comes to this place, very sad, and beautiful, more beautiful than Paris –'

'Than Paros?' Janet said. They were sitting in the back garden, drinking tea underneath an oleander tree. Marina said she liked it, but she wouldn't follow Janet and pour milk into it.

'No, no, no, more beautiful than Paris, you know, in France? But they don't come, not like ten years ago, you know it was on the Swedish television and then I don't see the Swedish television but it showed it here, how life is, you know, as beautiful, and then they all come so that there are not even beds for them and they sleep on, you know, the beach. *Ghorrible*.'

Marina shuddered again. Perhaps it was at the lack of Swedes now, which was sad, or at the abundance of them before, which had been horrible. Janet looked around, comparing her little garden to Paris; it was an odd comparison, but Marina was probably right, this was more beautiful.

Janet had stayed only two nights in one of the hotels before seeing that it wouldn't do. It was the chambermaid, the niece of the owner, with a moustache at eighteen, that persuaded her. The girl was going to university in Salonika, and working for her uncle over the summer, a man she found slightly unreasonable. (She had plenty of time to sit down and talk to Janet.) Not that there was anything wrong with the girl, but even when Janet had unpacked her bags, the room was still swept clean and made orderly each morning. No detritus from the day before remained when she got back from the beach; she could not think that for a time this room was hers.

The island, however, felt right to her, immediately right. She walked around the headland outside the town after breakfast, her still pale legs shining in the vivid light like the bellies of fish. When she came to the first beach, curving away in a slow arc about a shallow bay, neat as geometry, she took off her shoes and walked through the water's edge, the sea like gin in a blue bottle, lapping at her feet companionably. With her discarded sandals peeping out of her bag like puppies, she went along two long public beaches before wading over rocks. There began a series of tiny sandy coves, none much bigger than a sofa, and, invisible even to anyone walking through the heather behind, she unfurled herself, stripped and emptied herself into the day.

It was early in the season, and she had been the only guest in the hotel – almost the only guest on the island, the only stranger – but the heat had arrived early. In a month or two the place would be busier, but it was hard to see how it could ever be a great deal busier, and for the moment she felt like a child bridesmaid who has sneaked early into a wedding breakfast and, unobserved, taken a bite from the immaculate cake.

On the third day, she met Marina. It was good timing on Marina's part, she felt afterwards, since it was the day when her skin had reached a pitch of complaint against the sun, and was as pink and fragile as the bougainvillea petals; when your body and your hotel setting are both somehow at odds with you, whatever *you* may constitute, it is a difficult day. A day or two afterwards, her skin would be smooth and brown; her room would be her own; but the day she met Marina everything seemed a little hopeless. It was in one of the two tavernas, the one with red tablecloths. Marina was sitting with one of what turned out to be innumerable cousins and uncles, and talking in her Morse-code briskness on a single note. Janet couldn't understand, but with her eyes lowered, she absorbed the insistent note of complaint in Marina's paragraphs. The uncle or cousin was concentrating on his plate, and occasionally muttering something downtrodden, three or four syllables. The querulous noise of Marina's voice, she heard it but in a foreign language; conversations had a knack of forming one strand of the sounds of the world, like the chatter of birds. She did not really listen.

'I was wondering to myself,' Marina was suddenly saying, leaning across the gap between their tables confidentially, 'why you are here on your own, and maybe you are waiting for your husband or your boyfriend maybe to join you in a day or two.'

Janet explained, politely, trying not to be stand-offish, saying that she was on her own but only that. She had not yet got to the point where she would set out the failure of her marriage for strangers in restaurants. Food came and went, and Marina continued asking questions, leaning across the table at more and more acute an angle. The uncle or cousin she was supposedly dining with sat stonily smoking one cigarette after another; some obscure etiquette of the place forbade him to go on eating while Marina was ignoring him in this way, and from time to time he threw a blaming look downwards at his half-full plate. 'Yes, I see, I know,' Marina said, and in half an hour Janet had got to the point where she had become the sort of person who sets out the failure of her marriage for strangers in restaurants. She felt that she never knew so much about anyone as Marina now knew about her. But by the end of the evening, the uncle or cousin had ambled off into the night like a weary transplanted bear, Marina had migrated to Janet's table, and Janet had a little house she was renting rather than a room in a hotel; was listening, too, to the first of many stories about Marina's life and her family, what had happened, what was happening, what might happen, as well as things which had never happened but which Marina clearly wished to have been real, and wished to be believed.

She liked Marina's stories, told as they were in the raucous garden. There was something about the landscape which called up stories, she saw that, and after a few days on the beach she found herself listening to her own stories, telling them deliberately in her own head. It was the land-scape. Beach, sea, sky; three unequal and horizontal stripes, just that, and more like the diagram of a landscape than a landscape itself. Both space and time were empty; the world reduced to three stripes, the passage of time to a single long hot stupid day. You filled them with yourself; perhaps spoiling the island, as Mary had predicted you would, but painting the day with silent stories.

She had not thought of Gareth for years. The job had been her fourth since leaving school, and a good one. It had more to it than where she had come from, a financial services firm in Slough, and at first she found it daunting and demanding. In Slough, she had known the full range of her tasks from the first day, both contractually defined – the controlling of the petty cash, the minuting of minor discussions – and more informal – fending off the attentions of the boy with the post, dismissing his increasingly lascivious reminiscences of his week in Ibiza. This one was less defined, her tasks requiring a knack of improvisation, as she was asked to do whatever needed to be done. But she told herself that a job worth doing would naturally seem like that at first. Even the journey to work seemed inspiring for a few weeks; living in London, her journey to Slough had been a lonely journey against the vast stream, but now, each morning and evening, she was swept along on the tide of important humanity.

Janet had worked there for two weeks when she started to notice Gareth. He had, as it were, shyly stepped forward from the indeterminate mass of suited men she'd been introduced to and promptly forgotten. He was not in her immediate milieu, and there was no particular reason why he should be wandering over and sitting on her desk from time to time, to ask how she was getting on; there were several men who were to call on her services, but he was not one of them. All the same, he did come over, and three times ask her the same question, how she was getting on, and then, self-consciously and with agonising restraint, permit himself one direct question designed to map out her life for him before murmuring 'Onwards and upwards' and backing away, his eyes fixed on hers, like a courtier leaving a monarch. She understood it perfectly, and thought, as ever, that it would have been easier if Gareth had quite simply marshalled all his questions into one urgent interrogation, and she had given him five minutes of her time. 'Where do you live? Where do you come from? Do you have a boyfriend? Would you like me to be your boyfriend?' That would have been it; it would not have taken even five minutes. Instead, over the course of weeks, and a double handful of engineered encounters, he would move from a general observation about the volume of work at the moment, a lordly and yet pitiable piece of advice about life in the bank or even about the attractions and interests of living in London, though she'd lived here all her life, to a tentatively phrased observation about what her life might be like, offered for her to agree with or correct. 'I suppose you're still living with your parents?' he would say, and on learning that this was not so, would wander off for, no doubt, days of pained speculation before he felt he could return to wonder out loud whether she preferred living with flatmates, and then a difficult weekend for Gareth before he could establish whether the flat she lived alone in contained a bathroom cabinet with a boyfriend's shaving foam and toothbrush or whether – as he finally put it – she ever went into the West End for a drink.

She formatted her document, blocked and saved it for transmission, but she had long ago decided she would take pity on him. She suggested Friday night. An hour or two later, she had a note from him, on paper, saying no more than what they had agreed; a habit, she supposed. She examined the note. The hand was round, crabbed and unformed, unused to writing, but at the foot Gareth, instead of signing it, had written his three initials with dash and elaboration and underlined them. The handwriting was that of a child, and so was the signature; a child working out what he is going to become. She felt she knew him now.

She was probably right, and over the next three years her sense of him became more elaborate but unchanged. That Friday, he told her how much he earned, he told her the plot of the last film he had seen, he told her about every girlfriend he had ever had and what had been wrong with each of them, he told her about his school results, and at the end, having drunk too much, he set out the conditions under which Britain should enter the European Monetary Union. She nodded; she realised that it would be a good long time before this man discovered anything at all about her. But she went to bed with him anyway. Gareth's clothes, too: they were lamentable. He bought his shirts in airports, his socks at train stations, his unfitting suits from a posh catalogue, never looking or planning; he wore the same pair of shoes every day until someone made a crack about them, and then he threw them away and bought a new pair. His wardrobe was a wilderness of whim and despair; his socks, his pants, his ties formed a terrible anthology of bad jokes; his cufflinks were unforgivable. And that was for the week; Janet almost wept with pity when, that first morning, she sat in bed and looked at what he was seriously proposing to wear, that Saturday.

But still: three years. She sat on the empty island, and in those empty days she told herself the story. There seemed to be something in it for her. For those three years she was not asked to examine the basis of this. To the outside world, it was the most ordinary story. It was an exchange of money for beauty, and no one questioned this, even though the terms of the exchange were not universally apparent, some people calling Gareth lucky, some Janet (her mother, in her Battersea sitting room, looking resolutely at the wall and congratulating her: yes, she was sure Janet had by luck got more than she deserved). Janet was grateful for the ease with which everyone accepted this story, even though it was untrue. The alternative was the real story: and that she did not know.

Nobody knows what the real story of a relationship is: that was what Janet thought. Nobody ever knew what bound two people together, when it might be the look in her eyes when he shut the bedroom door, or the touch of her hand on his stomach. But they knew: surely they would know. And Janet did not know. She could identify the moment that somehow was at the root of her need of Gareth, or her acceptance of him, but she could not understand why that moment should so cement things. It was a bedroom moment; it was the look in his eyes when she turned from unhooking her bra, unhitched her knickers with her two thumbs, stopped talking about her day, and slid in a single movement on to the bed where always he lay waiting. That look in his eyes: it was so undignified, going beyond open gratitude and suggesting, of all things, mild fear. In his big eyes, there was the look of a dog anticipating a blow from his master; always there, at that moment before his incredulous hands began to wander speculatively towards her body, more like a fondler in a cinema than a husband.

That was at the root of it, and Janet wondered why her contempt for him was what it was all about. She needed someone, she always felt, for whom her contempt was complete, and an important part of it was a series of single facts about Gareth, each of which made her shiver with distaste; it was that his two front teeth did not quite meet, and the gap repulsed her inexplicably, whether she looked at him smiling or felt the absence with her tongue; it was that when he said, say, 'I put it on the table,' he pronounced the word 'put' as 'putt', a refinement or a modification unknown to any English dialect, something he apparently believed marked him out as distinguished, and which in her eyes indeed distinguished him, marked him out as repulsive. Could you be fundamentally repulsed by a man on the basis of a gap in the front teeth and a single mispronunciation? Could you stay with him for those reasons? Apparently so; but then she met John.

She started saying these things to Marina, after a week or two, but they clearly puzzled Marina, and she stopped. It seemed as odd to Marina as her confession that, from time to time, she had been phoning John, her husband,

and pretending to be travelling around the world, phoning him from steadily more distant places, when in reality she was still on this small island.

'Have you seen those girls from Japan?' Marina said one day.

'No, I don't think so,' Janet said. They were on the beach together; by now Marina had started coming down with her, not just waiting for her to come back and talk over lunch or dinner. It was an unusual thing for her to do, you could see that. There were no other Greek people on the beach. It wouldn't be their style. Marina had started putting on an old-fashioned swimsuit, black as a widow's veil with some sort of mock-modest skirting around the waist. Where she had got it from, and when it would have been used, it was difficult to tell; her stubby white legs started from it, ill-shaved and startled-looking in appearance.

'Two Japanese girls,' Marina said. 'They came three days ago, and they stay at the hotel; they come out with an umbrella over them and they walk along the harbour and then they go back.'

'They don't go to the beach?'

'No,' Marina said. 'I don't know why they come here. Japanese, they don't come here. The Swedish, yes, they come, but the Japanese, no. I think they are bored, but three days, they are still here.'

Janet got up, shook herself and went for a brief swim in the warm clean water. She held her head up like a seal. As she swam out, the light on the water spurted white and hard, blinding her; as she turned, just at the point where you could no longer touch the shallow decline of

the sand with your feet, Marina was there, a little discon-
solate figure in black, gazing out with her knees together.
Janet trod water out there, huffing and puffing, discreetly
weeing into the sea. Then she suddenly imagined a rare
Mediterranean shark, attracted by her salty odours,
coming to get her, and sprinted back towards the beach,
her Olympic arms arcing overhead.

'It's nice to swim,' Marina said.

'Go ahead,' Janet said.

'Oh, I swim later,' Marina said. She shook her head
and looked at Janet, almost angrily. 'No, why do I say
that? I don't swim later, I don't know how to swim.'

'Did you never learn?' Janet said.

'No, never,' Marina said. 'Strange, yes, that I live on
an island and I don't swim, but that is how it is.'

'Did you not want to learn?'

'Want, yes, but here, you don't swim, not in my family,
because one day you teach your daughter to swim and
the next day she is gone.'

'She's swum away,' Janet said.

'Yes, she swims away,' Marina said. 'And better that
she drown, you know?'

'But you couldn't swim very far,' Janet said. 'You could
only swim to Paros, even if you were good. And then
you'd only be in Paros in your swimsuit.'

'Yes, yes, but then, after that, what after that?'

'You might keep on swimming,' Janet said. 'I see that.'

'So I don't swim,' Marina said. 'But I want to tell you
that I swim, that later, maybe, I swim. That is stupid, I
know.'

Janet felt terribly tired, as if she had been the one strug-
gling through a foreign language, not Marina. Brushing
the sand off her legs, sticky with the sea, she remembered
how exhausting foreign languages were, even the sort of
foreign language you made up, talking nonsense to yourself at the end of the garden when you were six, calling
it French; as exhausting as emotion.

One day, a man approached her. She was sitting on the
side of the stone quay, her legs dangling over the sea child-
ishly; in the late-afternoon light, the tiny fish in the clean
blue harbour glimmered like the threads in shot silk. It
had been holding her attention for some minutes. She
looked up at the shadow.

'You don't want to go to the cave?' the man said, squat-
ting down beside her.

'Hello,' Janet said, happily.

'Marina, you know, my cousin, she says you don't go
to the cave, in two weeks, two weeks you are here, OK?'

'No, that's right,' Janet said. 'I know about it, though.
There's plenty of time.'

'I take you in my boat,' he said. 'I am Panos.'

'Hello, Panos,' Janet said. 'That's nice of you. Maybe
another day.'

'I don't charge you,' Panos said, prematurely affronted.

'That's OK,' Janet said. 'But maybe another day.'

'Very beautiful and interesting, the cave,' Panos said.
'And every day, you only want to go to the beach?'

Janet considered. A bright thought came to her.

'You know, Panos,' she said, 'I don't know that I want
to go to the cave today. But perhaps we can go out in

your boat anyway. Do you just want to take me out to
sea a little?'

'Out to sea?' Panos said. He was really not much more
than a boy; it might be a good idea to make sure Marina
really was his cousin.

'I just want to see the island,' Janet said.

Something dawned on Panos. 'OK, OK, I understand,
yes, good, good –' and he was off, quite cheerful. She didn't
understand, but, woozy from the sun, she raised herself
and followed him down to the quay. He was already
leaping into his boat, a little open vessel, hardly bigger than
a rowing boat with a tiny shed at the front, painted and
repainted in blue and white. Less securely, she stepped
across the little gap between the stone quay and the wooden
deck, and quickly sat down. The boy dashed to the back,
busy with luck, and started up the engine, uncoiled the
ropes, and with his brave face to the sun like a hero, steered
away from the island.

It was an impulse; she had no interest in caves, but
now she did want to see the island properly, now that
she knew it and it had lost the strangeness of her first
arrival. She could see now how small it was, so small
that it had a single shape like a long-spined dinosaur.
She knew the curves of it and its detailed life, but a
hundred yards out to sea, and it was strange again. The
boat swung to the right, towards her customary beach,
and chugged away into deeper waters. Janet kept her
eyes on the land, and in a moment or two the long curve
of the beach emerged from behind the headland. There
was nobody on it, just one figure; as they continued,

you could see that the figure walking up and down, back and forth, like a chained dog in the heat of the afternoon, was fully clothed. Janet felt a little flush of shame when she recognised the miserable pacing, and reproached herself for spying on Marina in this way. No one would walk like that if they thought anyone could be watching them.

The engine slowed, stopped. The boat settled into stillness, out there in the blue gulf.

'OK,' Panos said. Janet had almost forgotten he was there. 'You want maybe to sunbathe, swim, maybe?'

'I don't know,' Janet said. 'I hadn't thought about it.'

'Here, you know, very quiet, very private, no one looking at you,' the boy said. 'You like Greek boys?'

'I like everyone, if they're likeable,' Janet said. She saw it now.

'If they – yes?' Panos said. 'You want take off your clothes, very nice, swim with no clothes.'

'And you?' Janet said. 'Are you going to take off your clothes, too?'

Panos considered; the sense of a joke against his dignity was making itself clear. 'If you like,' he said, uncertainly.

'Go on then,' Janet said. 'You first.'

The boy reached for the button on the waistband of his shorts, all he was wearing, but his hand hovered indecisively, and finally replaced itself on the rudder.

'We can stay here, though,' Janet said. 'It's nice.'

Panos stood up quickly, grinned, and shucked off his shorts. Janet grinned back; he was a well-made boy. But she stayed where she was. Ridiculously, Panos dived off the boat backwards, sending it into a spasm of rocking, surfacing a showy distance away. He puffed like a spouting whale, his black hair shining.

'Nice,' he said. Then he was under again, diving, surfacing, all the juvenile tricks which English boys perform in swimming pools. Janet watched, amused and rather tempted. After all, why not? she thought. I could get out of my clothes, I could jump into the sea, I could have sex with a handsome and nice-mannered boy in the water, on the deck, and I could enjoy it. But behind the cavorting boy, all that time, there was the distant dark figure of Marina, pacing to left and right, her head lowered. She let him finish, get back into the boat, smile regretfully. They started back to the harbour.

'OK, I put back on my clothes,' Panos said, as they approached the quay, and wriggled into his shorts again. She let him put an end to the little adventure.

Marina was still on the beach. Under your bare feet, the tight sand, and the air fragrant with hot salt; Janet came up to her smiling, and without saying anything, they both sat down. Perhaps Marina had seen them, in the boat; seen them watching her, known that anyone now would understand what Marina went through, from the way she paced the beach. Janet said the first thing – any other thing – which came into her head. As if continuing the thought, she started to talk about her husband.

'Do you remember –' she began, but that was absurd; she started something else. 'You know, where we live in London, the house, it used to be a bed and – I mean, a sort of hotel, a long time ago, before we lived there. People still turn up asking for rooms sometimes. It makes you wonder, they've got such out-of-date information, it must be fifteen years since it stopped being a hotel. Someone turns up at least once a week and we have to tell them to go away.'

She saw, as if walking away from her across the surface of the sea, the graceful figure of her husband; his graceful walk, his grey suit, kindly walking as he accompanied these disappointed figures back to the front gate of their house, to point them on their way. It happened so often, she could see it without effort. He did it so kindly.

'You tell them to go away?' Marina said.

'Yes, of course,' Janet said. 'What else should we do?'

'You could take them in,' Marina said. 'They'd pay you, they'd be happy. Why do you turn them away?'

'Because we're not a hotel,' Janet said, puzzled.

'It could be good, good business,' Marina said. 'And you never think, take them in, take their money?'

'I couldn't afford the chocolate,' Janet said, but then she felt herself crying at what she had said. Why had she said that? Said it to Marina, who could not understand it; of course she could not, since it made no sense at all. It was what they said to each other. It was an ancient joke that was once funny, but for years now had been a token between John and her of their marriage. Whatever the first occasion of the remark, the moment when it had actually been funny, now and for many years it had been something one of them said to the other when the right situation or remark arose. It was just something they said to each other. They never said it in front of anyone else; it would have needed too much explanation, and neither of them could quite explain it, or remember the history of the remark. And by now, too, it was private. It was terrible to say it to Marina, a terrible betrayal, and pointless, since she would not understand or appreciate it. In Marina's puzzlement, Janet saw how grotesque it was to have abandoned her husband, and how bleak the future she seemed to have chosen. Marina had never had all that. Janet's marriage; a houseful of things which needed no explanation, a tone of voice, a movement of the head, a familiar phrase. She was here, abandoning all that, and if her life was to go on, sooner or later she would have to begin to accumulate all those things all over again with someone, perhaps, she had not yet met.

'John thinks I'm in Australia now,' Janet said.

'Your husband. It is so strange that you pretend like this,' Marina said. 'I don't understand.'

'I'm not in Australia, though,' Janet said. 'Obviously I'm not. I'd be upside down if I was in Australia.'

'I had an aunt,' Marina said, after a long sea-filled silence. 'She was like you, I think. She did not marry, she lived over there, on Paros. She comes here, when I am a little girl, every month, about that. And one day she comes and she tells us that she has met a man, a rich man from Germany, who loves her and who maybe will marry her. So we are all a little surprised, because my aunt, you know, not beautiful, not rich, not young. We don't say this but I think she understands this. So she comes again and she tells us more about the German man, how handsome and rich he is and how he loves her. But she sees that her brother, my father, you know, no one believes her. So the next time she brings letters which she says are from the man who will marry her. She shows us these letters, long, long letters, very sexy, you know, but it is sad, because they are written all in Greek and anybody, even me, and I was a little girl, they understand that she has written them herself because, you know, my aunt, she only speaks Greek. And we say nothing, but still she becomes cross and shouts that we do not believe her, that he is going to marry her, and even though no one says anything still she walks away and says she never comes back here.'

'That's a sad story,' Janet said. It was: it was a sad, sad story.

'Yes, but that is not the end, because I don't tell you what she wrote, my aunt, in these letters about herself. She reads these letters, and we listen, and in them there is love, OK, there is something about how she is the woman like no other woman, but she doesn't stop there. These letters she reads to us, she writes them herself, and they say too that she is old, she is ugly, she is not so clever, she has no money, she must be surprise, yes, that he wants to be married with her. She writes all that, about herself, and now I think why does she do that? She is writing love letters about herself, and she writes sometimes that she is a wonderful woman, but sometimes that she is old and ugly, and she comes and reads it all to us. I still ask myself why she does that. But I never see her again, my aunt.'

'Did she move away anyway?' Janet said. She under-

stood this story very well. She knew that Marina understood it now, too.

'No,' Marina said. She hugged herself, there in the heat
of the day. 'No, she is still living where she lived then,
but she doesn't see my family, none of them.'

'You could go and ask her,' Janet said. 'You could ask
her to explain.'

'You don't understand,' Marina said. 'You don't understand how Greece is.' And then, with a shudder and a low
pained yelp, in one of the many strange and undignified
ways in which people can start to cry, in one of the many
strange and inappropriate places where human beings can
grieve, she started helplessly to cry. She should not be
crying on a sunny day, on a beautiful empty beach, but
sometimes there is no time to organise a suitable setting
or the weather to match your falling tears. Janet waited
until the first gust of crying had subsided, and reached for
her bag. There was nothing helpful there but a bottle of
water, now warm as blood, but Marina took it and drank;
Janet took up her sweat-stiffened beach towel, the cartoon
image on it seeming cruel and ugly, and wiped Marina's
face gently. She made no resistance, the grains of sand in
the towel rasping her face. There was nothing else Janet
had to soothe the poor woman but a bottle of sun lotion,
and uselessly she anointed Marina's face with a few drops,
rubbing it in gently. It seemed the right thing to do.

'I am so stupid,' Marina said, after a long time. 'I don't
cry, never. People are bad to me and they hurt me and I
don't cry. People laugh at me and I don't cry. For years
and years I hurt and I don't cry. But when someone is

kind to me, like you are kind to me, then I cry. OK, please tell me why?'

'No,' Janet said. 'I don't understand that, either.'

Behind them, there was a sudden hiss; it was the stiff leaves of the palm trees, stirred by a breeze, but it had been still all day, and it made them turn. There was no one else on the beach; a solitary nudist at the far end had dressed, disappointed, and gone to find some lunch, or company. The sluggish little ferry from Paros was making its laborious crossing, and, coming to meet it, as if tied on the same piece of string, its identical twin crossing in the other direction. It was so short a strait, a journey of five minutes, and across the sea, from the steep hillside facing the little island, the faint tinny clank of bells, a herd of wandering goats calling to their sleeping goatherd. If you got into the sea, and swam, and swam, and swam, and never got tired, through day and night, from one sea to the next, from this blue sea to seas colder, greyer, deeper . . .

'You have a problem,' Marina said. 'Your husband thinks you are in Australia. So now you can't go any further. If you go any further, you start coming back towards him.'

'Yes,' Janet said. 'I suppose that's right.'

'So you pretend, now, you are staying in Australia when you talk to him?'

'No,' Janet said. 'I'm going to carry on going forward.'

'But you'll get back to him in the end if you go on forward.'

'Yes,' Janet said. 'Yes, I will.'

31

Afterwards, when I thought of Wasia's white rooms hung with photographs of me and my family, it seemed to me that there might be something here for me to deal with. In the weeks after the event, I searched out and found a good deal of admiring commentary in the newspapers about the exhibition. Wasia, it seemed, had portrayed a family with a dark secret with candour and surprising humour. Oh, and compassion: she had photographed us all with compassion. I thought of that, and then I thought of a wall of photographs of me at the Streatham nightclub, confused, sweating, dishevelled, trying to get the hang of grinning and not succeeding. Those photographs in particular were much admired in the press. Some critics said that I had been photographed in the same nightclub Franky went to on the night of her death. Which would be poignant. That poignant situation happens, too, if you believe what you read, to demonstrate the disillusioned but always human and sympathetic irony which characterises the remarkable and bold work of. But it also happens not to be true. I wonder who told them that it was.

Wasia, it was clear, made a great success with this exhibition. With our innocently lent faces. I never saw her again. Let me make that clearer. I never happened to see her again. I would not do her the compliment of evading her. I had stood in a crowded room, being recognised silently by strangers. 'Is that –?' one person after another would murmur in my hearing, and then, falling silent, inspect me like a monotype, held at arm's length. You don't want to see someone again, once they've done that to you. But as I left the gallery, I made a sincere wish for Wasia. I wished her exhibition a great success. As successful as it possibly could be. I did not want her to fail. If it failed, I would still not know how badly I could be hurt. Only a success could show me that.

It came true, my wish, and in Wasia's world she quickly achieved everything she could achieve. Her 'snapshots' were bought, every single one, by the same man, a Swiss collector, and had been bought before they were even placed on the wall of the gallery. My mother's face and my father's and my sister's in a wedding dress, and me and Mr Tredinnick and a sheet of howling newspaper, years old, elegantly framed, all of them in a Swiss chalet halfway up a mountain with the most expensive view in the world. I like to think of that. In reality, they are probably in a vault somewhere, awaiting a decisive upturn in the photography market. Anyone who had the time to pay attention to exhibitions of photography knew who she was. You, reader, may know who she is, if you are such a person. And with all that success, she had no power to hurt me. It was as if Wasia's curiosity in us was, in reality, desultory, and so was the curiosity of her photographs, of her publicity, of the stubby reach of her celebrity. I could no longer be hurt.

Here is a story; one garnered from a book I once indexed. It was the end of the day, and I suppose I stopped indexing and just read. I don't know why this story stayed with me. Once, long ago, a great prince of the Paris stock exchange, a Rothschild baron, was done a great favour by a young man of no fame or reputation, a junior broker – is that the word? – in his firm. The Rothschild wrote a note thanking him for this favour, and said casually in it that he would be happy to be of any service to him in his career. The young man, who had performed the favour in the hope of getting such a note, showed it to his wife, and to his wife's parents, who happened to be at his house for dinner. They all agreed that a Rothschild offering help like this might usefully be asked for some solid information, a tip in short, about promising shares in overlooked companies. The young man wrote a daring note to that effect, and sent it off rather nervously by messenger – actually, the young son of the concierge downstairs, who would subsequently boast of taking correspondence to Rothschilds later and steadily increase the size of the tip in the retelling. The Rothschilds were not dining out that season, having gone with the English court into deep mourning for the Duke of Clarence and Avondale, and in an hour the son of the concierge returned, flushed, with a reply. The young man opened it in front of his wife, her parents, the concierge's son and the concierge herself, who, clutching at ribbons, had been drawn upstairs. In his characteristic sloping hand, on vellum-thick, crackling paper with a border an inch wide, Rothschild had cordially written, '*Sir, I cannot do as you suggest, but perhaps I can be of more help to you. I shall walk with you across the floor of the Bourse on any date convenient to both of us. I remain, sir –*' but some of his last words ran into the inch of black border, and were lost to the young man and his audience.

The story goes that the Rothschild, still in deep mourning, did exactly as he suggested. The young man became very rich, in a very short space of time. That is the story.

And I tell this story because –

I tell this story because –

I tell this story because –

Listen. That was all I wanted at the end. I wanted to be guaranteed like this as the world looked at me. I wanted Janet to take my arm, and walk with me across the great trading floor of the City – no, the city. I wanted her even in pretence to walk through the city with me and talk as if in civility. For the men and women of the city to see this and see what manner of man I was. The shape of me, it was only to be painted with Janet's outpourings, her love for me. When she was not there I had no sense of what my own self might look like, where the boundaries of the self might actually lie. At the end of that hiccup-ping month, what I understood was that I had no notion of myself other than as the object of Janet's love. I put it harshly, and it may seem pathetic. But in the end, what are we, any of us, apart from the construct of other people's love? Don't the flattering panegyrics of a lover teach us what we might make of ourselves, to go on pleasing? What do we make of us, if there is no one to make anything of us, no one but someone we trust? The shape we have in the world is made visible only by the spume of love and regard playing over our indeterminate borders. Without that, we are nothing, shapeless, nothing; clay in the hands of people who hate and despise us. And this story haunted me.

The last days of my illusion ended with Wasia's exhibition. It had been a hot night. I hadn't slept well. I was still asleep when the doorbell rang, about nine o'clock. It was the postman. When I opened the door to him, me still in my pyjamas and sleepy, he was holding a large envelope. I took it upstairs, and while the kettle boiled for a cup of coffee, I phoned Mrs Grainger to say I would be a little late and then opened it. It contained an invitation, which was quite an unusual event. I don't think I had received an invitation since the one to my sister's wedding. The invitation was to an exhibition of photographs. I was puzzled for a moment, and then saw, at the bottom of the card, Wasia's name. I realised that it must be an exhibition of her photographs, incredible as it seemed for about ten seconds. The only other thing on the card, apart from the time and the place of the party, was my name, written in a superior, spiky, arty sort of hand which I suppose wasn't Wasia's. The name of the exhibition was *En Famille*.

I thought for a while about this. It seemed to me that I had reached the end of my relationship with Wasia, and she would probably now prefer me not to come to the party for her exhibition. I had so solidly concluded that I wanted my marriage back, I had hardly given Wasia and her showy departure any further thought. The party list, too, had certainly been drawn up before we had had our final argument. I remembered, however, that she had said in the past to me that I could be more supportive, and decided that it would be a good thing if I went. I could show her that I bore no ill will, that I was looking forward to my wife coming back, and that if she did, I hoped we could become friends again. As I made my cup of coffee, this seemed to me very much the best solution, and one which would make Wasia see that there was something, after all, to admire in me.

The day of Wasia's exhibition soon arrived. By then, I felt buoyed up rather than doubtful about what I started to think had been her change of heart about me. I didn't mind that I hadn't spoken to her. She would be pleased to see me, in any case, at her party. My life had gone up a gear, and though Wasia had for a moment fallen out with me, she had thought about it and changed her mind. The invitation was an apology in disguise.

As I began to prepare for Wasia's party, I looked out of the window. In front of the house, somebody was sitting on some kind of pile. It looked almost as if he was sitting on a rough boulder, but of course that could not be right. This was a street in Wandsworth, not the middle of a wild moor, where you might sit on a boulder and think. I dismissed it, and went to shower, shave and clean my teeth. From the wardrobe, I took out a white shirt, a pair of underpants, a pair of matching black socks, a suit and I dressed. Each was the last example in the wardrobe. I had no idea what I would do the day after. I brushed my hair, put on the shoes which I had effortfully shined the night before, and in the mirror I looked as I had always looked.

It took about half an hour. Outside, the figure was still there, and had not moved, or so it seemed. It was still facing away from the house with its chin resting on a fist, thinking deeply, or seeming to think deeply. I gave way to curiosity, and went outside. It was a beautiful day; not hot, but sunny and clear, cloudless and airy. The weather had been like that for weeks, but only now did I really feel the beauty of the London sky. But there was someone sitting outside my house.

I walked down the path, towards the figure. As I did so, the shape of the figure did not change, and it did not move. But all the same, what I was walking towards seemed to change with each step I took. It was a boy, that small figure, then, no, a pointy hunched black dwarf like a conifer, then it seemed to take on the potential of great glamour, facing away from me, perhaps a small beautiful woman in a coat too large for her. The path was flanked with white flowers, like votive candles; the glow dimmed the garden around them, like flames in a cathedral. At the end of it, the figure became more specific, and the beauty which turned away from me unaware of my approach more meaningful. With a series of surges, I realised that it must be Wasia, in an urban borrowed anorak; no, must be Susie, the girl who had come once into my garden with a message in a bottle and never returned, Susie in a brother's duffel coat; no, not her either, as I opened the garden gate which always creaked, which I never oiled because in my world garden gates should creak and announce the happy visitor and the happy departure from home into the street, into the world. It was my wife in a sable coat, sitting on her pile of luggage, come back to me.

But it was not. At the creak of the gate, the figure turned its head. I did not know the person. The face was old and sexless in the way women grow when they have no home. It was wrinkled and dark brown, as if oiled with furniture polish, filthy and bronzed with the sun in the streets. The look in her eyes was one of fear for a second, before even the thin rationality of fear was replaced by a mad sort of hatred. It was aimed at me, but I wondered what the world had done to her. I was standing there; she was looking at me with black-lashed intimacy. I had to say something.

'Can I help you?' I said.

'No, you can't,' she said. Her voice seemed like a shriek; it was, in reality, a forced whisper, her vocal cords shot to pieces. She broke out into a dirty smirk, very pleased with what she had said. For one delirious moment – I had by now drunk my daily bottle of champagne – it crossed my mind that this crone could be Hope after a particularly heavy night. She folded her arms, planted her feet on the pavement. She had no intention of moving from here.

'I just wondered why you were sitting outside my house,' I said. After all, though this was clearly not the case here, people did turn up having mistaken us for a bed and breakfast. I might have been trying to be helpful.

But it did not sound helpful to her. She broke into a shrieking yell at this. 'You don't own the street,' she said, shrill, broken and angry. 'You don't own London. You might think you do. But you don't own the whole world. I'll sit where I like. You don't own the world —'

It is hard to describe what happened then. All I can say is that I realised something very powerful, and it was like an opaque window shattering, silently, in my head. I found I was walking away, very fast, the harangue following me as I went. It was a gleeful noise, that shriek, as if she had happened on a truth and was insisting on it exuberantly for as long as I was in earshot. I walked away from my house, leaving the front door and the garden gate wide open. I was not upset or alarmed. That is the indescribable thing. I felt that I had been shown something, and at that exact moment, I needed to go very quickly to a place where my insight, or hers, could be tested against the evidence. The evidence was people. The street I lived in was empty of people, just at that moment. The streets beyond that would provide the evidence, and beyond those, Wasia's party. What I realised was simply this: the world did not belong to me. I belonged to the world.

I walked past Mr Patel's shop, and on, past the Ethiopian church, and on. By now I was walking along busy, tunnelling roads, but there were few people about. The people that were there were alone in their cars. That was no good to me. I needed a crowd. In London you can find a crowd somewhere, any time of the day, any hour of the week, if you want or need one. There is always a crowd, somewhere in London, and though people complain about this and say you cannot escape from crowds, that day the idea of a crowd seemed ecstatic with promise to me. I had to go in search of one. I found mine on Putney High Street. I paused at the top of the hill, by the train station, just where the flower stall is, and looked down the full length of the street towards the brave glittering river. There were people there, in their hundreds, too many to count, too many to know. But I looked at them and I saw I was right. Every one of those people had a mother. Even the old ones, walking sadly alone or in pairs, in fear or tolerance, they too had had mothers. They had all been born, too: that boy standing there, feeding small change placidly into the orange ticket machine outside, his joints loose as if they had not quite melded yet, his rounded shoulders and hunched head getting slowly used to his new spurt of height. He had a mother. The woman in a pink suit and dyed hair, bold and orange in the bright sun, tapping impatiently with her wallet in the queue behind him. The fat businessman with the sad face of an overfed Labrador dreamily surveying the windows of a stationer's, looking at pink unnecessary pencil sharpeners made floral and painted with puppies so that twelve-year-old girls would love them; look at him, look at him, the trousers and the jacket he wore from different suits, making it plain that he dressed alone and could not look at his own sad appearance in the mirror. But he had a mother. He had been born and held in his mother's arms and had cried at the new air.

Of course, I had always known this. Everyone knows it. It would have been mad and ridiculous to have gone up to one of those strangers in the bus queue and told them that I had just realised that everyone in the world had a mother. But it had been an explanation until now, not something I overpoweringly felt. It was the difference between listening to a teacher explaining, say, the exports of a country, and remembering the smell and sound and rhythm of that experienced land. What washed over me in a wave was the understanding, not just the acceptance, that everyone I could see had their own lives, that they had been born, grown older, learnt skills and acquired knowledge, that their hearts had leapt and been bruised, and that they had led lives which were entirely different from each other. If each life was only precious and distinctive to the bearer of it, that afternoon all of them seemed precious to me, and I seemed to see the long rich paths which had led those five people, say, waiting for the bus in boredom, impatience or reflection to exactly this ordinary moment, and the rich paths which lay in front of them. I felt that with a gulp, as if I had been shown the full depthless infinity of the summer sky.

I crossed the road, unsteadily, almost drunk, and stood where the man in the unmatching blue suit had stood, in front of the stationer's. He had gone now, though I hadn't seen in which direction. I stood there as if I could absorb and understand at least one of these lives whose energy I could feel buzzing and humming about me in great golden choruses. But I could not feel it. I loved that: that their lives were closed to me; what they saw and felt. It could be understood but not shared. I looked at a window full of pink, gold, silver, purple letters, paper butterflies, bright cardboard birds dancing with bright cardboard fish, of pencil-end rubbers in the shape of toucans, pencil sharpeners like pineapples, blazing tinsel garlands, party poppers, plastic rainbows, sticky-back menageries, moons, suns, stars, dancing and shining behind the shining glass, and I felt I had understood something which did not need to be shared. One day soon, my wife and I, we were going to be dining together by candlelight, under a sky of rainbows and stars, and in front of us, there was a great pile of lobsters, artichokes, pineapples, everything.

In this state I took a taxi to the private view. It took some time, and the fare was such as to make me wonder whether, what with all the champagne and cigarettes I had been getting through, there was anything much left of my small savings. I got out and paid the driver. I stood outside the gallery and let the taxi drive away behind me. In the dark street, the huge blank gallery window was brightly lit, and filled with people. There was no one there I could recognise. Wasia, I knew, must be there somewhere. From outside, you could hear that the noise was deafeningly loud in there. I went towards the door, my invitation in my hand. In there was my act of reconciliation and forgiveness, waiting to be easy for me. In there, somewhere, was Wasia, penitent, grateful, ready to play a part of cosy kindness in my future which she held out to me on behalf of another, like a sparkling glass bowl. As the door was opened in front of me, it occurred to me for the first time that I had no idea, really, what Wasia's photographs were like.

Pink Suit One

It must have been about – well, roughly speaking – I guess around eight years, seven months and three days ago. Roughly around that.

'Why don't you try it on?' I said.

'It is beautiful,' she said. We were in a miraculous clothes shop; one of those mausoleums of silent expenditure lifted bodily from a golden Paris street – stock, staff, air and all – and placed down in Bond Street. It was not somewhere I had ever been, nor the sort of place Janet often went. We were making an effort not to speak in whispers.

'Why not?' I said.

'I couldn't possibly afford it,' she said. 'I don't need even to look at the price.'

'There's nothing to stop people trying clothes on,' I said.

'And, after all, I am going to buy something,' she said. 'I'm going to buy the belt.'

It was a week after her birthday. I had met her from work, and we had walked all the way down Fleet Street, away from the City, westwards. We had walked in the same direction as the rest of the crowds, mostly, but at some kind of different pace, and the dark busy floods of London swept by us like a river. It was a dry, weary day, the end of a London summer which had overstayed its welcome; we had had no holiday that year, like the year before, and that afternoon, we were tired of the summer, tired of the long demanding day, disenchanted.

Janet had a hundred pounds in her pocket, or the idea of a hundred pounds. It was her birthday present from her mother, who never troubled to think of anything Janet might like, but had always given her a sum of money, slowly increasing from a twenty-pound note for Janet's tenth birthday, up to a hundred pounds for the last five years. She never asked afterwards what Janet had done with it: if she had been interested, she would have chosen a gift herself. But Janet always tried to spend the money on something, a present which a different mother might have chosen.

She had seen a belt in a magazine, a simple thing, but in the photograph dense, heavy and punctuating; it bore, discreetly, the symbol of a great shop, but was a beautiful belt, a beautiful swathe of leather. The magazine indicated it cost a hundred pounds, a lot for a belt, but Janet had a hundred pounds; and to mark this purchase, I agreed to come and meet her from work, and help her buy it.

She had the belt in her hand. It was a lovely belt, she had been clever to identify its quality from a magazine photograph. The shop assistant hovered by us: a French girl, her surfaces powdery and glistening, her hair a lacquered helmet, she was, despite all effort, much less beautiful than Janet, I noted with pleasure, and could not rival the exquisite touch of disorder which the long hot day had brought to Janet's beauty.

The belt might have been enough, but we stood, now, in front of a suit. It was pink; the colour, even on a hanger two feet away, brought a kind of warmth into Janet's face. It was Janet's suit. Anyone could see that.

'You should try it on,' I said.

'I'll only regret it,' Janet said. But the shop assistant had come forward and, with a swift, approving survey of Janet's figure, picked out the right size, and held it temptingly. Janet gave way, and followed the girl to the changing rooms.

'Does she wear pink often, your wife?' the shop assistant asked me, having left Janet.

I looked at her, surprised; this was before we were married, and it seemed odd to refer to Janet as my wife so confidently. 'No,' I said, not correcting her. 'Not often.'

'She should,' the girl said. 'She looks beautiful in it. Look –'

She was right, I found; Janet, standing at the far end of the shop, shoeless, in her perfect suit; she was beautiful in anything or in nothing, but this stretch of cloth, cut and sewed and shaped, paid so apt a compliment to that beauty, no one else could deserve it.

'You look –' I said.

'I know,' Janet said. 'I've got to take it off. If I keep it on one minute more, I'll have to buy it, and I can't.'

'You've got to have it,' I said. 'I'll buy it for you.'

'You can't afford it,' she said. 'Don't even think about it. I've seen the price.'

'I mean it,' I said. 'You have to have it.'

'When would I wear it?' she said. 'I'd never dare to wear it.'

'You only need to wear it once,' I said.

'What do you mean?' she said.

'You only need to get married in it,' I said.

'Be serious,' Janet said.

'I mean it,' I said. 'Shall we get married?'

'Yes,' Janet said. 'Yes, I don't see why not.'

'Just that?' I said.

'Yes,' she said. 'I don't see why not.'

There seemed nothing more to say. Janet went back into the changing room to take the marvellous suit off. Not that there was anything more to say. But even though I knew she would, and I knew perfectly well that I wanted to marry her, there was no real inevitability in my feelings, which bounded up in me like a Roman candle. Our lives would not change with marriage; we would live in the same house, we would sleep in the same bed, we would talk about the same things, we would continue with the same occupations as before; not much would alter at all. But it didn't mean nothing. I could feel what it meant. And I wasn't alone, it seemed, because as she came back out, she was grinning absurdly, her dark head turned away from me to keep her response to herself, just for the moment.

And then I bought the suit.

'You shouldn't have,' she said later. 'I'd marry you in anything.'

'I know that,' I said.

'You've got to let me buy you a suit, too, then,' she said.

'Well, all right,' I said. 'It won't be so much fun.'

'We can choose it together, can't we?'

'There's no choosing to do,' I said. 'All you need to do is phone up Mr Bradman in Hackney and tell him that I want a new suit. He's got my measurements and everything. Tell him it should be the same cloth as the last winter suit, same specifications, everything.'

Janet looked at me, half amused. We were in bed, though it was only seven o'clock in the evening; we had gone to bed as soon as we were home.

'It won't be that expensive,' I said, misunderstanding her expression.

'Come on, I can't start saying it's too expensive,' Janet said. 'You're sure that's what you want? You don't want a suit from somewhere flash?'

'No, just that,' I said seriously. 'He's really good, Mr Bradman.'

'You make me laugh,' she said.

So that was how it happened, five weeks after the day we bought the pink suit, and the shop assistant thought that Janet couldn't be anyone else but my wife. We went to a registry office and got married. It was a rainy day, and my wife lit up the room. One witness was a friend of Janet's from work, and the other was my sister Sarah. She came, and saw me married, and kept her promise not to tell anyone else about it, not even my parents, and she cried happily all the way through the short event, and afterwards in the pub. That was our wedding, and it was the only wedding I ever wanted. But at the end of our marriage, all the same, Janet left the clothes she had been married in hanging in the wardrobe, and set off without me, to travel round the world.

33

The next day I got what I wanted. It came to me in the garden. In the course of the previous month, I had hardly been into the garden at all: the last time, pretty well, had been the day Janet had left me. Since then, the weather had been the same, day after day; a policy of blue skies and comfortable heat; no rain had fallen. But even though the garden had been neglected, it looked now, if anything, even glossier and more healthy. Clambering over adjacent growths, bursting so vividly into flower, it was as if it was doing it in front of your eyes, the plants and the life of the garden seemed to have some unknown resources of their own, when all the time you thought they were depending on you. Even the lawn, though no velvet-striped marvel, was thick and green. I sat in the garden, just as I had, and enjoyed it; the several humiliations of the last few days had sobered me, and, slightly painfully, I looked properly at the garden. In front of it was Susie, the girl who was there at the beginning.

'You've changed,' she said.

'You haven't,' I said. '!'

'So it didn't work, then, the champagne,' she said. 'Did you keep it up?'

'Oh yes,' I said. 'I kept it up.'

I reached for a cigarette, but somehow my hand closed the packet instead of opening it.

'I didn't know you smoked,' she said. 'Did you try anything else?'

'My wife didn't come back, either,' I said.

'I can see that,' she said. 'I'm wagging it off work again today. Shall we tidy up the house together, you and me?'

'Don't talk to me as if I'm an invalid,' I said.

'Actually, I got the sack,' she said. 'I don't care, though. I'm still getting fed by my mum, and it's not like I go anywhere.'

'Was it all the skiving?' I said.

'Are you just going to sit there?' she said. 'Or are we going to tidy the house?'

It took five hours. We picked up everything that was on the floors, and put them in the cupboards where they belonged. We put the dirty clothes which were scattered about, not just on the bedroom floor but in odder places in the house, like the first-floor landing, in the laundry basket or in the washing machine, three entire loads washed and hung out to dry. We washed up every plate and glass and cup and pan which I had, because every one was dirty. We washed the floors and we vacuumed the carpets. We put all the rubbish into one set of bags, and forty empty bottles of champagne into another set of bags, and put them aside to be taken away.

Susie talked, all those five hours, telling me a long

marvellous story: it was the story of her family. It was a story of great-grandparents who had fled from distant countries with nothing but a clock and a diamond; of distant cousins perishing heartbreakingly in the snow. It was a story of modest fortunes made and lost, of spinsters whose savings were depleted by handsome cruel English rogues, of uncles who lived unmentionably happy lives with gentlemen in London suburbs, of an aunt who was discovered on a city break to Paris in the 1960s and was next seen modelling for Courrèges, of uncles who were nearly murdered by the Krays, of cousins who went to university at thirteen and by eighteen had retreated to an ashram for decades to come, of failed quail-farming, long-lost millionaire relations, of prodigies and the human visions and a treasured family emerald which turned out to be made of paste. I was enchanted. It was the best story I ever heard, that story of Susie's family. It was too good to try to recount. You had to be there. And at the end of it, the house was looking like the beautiful gift it had always been. We took the last of the rubbish bags out, and Susie looked at me and wrinkled her face.

'Better be off,' she said.

'I don't know – ! – what to say,' I said.

'Don't say anything, then,' she said. 'I didn't mean to go on like that.'

'Oh, you,' I said.

'You've still got the hiccups, though,' she said. 'There must be something we can do for that. Bye, then.'

She went, and I went back inside, and shut the door. She didn't seem to have said goodbye, not properly. I thought she must be coming back with the cure, whatever it might be. The house looked wonderful. Its surfaces shone now like Mrs Grainger's. I sat in a chair and took pleasure in it, just as I had taken pleasure in the garden.

So it was that when the doorbell went, I thought it must be Susie. But it was Janet.

'Hello,' I said.

'Hello,' she said. Her three suitcases were by her, just as they ought to be. She pulled a funny face, protruding her upper lip, not quite sure what I was going to say and making herself look vulnerable, just in case.

'I'm glad you're back,' I said.

'Yes,' she said. 'Listen, I've got to tell you all about it, because in the end, when you leave what you've got, it's only then that you see what you've got, it's only then that you see what you're on the point of losing by doing what I did, so, I have to tell you, I may not look it, but this is a really hard and difficult thing for me to be doing now, just standing here and trying to explain, with my suitcases not even unpacked or knowing if you're going to let me unpack them even –'

I stepped forward and I kissed her.

The kiss went on. We went on kissing even through the hiccups. Not even the kissing could cure them. Not even the hiccups could stop us kissing. But in the end we separated, and found that in the course of our kiss I had walked backwards into the house, like a tango dancer being expertly led. One of us had shut the door as we went, feeding on each other's faces, finding out what the shape of our mouths were by pressing them up against me. But in the end you separate, and look at each other, shiningly. The shine of her regard, however, had a forensic aspect to it.

'!' I said. '! ! !'

'It's been going on all this time?' she said.

'Since you went away,' I said.

'Poor baby,' she said. 'I know how to get rid of it.'

'I've tried everything,' I said. 'Everyone knows how to get rid of it. Nothing works. Everybody I've met in the last month has had a brilliant idea for curing hiccups, but no one's been able to do anything.'

'What have you tried?' she said.

I sighed, and hiccupped, and sagged helplessly, and hiccupped again. I had the index of the failed cures ready. 'I've been startled by people jumping out of the shrubbery. I've taken to drinking a bottle of champagne every day. A girl called Susie suggested that. Then I started smoking. Then someone took me to a nightclub where I snorted cocaine and swallowed some ecstasy tablets. Then I was subjected to total humiliation in the press and on the radio. Then I drank out of a glass backwards. Then someone mounted a photographic exhibition about my life and my family and gave me the shock of my life by not telling me but just asking me to come along to the opening night. Then everyone stopped telling me that they loved me.'

'Poor baby,' she said. She ran her fingers along the table in the hall, mildly marvelling, as well she might, at its perfect dustlessness. Should I have left the house in a complete tip? Should she not have been able to feel flattery at what was true, that I could not cope without her, had fallen into a complete slough?

'So I tried everything,' I said.

'But you haven't tried this,' she said. She stopped running her fingers along the table; she began to run her fingers up my side. I had never been ticklish; you cannot be ticklish at a truly familiar touch, any more than you can tickle yourself; and yet I felt the beginnings of a tickle as my new-familiar wife stroked me.

'It won't work,' I said. 'No one else could do anything at all.'

'But,' she said, a shine in her eyes like what she must have seen, the sun setting over a tropical sea, 'none of those people were your wife. Watch.'

She wet her finger; not like a mummy coming to kiss a bruise better, but with slow grace, her eyelids falling heavily over her wide drowsy eyes, a gesture as lascivious as she could make it. Cor, I thought. 'It's a Spanish trick,' she murmured; stagy, slutty, not quite convincingly, but it seemed to be having the right effect, all the same.

'Cor,' I said.

She brought her wet finger up to my forehead, and started to trace a line downwards. 'I'm writing a word,' she said. 'Concentrate hard. What am I writing?'

I concentrated. Her wet finger went down, and across. It lifted, and placed itself at the top again, tracing a curve down and up. She went on, and there were four letters, I think.

'I don't know,' I said after a moment. 'Do it – again.' My voice was low and quiet, and it dried and broke as I tried to say what suddenly seemed the sexiest word imaginable, the word *again*. To lose your hiccups and acquire a stutter in its place.

'It's not so hard,' she murmured, going back to the beginning, and this time her finger was wet not from her licking, but from the damp response of my forehead to her touch. As she pressed with her finger, I walked backwards, and she followed me, until we found ourselves in the sitting room. I tried to see the slow movements, concentrating. She finished, stepped back, and from the way she looked at me I might have been as transparent as a glass of water. Her gaze; it drank you backwards.

'It isn't so hard,' she said.

'The first letter was L,' I said. 'It was definitely L.'

'And then?' she said.

'There were four letters,' I said.

'That's right,' she said.

'But I only got L,' I said.

'It isn't so hard,' she said. 'And did it work?'

We both listened, as if for something quite outside, like truced soldiers waiting for the resumption of gunfire. We stood in complete silence, ears cocked, for nearly five minutes. London is never really silent; it was only the resumed quiet of my body which made it seem like that. The French windows were open, and you could hear a quiet chorus of activity around us. At first, you heard the mechanical noises; in the road, a metal grunt as a learner driver attempted a three-point turn; a few houses away, the merry Bronx cheer of a petrol mower; from next door's kitchen window, a radio chattered – but there were people, too, voices; the radio was being sung along to by,

I supposed, a pair of builders; further away, a woman calling an out-of-sight child to her, the name indistinct but the quickly summoned tone of anxiety clear in her call. The hiccups had gone. The longer you stood there, the more you heard: a murmur, a little further off, of two people walking and talking easily; the clockwork rattle of a taxi passing in the road; and then, all at once, I heard what had always been there: the birds of London, singing in the silence where my hiccups had been, singing and singing over the gardens of London, all the birds of Lambeth and Wandsworth, of Putney and Barnes, of Clapham, Streatham and Brixton.

'Go on, then,' a voice said, quite clearly. 'She'll have your guts for garters, though.'

It was one of the builders, next door; and at once over the fence came the decisive pluck of a bottle of champagne being opened.

'They deserve it,' I said, meaning not just the pilfering builders, but everyone. I meant it.

'They do,' Janet said. 'Gone?'

'Gone,' I said. And the hiccups never came back, never once, all the rest of our life. Once, years later, in the spring of 2035, one morning after a hasty breakfast, she was to hiccup, just once, it's true, but I leant over and kissed my beautiful old wife, and she never hiccupped ever again. And nor was I to. The word she wrote on my flesh worked a spell, though the letters melted in my sweat and were gone before they could be read. What the word is that works the magic, I didn't ask, and never knew. It began with L, though. It definitely begins with L.

Subject Index